Ralph Compton
Stagecoach Revenge

A RALPH COMPTON WESTERN

RALPH COMPTON
STAGECOACH REVENGE

D. B. PULLIAM

THORNDIKE PRESS
A part of Gale, a Cengage Company

GALE
A Cengage Company

**LIBRARY OF CONGRESS CIP DATA ON FILE.
CATALOGUING IN PUBLICATION FOR THIS BOOK
IS AVAILABLE FROM THE LIBRARY OF CONGRESS.**

ISBN-13: 979-8-88578-493-1 (hardcover alk. paper)

Published in 2023 by arrangement with Berkley, an imprint of Penguin Publishing Group, a division of Penguin Random House, LLC.

Printed in Mexico
Print Number: 1   Print Year: 2023

For my mother, who always believed in me

THE IMMORTAL COWBOY

This is respectfully dedicated to the "American Cowboy." His was the saga sparked by the turmoil that followed the Civil War, and the passing of more than a century has by no means diminished the flame.

True, the old days and the old ways are but treasured memories, and the old trails have grown dim with the ravages of time, but the spirit of the cowboy lives on.

In my travels — to Texas, Oklahoma, Kansas, Nebraska, Colorado, Wyoming, New Mexico, and Arizona — I always find something that reminds me of the Old West. While I am walking these plains and mountains for the first time, there is this feeling that a part of me is eternal, that I have known these old trails before. I believe it is the undying spirit of the frontier calling me, through the mind's eye, to step back into time. What is the appeal of the Old West of the American frontier?

It has been epitomized by some as the dark and bloody period in American history. Its heroes — Crockett, Bowie, Hickok, Earp — have been reviled and criticized. Yet the Old West lives on, larger than life.

It has become a symbol of freedom, when there was always another mountain to climb and another river to cross; when a dispute between two men was settled not with expensive lawyers, but with fists, knives, or guns. Barbaric? Maybe. But some things never change. When the cowboy rode into the pages of American history, he left behind a legacy that lives within the hearts of us all.

— Ralph Compton

CHAPTER ONE

"You make this run often? Ever have any problems on the ride?"

The knock of his knuckles against the wooden bench of the driver's box made it clear what he meant by problems on the ride. It was the third time one of these passengers had asked some version of that question, and Jasper Duncan was getting mighty tired of it.

This question was at least better than the first. "Are you entirely sure this thing is safe?" one of the passengers had asked, wire glasses on his nose and starched shirt buttoned up all the way to his neck, which looked as thin as the stubby pencil he'd been scribbling with before he boarded the coach. Oh, for certain the man's tone was polite enough, but Jasper would have preferred a plainly spoken insult to one that hid inside a question. A question he hadn't answered, just like he hadn't answered the next variation and didn't intend to answer this latest one.

He had five passengers this ride, four in the coach and one who wanted to act like his shotgun messenger, perched up beside him. The man had a shotgun laid across his knees, and he carried it like he knew how to use it, so that was helpful even if he didn't understand what made a stagecoach reliable. *His* stagecoach was as reliable as they came, even if she might not look as showy as one of the newly painted Wells, Fargo, and Co. vehicles that ran routes all over California these days.

"I rode out to California on Butterfield's Overland, back in sixty-one? I'm no stranger to a rough ride."

Jasper didn't think this ride had been particularly rough, though the road had certainly been easier before they'd started climbing up into the mountains. This man had come on at Sonora, where the countryside was pleasantly hilly, not rocky like the land they were traveling now. Jasper wondered what was sending him up and perhaps over the Sierra Nevadas, but he had made it his business to transport folk, not ask them about why he was doing so.

"I must say, this scenery makes for a more enjoyable ride than that one," the man continued. "Through the desert for weeks!"

Jasper also preferred this country to the desert. He'd traveled through deserts before, felt the sand and dirt in his nose, in his hair. The Butterfield Trail, well traveled as it was, at least had water in regular intervals along the way. But driving a stage through a desert on a windy day left one feeling half scalded by the tiny hot grains of sand. This . . . this was better.

Folks said that in these parts, the air was cool and tasted sweet. The sky was blue and the clouds rolled and billowed, and each day was more lovely than the last. Jasper supposed they were alright, but he hadn't gone to California for the scenery.

"How long you been a jehu, friend?"

"Four years," Jasper answered.

"Seen any trouble?"

"Depends on what you mean by trouble," Jasper replied dryly. He'd seen passengers heave their guts out after the wind shook the stage as much as the rough road did; he'd had a horse slip in the mud and end up beneath his stage, the passengers evacuating quick as they could.

"You ever been robbed? There are bandits round these parts, I hear — Black Bret and the Casey Gang."

Jasper hadn't seen hide nor hair of the Casey Gang. He'd been looking.

"Ain't as dangerous as all that," Jasper said. If his voice sounded a little more bitter than a stager's should, his companion did him the courtesy of not mentioning it.

"Three days ago, Casey's gang hit a stagecoach carrying payroll just north of Modesto. Killed two of the passengers. Not sure how that's not dangerous."

Those words hit Jasper like a punch to the stomach. News generally took more than a couple of days to make its way to him. Even the more populated end of Jasper's run was barely a city, despite being the county seat. But Jasper sought out any news of the Casey Gang wherever he went. He wondered how he'd missed this. Three days ago . . . !

"If the Casey Gang strikes on this road, I reckon you'll be happy to have my gun along," the man continued.

If the Casey Gang struck on this road, Jasper had his *own* gun to deal with them.

"North of Modesto," Jasper said. "Whereabouts exactly?"

The man had just started to speak when the crack of gunfire rang out.

The lead horses both let out shrill whinnies and one of them reared up, bucking and then shying backward.

That gunfire had been *close.* Jasper looked

12

all around, and beside him, the man riding shotgun did the same. But despite the talk of outlaws, Jasper didn't see whoever had shot nearby. A hunter, maybe — plumb stupid, but not an outlaw.

Most teams that ran stagecoaches for any length of time learned quick to ignore the sound of gunfire. This one should have been no exception. But the lead horse was acting like someone had taken a shot at her, and she was looking likely to drive the whole stage off the road.

Behind him, Jasper could hear the passengers cry out as the stagecoach gave a jolt. Jasper rode it out. They'd been going at a good trot, but with the lead animals panicking, Jasper was going to have to bring the stage to a stop. He shortened the reins of the lead horses, then went to do the same for the reins of the wheelers.

But before he could get them under control, another shot rang out.

The same horse who'd reared up gave another shrill whinny and bolted, and the other horses followed along. They'd been going at a good clip, true, but now they were flying.

Jasper felt the wind try to tear his hat off. If he hadn't needed his hands to drive, he might have shoved it down farther onto his head, but instead he kept his focus on the horses and the reins. The man next to him was shouting something. Jasper couldn't make out much beyond his panicked tone.

"Calm down!" he shouted back at the man, but his voice might have gotten lost in the wind and the sound of the horses' hooves as well.

Jasper knew every stretch of this road up through Tuolumne County, but going at this speed added some extra lumps and bumps. The stage hit a steep dip in the road and the whole stagecoach rocked violently.

The passenger beside him leaned in close. "We need to stop!" he shouted.

"I'm working on that!" Jasper shouted back.

They were about to reach a bend in the road. It was dangerous at this speed, but all he could do was try to slow them down, try to keep the stage steady until after they made the turn. After that, the road widened up, and it would be easier to bring them to a stop. Trying to do that at this speed, around a tight corner? Bad idea.

But instead of holding on and calming down, the would-be shotgun messenger reached out and grabbed the reins in the hand closer to him.

Jasper hadn't been expecting it. What sort

of fool tried to grab the ribbons from a reinsman?

"What are you doing?" Jasper demanded, trying to wrest them away from him.

The man was strong, though, and panic must have helped the strength of his grip, because Jasper couldn't get him to let go.

And then the man *pulled.*

The road bent to the right. The man jerked the horses to the left, and the horses didn't even want to listen.

Jasper could hear cries coming from the coach behind him. He hoped they'd all found something to hold on to. If they tipped on this rocky ground? He didn't think it likely that any of them would walk away without injury.

He couldn't think of anything else to do. Wrapping the right-side reins around his hand, trying to keep them steady, he threw back his left elbow, slamming his passenger in the head.

The reins fell from the man's hand as he clutched at his face. Jasper hurried to grab them before they could fly out of the driver's box. He almost lost the wheeler's reins but snatched them just before they fell. He gave the horses as much slack as he could, trying to let them gallop through the turn, but they were too frantic and the stage started to tip to the left.

There wasn't much else left to try. Jasper kept his eyes open but said a prayer anyway, and pulled the reins to lead the horses right as hard as he dared.

The horses moved the exact way he wanted them to, and the wagon righted itself with a thump. His lips quirked up in a smile, but it lasted only an instant. They were still only halfway through the turn, and the cliffside was rising up rocky and mean right beside them. They were too close. Jasper could feel it coming and winced.

And then the wood slammed against stone.

He could feel the impact in every part of his body. It sent him sliding down the driver's bench, knocking into his passenger, this time accidentally. Jasper righted himself quickly, trying to ride out the damage, get the horses calmer.

The bend in the road behind them, no more gunshots splitting the peaceful afternoon air, the horses settled down quickly. But the stage wasn't riding right, limping along. When they finally came to a stop, the wood frame around him groaning in protest or relief, Jasper looked over to check on his would-be shotgun messenger. He was moaning, but aside from some bruises, he'd be fine.

Jasper dropped down from the stage. He'd felt the impact of that crash to his bones, so it was likely the stage had too. And she definitely had some broken parts.

Voices came from the coach, and he suddenly remembered the passengers inside. He walked toward the door, but before he could reach it, it slammed open. The man in the white shirt and spectacles tumbled out. He looked green.

Jasper's eyes went from the bespectacled man up to the other passengers staring at him from inside the coach. Jasper took a breath. "Everyone alright in there?"

CHAPTER TWO

Indigo was not much of a town, but the road to the home station had seemed far longer than it ever was before, and the meager lodgings were a welcome sight as Jasper's horses shambled their way into town.

Jasper had managed to get himself, the stage, and all the passengers to the end of his run, up here at what passed for a town in these mountains. The passengers weren't too happy. The man with the wire-rimmed glasses had gone as white as his fine pressed shirt when Jasper told him to get back in the stage after the near accident.

Jasper had saved all their lives. He'd have thought they'd be a little happier about it.

In any case, the stage was in worse shape than the passengers — one of the horses was limping, one of his wheels was barely holding on, and the gouge in the stage's side looked bloody due to her cracking rust-red paint. *Just a little farther,* he thought, and then he could properly assess the damage without any angry passengers breathing down his neck or crying into their handkerchiefs.

Finally, they made it to the home station — a long, low rectangular building that housed stables and lodging for travelers waiting for a stage to take them on the next run of the journey over the mountains and into Nevada. Jasper climbed down from the driver's box and swung open the door to the coach.

"Welcome to Indigo. Food and lodging," he said, pointing to the station, then gestured down the road, "and the mine office is that way. Watch your step as you get out."

His emphasis on the last two words didn't go unnoticed, if the glares he got from the passengers were anything to go by. He didn't stay even to help the lady climb down; surely one of the men could do that. He had to check on the horses and the stage.

The hostlers had come over while he was talking to his passengers. "Give me a moment, boys," Jasper said, then went to the horse he'd noticed struggling.

She was one of the leaders, a quick, slight mare with clever eyes and ears that twitched with her annoyance or her amusement.

19

Stagers switched out horses at swing stations along the route, but some of them stood out more than others. This mare was one of his favorites. He always thought he could tell what she was thinking, her decision to bolt aside. Right now, though, he could tell she was in pain.

"It's alright, girl," he murmured, scratching behind one of her ears. But it wasn't alright. This injury might not cripple her, but she certainly wouldn't be running routes up and down the mountains anytime soon.

Not that she would be leading *his* stage anyway.

Jasper shook his head and looked up. The hostlers were watching him, waiting to take charge of the horses and stage.

"You'd best be careful with them," he said. "Had a rough go out there."

"Can tell that," one of them muttered.

Jasper thought about cuffing him on the head, but no good could come of that, not when he didn't have the cash to make any enemies. He followed them instead, stripping off his coat and rolling up his sleeves, waiting until the horses got unhitched to get up close to the stage.

He'd wanted a proper look at the damage, hoping it would ease his mind to know just what was wrong. But instead, his stomach sank lower with every broken piece he found.

Jasper's stagecoach was a Concord, which were the best, solid, reliable. She still had the same paint job she'd had when he bought her — black, red, yellow, now faded. The man who'd sold her to Jasper, four years before outside of Denver, said her best days were long behind her, but she had never done him wrong. And Jasper always tried to do the same. He might not keep up with the paint job like he should, but he kept the rest of her cared for and clean.

She didn't look so cared for now.

The body damage was disappointing; a gouge to the doors or the body panels certainly didn't instill confidence in the stagecoach or in him as a driver, but they could be easily sanded or painted over. But the rest of the stagecoach . . . As expected, the damage to the wheel was worse now than it had been immediately after the crash; three of the spokes looked like someone had taken a hammer to the wood. Chances were, the rest of the wheel was damaged somewhere too. Had the accident happened more than a couple of miles from town, they'd all have been walking. Driving the coach on that damaged wheel, with all the jolting when the horses had spooked . . .

Jasper dropped to his knees and poked his head under the coach. The rear axle had a crack through the wood.

He let out a string of curses while the hostlers finished stabling the horses for the night and left the barn. If news hadn't spread through the home station about his arrival, it surely would now. But they'd come in late. Maybe he wouldn't have to face O'Reilly, the division agent in charge of the California–Nevada stretch, until tomorrow.

Jasper was in charge of the route from Indigo down to Knights Ferry. He ran the seventy-mile route near every day, weather permitting — down the mountain one day, up it the next. Down where the land was a little flatter, the climate a little milder, the weather almost always permitted a full route. Get farther into the mountains, though, and that wasn't the case anymore. But it was spring now; it had been three full months since these roads had been near impassable with snow and ice. Even when the roads did act up on him, he was usually able to make it through. He was good at what he did, and his stage was as reliable as anything Wells, Fargo, and Co. could offer.

Or she had been until earlier that day.

Stagecoaches ran their routes through the

nights often enough, but not once this station was reached. The next stages over the mountain were rocky and the roads were bad, so Indigo's home station as often as not bedded down the jehus as well as their stagecoaches and all the division's horses. At this time of night, when people were bedding down in the home station's rooms or in beds above the saloon, or eating what was left of Missy Banks' food in the home station kitchen, the barn was deserted. Just Jasper and a dozen horses snuffling their way to sleep despite his colorful evaluation of his banged-up stage.

He hadn't managed to find much in the way of good news when the barn door creaked open. Jasper looked up and his breath left him in a whoosh, one he barely stopped from being an obviously disappointed sigh. Bruce O'Reilly. It had been a fool's hope to imagine avoiding O'Reilly, but one he'd held just the same. He'd hoped he could do something with the stage before checking in. But it wasn't to be.

Most of the locals Jasper could stomach; O'Reilly was an exception. He was a large, lumbering man who was quick to smile and quick to laugh, but none of that gaiety seemed to ever reach his eyes or his voice. Being the division agent of this route made him Jasper's boss, in some senses of the word. Jasper owned his own stage, but he ran the route for the company, and O'Reilly worked for them. More than that, he owned the home station, which was the biggest building in town. After some treacherous winter runs, he owned more than half the jehus' stages. He'd probably have liked to own them all. He was the kind of man who was satisfied only when he'd bled everyone around him dry.

O'Reilly looked Jasper up and down. Jasper knew he didn't look like someone to be reckoned with. He wasn't tall, and his hair was shaggy and too long. If his mother were here, she'd tell him to get a haircut. He'd get around to it eventually. He was dusty from the road and he thought he'd probably have bruises ringing his wrist in the morning from wrapping those reins around it in the struggle.

O'Reilly kept his gaze on Jasper long enough to let him know he'd been found wanting, then transferred his gaze to the stagecoach. "Home station is home to some angry folks this evening."

Jasper scowled. "Are your accommodations as lacking as all that?"

O'Reilly chuckled. The man could laugh and smile even while being insulted; Jasper supposed when you had as much money and as few problems as he did, insults could roll off ones back like stones down a mountain. "We have the best coffee between Stockton and Carson City. No one has cause to complain about that."

"That crash wasn't on me." Jasper tossed the splintered piece of wood he'd been holding into the driver's box. "If anything, I stopped it from being worse. Who is that man who was sitting shotgun? Fool nearly killed us all."

"Some muscle the mine folks sent up with the accountant," O'Reilly offered easily. Jasper wasn't sure exactly who the accountant was, but he could make a fair enough guess: the one who looked like a copyboy in the white shirt and glasses. "Someone said he was a Pinkerton. I don't believe it myself."

An accountant wouldn't need a Pinkerton, and that was good, because now he wouldn't have one. The fool was the only one who'd been truly injured and it was his own fault; the rest were just hit with aches and pains. Couldn't do much guarding if one was dizzy from a conk to the head.

"If he is a Pinkerton, they need to reconsider who they hire. Not a lick of sense under pressure," Jasper grumbled.

He'd gone over it again and again in his mind. A shot from far off, the horse spooked, and the Pinkerton had grabbed the reins and pulled. It was the jolt and the tangle with him that had caused the stage to hit the rocks. Jasper had done what he could to right the mess and stop the horses from galloping them all off the side of the road, but what if he had kept the reins closer to him, or not let the man ride in the driver's box, or . . .

O'Reilly was still there, watching him like he was waiting for Jasper to say something else. So he did. "These things happen along the route all the time. Like I said, nothing else I could have done."

"Sure, sure," O'Reilly said, but Jasper knew he didn't truly mean it. "But now you have a problem, son."

Jasper ground his teeth. O'Reilly was familiar with everyone, the way a muggy day left everyone hot and sticky. "I'll fix it all up."

"Will you?"

He tilted his chin up. "I will."

"There's a stage coming over the mountains tomorrow. I'll need someone to bring them on down the mountain the next morning. Think you'll be all fixed up for that?"

Jasper clenched his jaw. O'Reilly knew that

was unlikely without some help, of course, but his sort of help always came with enough string to make a rope — and enough of that to hang yourself with.

"But you know, I could offer a solution. An easy one too. You could sell to me," O'Reilly said. "I'll let you keep running the same stage, same route. Only difference is who owns the thing."

O'Reilly had tried this before. But even when things were rough — and they had been rough a time or two over the winter, certainly — Jasper had barely been tempted. His stage hadn't just seen him through those rough times; no, his stage had brought him into California, down south at first, then up the coast, until he'd finally landed here in Tuolumne County two years before. If he sold out to O'Reilly, he could still leave, but he'd leave without the stage, and it would make setting up in the next place twice as hard.

The next place. Each time, he hoped there wouldn't *be* a next place.

He thought of the Casey Gang's payroll grab. Just north of Modesto.

"I ain't interested," Jasper said.

"Don't be a fool, Duncan. I can have that back up on the road in two days. For you to replace that wheel, fix the axle? It'll take

27

longer, and you don't have that sort of time, do you?"

O'Reilly was right. He didn't have the time, not if he wanted to keep his job. Keep his stage or keep his job. Maybe he didn't want to keep either.

"I'm trying to help you, you know. You ain't got a good reputation around here, and stunts like this don't help much. All you gotta do is let me help."

Jasper didn't say no again. He'd already turned the man down; he wasn't going to do it twice. He turned his back and continued his inspection of the stagecoach. He'd found all the damage already, but he looked it over again while O'Reilly muttered about him being a stubborn fool and walked out of the barn.

Jasper almost kicked at the wheel, then realized that would have been a bad idea with as much damage as there was. Instead, he collected the flask of whiskey from his bag in the driver's box and swung up into the coach himself. He settled on one of the benches — smooth from years of long rides and meticulous care; let no one say they had stabbed themselves on a splinter in Jasper Duncan's stagecoach — and took a long swallow. His body ached from the ride, and his mind ached already from trying to decide his next move. *Tomorrow,* he told himself. He'd just face all of it tomorrow.

CHAPTER THREE

One of the hostlers whistling woke Jasper.

He was curled into the side of the stage-coach. His mouth tasted like someone had shoved a dirty shirt inside and left it there, and he wished there had been water in his flask instead of whiskey. Jasper stretched out his neck and wished instead that he hadn't fallen asleep sitting up. He'd been aching the day before from the jolts and jerks of the crash, and sleeping on this hard bench hadn't done his back or neck any favors.

Jasper pushed the door open and winced when the hinges gave a whine. Had he slammed into those rocks hard enough to damage the door? He clambered down, then grabbed his canteen from where he'd left it in the driver's box, and downed the rest of the water. It tasted as good this morning as the whiskey had tasted last night.

The barn was brighter now, with morning

light spilling in through the open doors, than it had been the evening before when they'd dragged his coach inside. He'd slept all night on that bench. He hadn't meant to.

Tomorrow, he'd told himself, and it looked as though tomorrow had come.

He circled the stagecoach again, mentally listing all the damage. This time he added the door. Creaks and moans could be dealt with on a stagecoach ride; the passengers were used to that, and used to jostling around in their seats for miles. They were usually a hardier bunch than the ones who'd take one look at an old paint job and decide they would never reach their final destinations alive. No, the trouble was the wheel and the axle. The wheel he'd have to replace, but could the axle be fixed?

He crawled beneath the wagon to assess the damage, but regardless of the morning light, the situation seemed as dark as it had the night before. That crack in the axle . . . He let his hands fall to his sides and closed his eyes, wondering whether he should have taken O'Reilly's offer, if he should have sold and then quit. He could have taken a horse, struck out toward Modesto.

"There's a room above the saloon that would likely have been more comfortable

31

than this floor," a voice said from above him.

Jasper turned his head and saw the bottom of a skirt and two worn boots, one of the toes tapping the hard-packed dirt. In his sore condition, it took him a moment to wriggle out from under the stage.

Charlotte Hawthorn owned the saloon in Indigo and was one of the few Jasper called friend in town. What he never called her was Charlotte, though; she went by Charley. She couldn't have been more than thirty, he thought, or maybe she'd just aged better than most. Charley wore a long, dark skirt and a white blouse, with her gun belt on her waist. Her dark hair was pulled back into a knot at the back of her head. He'd never seen it done any other way. She wore gloves, and he could see where there were no fingers to fill the glove. Her right hand. She shot with her left now. One night she'd told him she'd been right-handed before the accident that left her injured and ended her days driving a stage. She'd set up shop in Indigo then, with a watering hole for miners, stagers, and their patrons. When Jasper had landed here, she'd been the first one to welcome him properly, with a shot of whiskey and not a single question. Since then, they'd become friends, and he found it was easier to talk to someone who wasn't prying into his business for curiosity's sake.

He smiled up at her. "I've slept in that room, and I'm not sure about that."

Charley's lips flattened into a line, but the eyes above were playful.

"And I didn't sleep on the floor," he said, climbing to his feet.

"Oh, no? Just fancied laying in the dirt?"

He almost laughed. "I slept in the coach."

Her nose wrinkled. She'd been a jehu for near ten years, she'd told him once, and would do all she could to avoid riding *in* a stagecoach. Apparently that feeling also included sleeping in one. He didn't blame her. He hadn't meant to fall asleep, after all.

She held up the small bundle she was carrying. "I brought breakfast. Unless you have that in there as well," she said with a quirk of her brow.

He did have some dried fruit and jerky in there, but nothing that would count as breakfast. He swept a hand toward the hay bales against the wall.

They both sat down, and she opened her bundle. Biscuits, a wedge of cheese, and a small jar of jam.

"Well, this is a welcome way to start the morning," he said, spreading a generous layer of jam on one half of a biscuit.

"I thought you could use something nice after the day you had yesterday."

"Ah," he said. "You heard." She'd probably known last night. She always knew everything before anyone else.

"I heard."

"That crash wasn't my fault," he said before she said another word.

"I believe you," Charley replied easily, and left it at that; just like that first day, she showed no interest in questioning him.

Just like then, it made him want to talk. "Those passengers staring at me like I done something on purpose to nearly kill them. Why are they heading over the mountains if they want a cushy ride? They should take a steamboat around the Horn if they want to go east so bad. Heaven knows a trip across Panama would kill them all. I bet that one with the stiff white shirt hasn't so much as seen a mosquito." He put the rest of his biscuit down and started to pace, angry.

She let him run himself out of steam before asking, "Has O'Reilly been to see you?"

"Last night. Offered to buy her again." He tapped the door of the stage with his knuckles. "I told him no."

Charley nodded. One time — during one of those rough patches of his in the winter

— she'd asked him why he didn't want to sell, one of the only times she'd ever really pried into his affairs. He'd been drunk enough to answer her. "He doesn't like being told no," she said.

"He's gotten pretty used to it from me," Jasper replied, but he didn't need her to elaborate to understand what she meant. Right now he could have used O'Reilly's goodwill, and he'd all but made sure that was all dried up. "You come down here to look at the damage and bring me food or was there something else?"

"Something else," she said, but then she was silent for a moment before continuing. He raised his brows, waiting. "Mail came in on the last Overland stage."

He felt colder than when he was curled up on the bench without a blanket. "Something for me, I take it?"

"Yes."

"Well, you leave it with the rest of my mail, and I'll see about collecting it."

Her face told him clearly that she knew that wasn't going to happen. He might not keep that room above the saloon for his own, but he kept many of his things there, including a stack of mail he'd never seen beyond a quick glance. But his refusal to read through it never dampened Charley's eagerness to tell him when he got a fresh letter from Nebraska Territory — *Nebraska now,* he corrected himself. He'd never even been to the state of Nebraska, even if it was his home. She understood a lot about him, but she never seemed to understand his unwillingness to read letters from a family he hadn't seen in going on seven years, even if she never pushed. He hadn't tried to explain it to her. If she were going to understand, she'd have understood already.

"Say, Charley, do you think Barman Jack would be willing to give me a hand with this axle?"

Charley snatched up the last bite of his biscuit and popped it in her mouth, then tied her bundle of food back together. She knew he wouldn't settle back down to eat, not when he was thinking like this. "Your guess is as good as mine, but as long as you don't keep him past when the miners knock off work, you have my blessing to ask him."

Jasper gave her a nod in thanks, and instead of collecting his letters or going back to deal with O'Reilly, he went to hunt down Barman Jack, who — in addition to serving drinks at the saloon — was a clever hand with repairs and generally didn't begrudge Jasper his help, even when he couldn't pay much.

He spent the day working with Jack and avoiding anyone else. He didn't much feel like talking, even to Jack. Luckily the man didn't seem to mind; they mostly worked in silence, punctuated with stories from the saloon — O'Reilly was a dab hand at the piano; one of the jehus nearly lit the place on fire with a cigarillo; a miner had tried to lay Jack out three nights ago when he'd refused to pour him another drink. Charley had been ready to shoot him, and he was saved only by a shift boss' intervention, a man called Brady who'd gotten himself fired only yesterday.

Jasper ventured out in the midafternoon to get a plate of stew from the home station dining room, waiting until after most would have already taken their midday meal so he'd be able to sneak into the station without bother.

Indigo was busier this time of day than the evening before, but it wasn't anything like a bustling town. There were a blacksmith and the general store, but the latter was no bigger than the passenger coach of Jasper's stage. And there was no real post office, just Charley's system of annoying folks who didn't even want to take their mail. As far as Jasper could see, the town had only three things going for it: the mine, the way station, and the scenery.

That last, at least, was truly beautiful. Greenery stretched up the mountainside, a dozen kinds of trees standing in the distance. Up close, some of these pines seemed like giants, but far off, they were dwarfed by the rocky peaks. The first time he saw this country, Jasper felt like his breath had been taken away. By now he knew it was just that the air was a little thinner the higher up you went in the mountains.

The home station was near as deserted as he hoped when he snuck into the kitchen. Missy Banks, a woman too good-hearted to be working for O'Reilly, sent him back with not just the stew but a square of corn bread as well. He split it with Jack, who thanked him through a mouthful of golden crumbs.

But whatever good mood the corn bread and stew had put him in, it faded shortly after. Even with Jack's help, there wasn't much more he could do without parts. And for parts he needed money. For parts he needed time as well, and O'Reilly was right that he didn't have much of that.

Jack left before the sun started to fade. The miners would be knocking off work soon and the saloon would need their bartender. The stagecoach O'Reilly had mentioned came in; it was more of a mud wagon than a proper stage like his, suited for rough country like the mountain route. It'd be heading back east, taking most of his passengers from the day before with it, and Jasper wondered who O'Reilly would get to run these passengers down to Sonora the next day, since it clearly wouldn't be him.

He'd have to sell. That was the only option there was. O'Reilly was right. His reputation wasn't one to be celebrated, and what did it matter if he cut ties? He could make his way down the mountain, leave off being a jehu. He'd never meant to be at it this long anyway. He'd never meant to like it. It was the means to an end, and since he didn't have the means, he'd have to end it. Maybe it would be for the best, considering what he knew now. He could leave on horseback. Head out, not stop until he'd found what he was looking for.

Three days ago, north of Modesto. Crash or not, he hadn't forgotten that.

Jasper left the barn an hour or so after Jack had. He didn't head toward the home station, no matter that the cook there almost always gave out johnnycakes on the house for stagers. No, instead he headed across the muddy street to Indigo's only saloon. He needed a drink more than he needed dinner. There was a chance at the saloon he'd get both, at least; the home station never served anything but coffee.

The light inside was dim, but the air was warm even in the chilly spring evening. A big warm stove was burning in the corner, and a group of miners was sitting around it, warming their dirty hands. A man played a mournful tune on the fiddle across the room until someone shouted for him to liven it up. Jasper preferred the mournful song to the jig. His eyes skimmed the saloon, searching. But before he could find Charley, a man stepped up beside him and spoke.

"Friend, you look in need of a drink."

Jasper couldn't say he'd ever particularly considered William Hatchett a friend of his, but the man was sorely right. He was one of the town deputies, older than Jasper by a decade or more, with a lined, friendly face and a penchant for speaking the obvious.

"You buying?" Jasper asked.

Hatch clapped him on the back and steered him toward the bar. "Why not?"

Jasper didn't take much to charity, so when their drinks arrived, he put down his own coin even though Hatch tried to wave him off. The price of a drink wouldn't save his stage, after all.

As if in response to his thoughts, he heard a flurry of voices start up on the other side of the room, the kind of whispers that weren't really anything of the sort, but were trying to pretend to be polite. He looked over his shoulder. Sure enough, drinking in the corner were two of his passengers, the Pinkerton who'd perched beside him and the stocky one with the blotchy face. The two hadn't been traveling together; likely the only thing they had to talk about was Jasper and the crash he'd prevented — though from the looks on their faces, they wouldn't put it like that. The Pinkerton didn't look *too* worse for wear — a black eye and some other, smaller bruises. Jasper supposed he should be happy about that.

"Hear you almost got those folks killed," Hatch said.

This, Jasper thought, was why he'd never considered Hatch a friend. The man talked too much and Jasper never liked to hear any of it.

"No one almost got killed," Jasper snapped, even if that wasn't entirely true. "And it was that shooter that caused the trouble, not me."

"I'm sure that's so," Hatch replied. His

tone clearly said the opposite.

Jasper slammed back his whiskey and let the burn hide his scowl. He wasn't sure what Hatch had heard, or how, or from whom, but if he'd already heard the tale, everyone likely knew it. That wouldn't bode well for him.

He glanced back at the passengers from the day before. They were still talking and the anger on their faces hadn't cooled. They caught him looking and the stocky man started to rise. One of his drinking companions made a halfhearted attempt to get him to sit down again.

Jasper didn't want whatever trouble he was going to bring over.

"Thanks for the drink," he said to Hatch, even though he hadn't let him pay for it, and slid off of his stool.

Jasper ignored the glares from the corner as he crossed the room. There was a door along the opposite wall, half hidden between a cabinet and a screen with painted scenes of rivers and steamboats. The door led to a narrow set of stairs, dimly lit by a lamp at the very top. There were three doors in the short hall, but Jasper had only ever gone inside one of them.

The upstairs of the saloon was closed to most of the patrons, including the room

Jasper went to. Someone had called it a parlor once, and the name had stuck. The room was warm and as dim as the hallway; the windows were shuttered and the roof low, and smoke drifted toward him when he walked in. There was usually someone in the room, even if most weren't allowed up here. It was by invitation only for the miners, and the only regulars with an open invitation to enter were the whips. Jasper was still one of those. At least for now.

Inside the room there was a card game going on. Four around the table: two jehus, one miner Jasper vaguely recognized as one of the men who'd found the vein of gold to begin with, and Charley herself. Now she kicked a chair out for him and jerked her head toward it in invitation.

He declined with a shake of his head. Even if Jasper were inclined to gamble, he didn't have the money to risk. But poker had never been his game; neither was faro, or blackjack, or whatever the men round this table were doing with their cards. Instead of taking the chair Charley kicked out, he parked himself in a corner, propping his feet up on a barrel.

Hatch had been only the first, he reckoned. He'd have to weather questions from all sorts. Maybe from Buck Simmons, the man in charge of the mine. The pale, stuffy fellow was an important sort; Jasper might have to answer for nearly killing him. Even if Simmons didn't hold the crash against him — though Jasper wasn't sure how likely that was with the rumors already swirling his reputation down the drain — a man couldn't be a jehu without a stagecoach to actually run his stage of the route. That was the problem he kept running into. He might need only a few days of good work or a little bartering for parts, but he didn't have a few days, and he didn't have much to barter with.

What worth did thinking about any of this have if he was going to sell? He'd made his decision. But decision or not, he'd never been very good at keeping the trouble from his thoughts for very long.

The door banged open and shook Jasper from his thoughts. He glanced at the door. O'Reilly lumbered inside, and Jasper thought about taking his leave. O'Reilly wasn't someone he wanted to see right now.

"This game's invitation only," Charley said. Her voice was mild, but that was when she was most dangerous in Jasper's experience.

"You wouldn't turn away a neighbor," he said, and held up a bottle. "Especially not

44

one who brings enough whiskey to share."

She waved him closer, though she didn't look too happy about it. She had plenty of liquor downstairs, Jasper wanted to argue, but didn't. It wasn't his business who she allowed up here. He was only glad he was still invited.

O'Reilly got himself settled, but Jasper stayed tense. He wasn't fool enough to believe O'Reilly was going to let the accident pass without comment.

Sure enough, after the next hand had been dealt, he spoke. "Heard some of our Charley's guests downstairs speaking about their troubles on the road." O'Reilly didn't look up from his cards, but the comment must have been directed at Jasper.

Jasper thought again about leaving, but everyone at the table save Charley and O'Reilly had swiveled their heads toward him, and if he stormed out now, they'd only talk more.

"I told you what the trouble was. That Pinkterton, for one. And a gunshot — two — spooked the horses," he said, though he didn't like to blame them. "I'd like to get my hands on whoever was shooting up the road." He'd break him like the shattered spokes of the wheel.

"Son, revenge is no good for the soul,"

the miner said.

One of the jehus chuckled. "But it sure is sweet."

"I'll drink to that," Jasper said.

Charley snatched up O'Reilly's whiskey and held the bottle out for him. Jasper took the bottle, poured himself a generous drink, and threw it back.

The conversation moved on from Jasper and his stagecoach. Each time a glass emptied, O'Reilly generously filled it back up again, and the men's tongues loosened as they played and drank. O'Reilly complained about the weather; one of the jehus complained about Pitt Randall, the local sheriff, and the two others quickly agreed. He was unreasonable; he was surly. Then someone complained about Buck Simmons, and the others followed suit again. He was cheap; he was cold. They'd be sorry they'd said anything when they sobered up, Jasper knew. Nothing said around O'Reilly would be kept secret for long unless it was in his self-interest to hold it back, and Pitt Randall was as surly as Simmons was cold. They wouldn't take comments about them with good humor. Jasper tried to steer clear of both of them best he could.

The miner shook his head ruefully, though Jasper wasn't sure if that was about the hand he'd been dealt or the comments about Simmons. "I tell you, friends, there's something rotten going on with those mine men. They laid off a whole shift of workers. You hear about that?"

Everyone at the table clearly had, though it was the first Jasper had heard of it. The miner continued. "Them businessmen act like she's all dried up, but we broke through to another vein of quartz not two weeks ago."

"Duncan over there brought us someone to help with the mine," O'Reilly said. "An accountant."

The miner cast Jasper a dark look, like it was his fault he'd brought the man to town, or like maybe he should have made sure the accountant had gotten killed in that accident. "Just what we needed."

He grumbled a little more, but then he won the hand and didn't seem to mind as much. If Jasper had any faith he'd do some winning, he might take up poker to get his mind off his troubles like the miner.

He was just about to leave when the back door creaked open and another man shuffled inside.

It was JD Valdez, one of Indigo's deputies, looking rougher than Jasper had ever seen him. It was rare to see Valdez without

Hatch; Valdez was closer to Jasper's age, but the two were fast friends, usually as inseparable as Valdez and his dog. The dog had come up to the parlor, trailing in behind him as always. Her ears drooped like she shared in her master's mood.

"Deputy," Charley said. "We've got a chair here."

"I need a proper invitation, but Valdez here can bust in the back and join the game?" O'Reilly asked. Jasper couldn't tell if he was actually offended or just causing more trouble.

"He looks like he needs a drink," Charley said.

The man sported a fat lip and his clothes were muddy, as though someone had shoved him right into a ditch. He clearly needed a drink as much as Jasper had. Valdez made his way to the table and slumped down into the open chair. His dog was cleaner than he was, though the mutt didn't seem to mind the dirt, sitting right beside Valdez with her head propped on his knee.

"I could use more than one," Valdez said.

"Problem at the mine?" O'Reilly asked.

Valdez shook his head. He clearly didn't want to talk about whatever had rendered him beaten and dirty, though from the pinched look on his face, Jasper would have wagered it was less that he wanted to be silent and more that he'd been ordered to. That pointed to something serious. Valdez was the silent sort; he didn't like to air his problems unless they needed airing. What use was it to swear him to silence? Jasper wondered. Whatever had happened would be all around Indigo by the time the sun slipped below the treetops. Maybe it would overshadow what had happened with Jasper's stage. If only he were so lucky . . .

"Come on, now," O'Reilly cajoled as Charley poured out a measure of bourbon. "If I'm sharing my liquor, you can share your story."

Valdez let out a breath. "We caught a man squatting in that cabin out by the mine." Jasper knew exactly which cabin he was talking about — it had been there before the mine, made from rough-hewn logs and half burned out from some fire. No one had lived there for as long as Jasper had been around these parts, and it was a surprise anyone would risk the charred roof coming down on top of them in order to sleep there.

"Some squatter gave you that lip?"

Valdez scowled at O'Reilly. "He ain't just a squatter. The man's an outlaw. And he didn't just pop *me* one. Drunk as a skunk and still laid two of us out flat."

49

"An outlaw? Fancy that. We've got our own criminal element round here."

O'Reilly knew as well as anyone that they already had a criminal element. All places did, didn't they? But it wasn't just him who perked up at the news of a captured outlaw. Jasper felt his muscles tensing, and he stopped pretending not to be following their conversation.

"Not for long," Valdez said. "Randall wants him gone soon. Gonna send a stage first thing down to Sonora, special run."

"A special run? Well, now, who could be so important as all that?"

Valdez picked up the shot of bourbon Charley had just slid across the table to him. "Alec Casey's brother," he said, and downed his drink.

CHAPTER FOUR

May 14, 1866
It was a fine spring day. The morning had been warm enough to burn off the dew early, and they'd gotten to work after eating a good breakfast of bread and bacon. Jasper was crouched in the dirt beside his father, the two of them pulling up weeds that had started to choke out his mother's vegetable garden. The weeds kept coming no matter the work they did. Jasper was complaining about it when the sheriff arrived.

Jasper scrambled to his feet when he saw the sheriff and gave the man a respectful nod, but his father took his time in rising. Was that because of the aches in his knees, or because he knew somehow what was coming?

"Ben," the sheriff said with a tip of his hat. "Jasper."

"What can we do for you, Sheriff?"

The sheriff looked uncomfortable, standing

in the vegetable garden. "You have a moment?"

Ben Duncan wiped his hands on his pants and stood. "We should head inside."

Jasper started to follow the men in. His father gave him a sharp look, but whatever he saw in Jasper's face must have made him relent. "Fine," he said, chuckling, cupping the back of Jasper's neck and pulling him into a half embrace.

His father had built their home himself, timber and stone hewed from their land. He sat at the table next to the sheriff, and Jasper wondered if he ever missed it, trading the life of a lawman to build a home and weed vegetable gardens.

"Thank you, Martha," the sheriff said when she poured him some coffee.

"Jasper," she said, "let's let your father and the sheriff talk."

"Pa said I could stay," Jasper replied. Worry flickered across his mother's face, but Jasper didn't pay attention to it. She didn't pour him any coffee, but he snuck one of the lavender cookies she'd served their guest, waiting until she was out of sight to take a bite.

The sheriff started to talk after taking a long, fortifying drink of his coffee. "There was a robbery out near Fort Kearny, and we've had some information come in that the gang's holed up not far from here."

"I ever heard of this gang?" his pa asked.

"May have," the sheriff said. "Alec Casey and his boys."

Strange how something can come into a man's life so quietly and then upend it completely.

If Ben Duncan knew the name, he didn't show it.

The sheriff brought out a handbill, a small one, and new. "WANTED," it read across the top. A drawing of Alec Casey was below that. He looked young and slightly snide, with his black hair inked in dark. Jasper couldn't see what was so frightening about this boy. According to the handbill, Alec Casey had been on the run for a year.

"He's robbed banks, taken some payroll stages, killed more men than he's left alive," the sheriff said. "Don't let that face fool you. He might be young, but he's bad as they come."

"What do you want me for?"

"We're riding out," the sheriff said. "We aim to bring them in."

"Dead or alive?" Jasper's father said.

"Alive's preferable," the sheriff replied.

"I'll get my rifle."

His father always seemed to tower above everyone. Jasper hadn't gotten his height —

he was near a head shorter than his father — but he'd always tried to stand like him, shoulders back, chin firm, and facing the world head-on. His pa hadn't been an active deputy for nearly a decade, but Jasper knew once a good man made a vow to keep a place and people safe, that vow wasn't so easily dismissed.

"Wait," Jasper said, brushing crumbs off his shirt and trying to look older than his seventeen years. "You'll need men for this posse."

"Jasper," his father started.

"I ain't saying I'm going to get into a shootout," Jasper said. "But don't you think you'll need some help?"

"The boy has a point," the sheriff said. "I'd like the numbers to be on our side for this one."

Ben Duncan nodded twice and pursed his lips before turning to his son. "You'll stay clear of trouble unless it comes right up to find you," his father said. Jasper nodded rapidly, but that wasn't good enough. "I want you to swear."

"I swear it," Jasper promised.

His father relented.

The sheriff clapped Jasper on the shoulder. "Consider yourself deputized, son."

Jasper didn't think he'd ever smiled so wide as at that moment, on the day his father died. He surely hadn't smiled so wide since.

CHAPTER FIVE

Jasper left to track down Randall before Valdez even finished swallowing his drink.

A special run down to Sonora. All thoughts about selling out to O'Reilly, leaving on horseback, were gone the moment he'd heard who that outlaw was. Alec Casey's brother. Six years, and this was as close as he'd gotten.

Alec Casey had left Nebraska Territory the year after killing Jasper's father, shooting and robbing his way west, striking his own sort of gold once he got to the southern part of the state. He'd moved around since, though he'd spent the last three years here in gold country, robbing payroll runs, banks, and anything else he wanted to take.

Jasper had been following him since shortly after his father's murder. The thing about the men of the Casey Gang was that it was easy to track them down but impossible to pin them. The lawmen hadn't been able to. Jasper didn't keep up with Casey's associates; the members came and went, the latter usually by way of a bullet. Sometimes the bullet was from Casey himself, rumor said. But the one constant in the gang was Alec Casey's brother, Slip.

Where the reward for Alec Casey had risen with each of his crimes, his brother's bounty had stayed much the same. He was older, though probably not by much, and Jasper wondered if it galled him to play second fiddle. Wondered if doing less to make folks want you dead was something to be ashamed of for the Casey brothers. Regardless of that, if the tales Jasper'd heard among lawmen and in saloons had it true, there were plenty of other things for Slip Casey to be ashamed of. By all accounts, he wasn't a very good outlaw, always blundering into one mess or another. No matter if that was true, where one Casey was, the other was sure to be close by.

Jasper didn't care about the other members of the Casey Gang, didn't particularly care about Slip Casey even. He didn't even care about the bounty. What he wanted was to look Alec Casey in the eye and do what he should have done six years before: shoot him through the heart.

And now Pitt Randall might give him the

key to finally doing that.

They called Randall the sheriff, but he was properly a deputy himself. Indigo wasn't much of a town. It was far enough away that the county sheriff himself never came round. So Randall was lawman enough, with his two deputies and a few others he might call on if there was a problem. There was a makeshift jail where drunks could be thrown until they sobered up enough to apologize to whomever they'd laid out or offended, but Randall spent most of his time dealing with the mine men. If they'd been dealing with some drunk, Jasper might have headed to that makeshift jail. But they would never put one of the Casey boys there in the middle of town. That would be just asking for trouble.

But he didn't need to find Slip Casey. He needed to find the lawman, and he knew exactly where to go — to wherever Simmons was.

The mine had gone up on the ridge three years earlier, before Jasper had made it out to these parts. The operation seemed ramshackle to him, sloping roofs and sluice boxes and carts and more men than could fit in the whole town, it sometimes seemed. Fewer men now than before, Jasper thought; he wondered if the miners who'd been laid off would lope on down the mountains, or maybe up them, trying to find a hole in the ground where there was still gold to carve out.

During the day, Simmons would have been at the mine. He'd been here nearly as long as the mine had, maybe even longer than the town had a name. He had an office there, though Jasper had never seen it.

Since it was late and the mine was closed for the night, Jasper went instead to Simmons' house, another place he'd never been.

It lay on the edge of town, on the way to the mine. It looked as orderly as the mine looked ramshackle: clean lines, a boxy frame with a strong, sloped roof, whitewashed and kept clean.

He strode up the porch steps, boots clomping on the wood, and thumped on the door before his manners caught up with him and turned the thump into a knock.

A woman answered the door. Her hair was swept back under a kerchief, and her eyes looked suspicious. *A maid, not the man's wife,* Jasper thought.

"I need to see Simmons," Jasper said.

"Mr. Simmons is busy with the sheriff and —"

"Good," Jasper said. He thought about asking her to get him, waiting for the man's reply, but *asking* for permission didn't always mean *getting* it, so he just pushed by her into the house. "I need to see the sheriff too."

Inside, the house was as neat and clean as it was outside. There wasn't much there to mark who or what Simmons was, just plain but finely built furniture. His office was near the front door, which made sense to Jasper; he was certainly not the first man to come stomping through this well-kept house with dirty boots and a bad attitude.

The maid took him to the office, though her face clearly said she didn't want to. She gave a knock, waited for a gruff call from Simmons, then opened the door. "Sir, a man's here to see you, said it was urgent, and —"

The two men looked up, and Simmons saw Jasper. He gestured for the maid to go.

Jasper remembered what the men in Charley's parlor had said — cheap and cold. Only one of those things was certain from the moment you looked at Buck Simmons. The man was as cold as winter on the top of the mountain. He was in his middle forties, Jasper guessed, with dark blond hair that he kept neat and short, and wide shoulders that spoke to a history of laboring. Jasper didn't know what he'd done before he came to the place that would be Indigo. He'd never given much thought to the man, except for avoiding him. Couldn't do that now.

Jasper walked in, sweeping his hat off as an afterthought. "Mr. Simmons," he said, then turned toward the second man in the room. "Sheriff."

Pitt Randall was near fifty, as far as Jasper could figure. All that was left of his hair were wisps of gray that he kept shorn, though Jasper could hardly remember seeing the man without his hat. Or without a frown on his face for that matter. He was wearing both when Jasper pushed open the door, and beneath his drooping brows, Randall's eyes narrowed at the sight of him.

Simmons didn't react to the sight of him, even though he'd just busted into his home without so much as an invitation. "Mr. Duncan. What brings you here?"

Randall might have been as good as the sheriff around here, but Simmons was as good as the mayor. Most of the men who lived in Indigo worked for the mine, after all, and Simmons ran the mine. He didn't own it, of course; no, the mine's owners rarely showed their faces in this town, not when it dribbled out less and less gold. But what gold it produced was enough to keep it running, and enough to keep Simmons the most important man in Indigo, though O'Reilly surely hated it.

"I want in," Jasper said.

"In? What do you want in on, Duncan?" Randall asked.

"I heard about the man you caught and that you need a jehu to take him down first thing. I want in."

"Now, how'd you hear about that?" Randall's face looked even surlier than it had when Jasper walked in the door.

It could be that Jasper had just gotten Valdez in trouble. He'd have felt worse about that if it weren't so important.

Simmons, on the other hand, was staring at Jasper, his blue eyes seeming to weigh him. "You have a lot of nerve asking for another job after botching one yesterday."

"I didn't botch that job."

"Oh? I have a stagecoach full of passengers who say otherwise."

Arguing that they were wrong wouldn't help his case. Jasper bit back his reply, though it rankled to do it. "All the better for this job, then, ain't it? No passengers to coddle on a prison run."

Simmons' lip curled up. "No passengers to coddle, but a crash could kill a criminal as easy as it could a fine upstanding soul."

"The reward on the Casey Gang has always been dead or alive. Still is, ain't it?"

"There a reason you're so well-informed about the reward on the Casey Gang?" Randall asked.

There weren't many around here who knew why Jasper had come to this part of California. Charley really was the only one. O'Reilly probably had a fair clue, as the man collected information as much as he collected other people's stagecoaches. Simmons might not care if he were hiring a man with a personal stake in things, but Randall didn't seem like the sort who would invite that kind of investment.

"I read the papers," Jasper said. "And anyway, no one's gonna die."

Randall and Simmons exchanged a look. They were going to say no. Jasper could see it, and he knew he had only a moment to change their minds. How to do that? This was the closest he'd come to Alec Casey since he'd gotten to this blasted town, but he couldn't think of a thing to say to change their minds.

"Mr. Duncan is correct about his job yesterday."

Jasper startled at the voice. All three of them turned their heads to look at the man who had just spoken.

It was one of the passengers from the stage, the prissy one in the fancy suit. The accountant, O'Reilly had called him. The man didn't look as fancy now, with his shirtsleeves rolled up and a smudge of ink on his collar. He sat in the corner, a small table in front of him that held a ledger of some sort and a mostly empty glass with the remnants of a shot of bourbon at the bottom. Jasper hadn't noticed him as he came inside, and from the looks on Simmons' and Randall's faces, they'd forgotten he was even there.

"I had my fears boarding his stagecoach," the man continued. "It certainly didn't look like much even before the unfortunate incident yesterday. But he handled it well, and I believe had it not been for his quick thinking, we passengers would have been much worse off than with cricks in our necks and a few aching heads."

Jasper stared at the man. He couldn't for the life of him remember his name. Had he known it? Likely not; Jasper didn't make it a habit to introduce himself to his passengers. The man stared back, then looked away, a pinch to his lips; a beat too late, Jasper realized he must have been waiting for a word of thanks. Well, he'd spoken nothing but the truth, Jasper thought, and looked back to Simmons and Randall.

"I told you I didn't botch the job," he said. "You let me in on this and you won't regret it."

Randall didn't look like he believed that for a second, but Simmons . . . Simmons was thinking it over.

"I'll take the job for half," Jasper said.

"We never discussed payment," Simmons said, his voice dry.

Jasper knew that he was being too eager, that he was showing too much of his hand — one reason why he didn't gamble at the card table. That offer he just made, that desperation, might get him paid even less than it would have before that, and worse, it might let Randall know he was out for more than just a job. In the corner, the unnamed man with the ledger made a small disapproving noise. Jasper wasn't sure if it was directed at him or at the books he was combing through.

"Westin, you wanted to head back soon as can be. This stage leaves at dawn. You reckon it's safe enough for you to be on it with Jasper Duncan driving?" Simmons asked.

Jasper felt a flare of annoyance even as he knew it was pointless to feel anything of the sort; Jasper wasn't sure if this was a test of his own temper or of the other man's, but the words were calculated, not an offhand insult.

Westin — the man in the corner, though the name still didn't sound familiar — didn't look up and his even tone of voice didn't change. "Assuming your outlaw has sobered up and doesn't try to bloody my lip as he did your poor man Valdez's, I would not be opposed. I do need to be back to the office as quickly as I can."

Simmons looked over at Randall. The lawman was as surly as everyone said; Jasper didn't know what he was going to decide until he grunted an affirmative at Simmons.

"Looks like you've got yourself a run, Duncan," Simmons said. "And we do appreciate the deal you cut us."

Jasper nodded once and started to leave.

Simmons' voice stopped him before he could reach the door.

"You sure your stage will be up for the ride? Heard you only barely limped back into town yesterday evening," Simmons said. "This run leaves at dawn, and if you can't do that . . ."

Jasper swallowed hard. "It won't be a problem," he said, and left the room.

CHAPTER SIX

Jasper made it out of sight of Randall, Simmons, and any of the other mine men who might have had their eyes on him before running a hand through his shaggy hair and letting out a deep sigh.

He definitely had a problem.

He could get the stage ready. That hadn't been a lie. She had good bones, and the work he and Jack had done that day had already fixed some of the problems. They wanted to leave at dawn? He could have the stage ready at dawn. Might not look pretty, might not last, but he could have those repairs done by the time the sun peeked its head out of bed.

Assuming he had the parts.

The axle still needed work, and Jasper was relatively certain he saw problems with the thoroughbraces, and the wheel . . . He needed a new one. He knew O'Reilly had one, but he'd spent all his goodwill with the man long ago. It all came back to money. He'd spent all of that just the same as he'd spent all his goodwill.

They were still serving drinks when Jasper made it back to the saloon, and though the fiddler had certainly livened up his tune, it sounded like he'd drunk too much to play it right. Charley wasn't anywhere to be seen and Jasper headed toward the stairs, wondering if the poker game was still going on, and if it was, how he'd be able to pull Charley away to ask for a favor.

"You!" a voice called. Jasper didn't stop walking. "Jehu! Stop!"

Each word had gotten closer, and then a hand on his shoulder spun him around.

It was the stocky man from earlier, one of the passengers. He'd kept drinking same as the fiddler, and it didn't look like any of his friends were sober enough to stop him from starting this fight either.

"I don't want to fight —" Jasper started.

The man swung.

Jasper darted to the side. The punch missed and the stocky man almost spun in a circle from the force of it. He ended up facing Jasper again, his color high, the patrons in the saloon shouting out encouragements, though Jasper couldn't tell for whom. Likely they just wanted a fight.

"You almost killed us," the man snarled.

"I didn't!" Jasper flung a hand out to where the Pinkerton had been sitting earlier. "Your Pinkerton friend almost did the killing. He ain't got a lick of sense and neither do you if you don't leave me alone." He turned to leave and then the man grabbed him again.

Jasper shrugged the man's hand off. "You touch me a third time, I'm laying you out, no matter how drunk you are."

"It ain't right," the man said. "You rumbling up and down these hills. You're dangerous, you know. I talked to others and you . . . you . . ." He stepped forward, right in Jasper's face, so close their noses were almost touching.

"Me?" Jasper asked, his voice a low rumble.

"You almost killed my son."

Jasper took a step back.

He remembered now, the stocky man climbing into the coach, a younger man with him. Maybe a boy. Jasper wasn't sure where the cut off between man and boy happened. This one had the makings of a mustache, too wispy to truly be called one. Jasper hadn't given either of them a second thought.

"No one died," Jasper said, his voice

calmer now with effort. "Go back to your friends. Complain all you want. I don't want a fight here." He held the man's gaze for a long moment until he felt the message had sunk in.

He turned around, and the man grabbed his shoulder again.

Jasper had warned him. He turned, just like the man wanted him to, and swung a punch of his own. His connected.

The stocky man crashed to the ground. His friends were on their feet as soon as the punch connected, tripping over themselves trying to get to them. The patrons who'd been cheering on the idea of a fight now seemed to want to participate, springing up as well.

Jasper really hadn't wanted a fight.

Before he could do anything else, the sharp blare of an out-of-tune bugle sounded from the bar. Barman Jack was holding the stage horn that Charley always kept behind the counter.

"I see one more punch, you're all out!" he roared.

Before anyone could realize he'd moved, Jasper went for the stairs. This time he reached them.

The luck that deserted him when he'd walked into the saloon came back when he made it upstairs; the poker game was over, and all the players had cleared out. That wasn't always the case. It wasn't unusual to find someone sleeping off their bad luck on one of the benches in the back of the parlor. Jasper had done it himself on occasion, though usually his bad luck wasn't in relation to gambling.

Charley sat at the poker table alone, shuffling her cards. She looked up at him. "I heard the commotion. Did you leave me a bag of nails downstairs, Jasper?"

"No," he said. "Chaos cleared up pretty quick. Might be a broken chair."

"Maybe a broken nose?"

He shrugged. He didn't think there was, but if so . . . "The other guy came at me."

"Sure," she said. She dealt out a hand of what looked like solitaire, then gestured for him to join her at the table. "I wasn't sure you'd be back."

Did she mean that he'd be back tonight or be back ever? Of all the people in town, she was the one who knew exactly what he wanted with Alec Casey. She'd told him once that she wasn't sure he'd come back from that confrontation. She didn't seem to understand that he didn't much care about coming back.

"I need a favor," he said, sitting across

70

from her.

Charley nodded like she had expected that. "You get that job?"

"I got the job," Jasper said. "What I don't have is a working wheel."

"I saw. That crash did your stage no favors."

"I didn't crash." His voice came out hot and louder than he meant it to, but he bit back an apology.

Charley arched a brow. "I didn't say you did."

"I know what happened out there. I told you, I told O'Reilly, someone was shooting near the road and spooked the horse."

"I believe you. I must say, I'm surprised that Simmons did."

"I ain't some town drunk making things up."

She scooped up the hand she'd dealt, shuffled her deck back together, and slapped the cards down onto the table. "No, but your shoulder's awful cold. And it seems to me you got a chip on it. That ain't a combination set to win you many friends."

Not many, no, but he counted her as one. "One of the passengers told Simmons the truth, and he gave me the job. But I need my stage in good enough shape to run." He swallowed hard. "O'Reilly wants my stage,

71

but I think if I make him a good enough offer, he'll sell me the parts to fix it. And if I get this job done, I'll have money coming in. Good money too." Even if it was only half of what it would have been, thanks to his eagerness.

"You really in this for the money?" Charley asked.

Jasper took a deep breath. He couldn't very well lie; she knew the truth, and lying to someone like that just made you look like a fool. Jasper had very nearly done that himself, rambling on about giving a good offer to O'Reilly and having money coming in. The end of that would have been him begging her for a loan, eagerly tripping over his words like a puppy tripped over its feet. He should have thanked her for interrupting, truly. He could bring himself to ask, if he had to, but to convince? To beg? The idea left a sour feeling in his stomach.

"You know I'm not. Look, you gonna help me or not?"

She swept a hand back along her hair. This late, wisps of hair had flared out from her braid, like curls wanting to escape. "I'm one of the only ones in this town who actually likes you, Jasper."

"That a yes?"

72

"That's a no. This job? It's no good for you."

"That isn't for you to decide," he snapped. All that time he thought she'd listened without pushing, been a sympathetic ear. Sympathetic maybe. But for all that she didn't push, she sure knew how to give him a shove when he least expected it. She opened her mouth to reply, but before she could, he held up a hand. "Forget about it. Forget I asked."

He wasn't sure if she said anything as he stormed out; he slammed the door to the back room loud enough to muffle anything she did say.

He went out the back of the saloon. He wasn't sure if anyone was fighting, but he wasn't in the mood to deal with them even if they weren't.

The barn was empty so late at night. Just him and the horses. His stage still stood where he'd left it, wheel off, axle partially repaired.

He walked toward the mare who'd hurt her leg on the run the day before and she nickered a little as he approached. She'd been brushed down, and she looked shiny and clear-eyed. Someone must have decided she'd heal up alright, though he wasn't sure from the look of that muscle that she'd ever lead a team up and down these mountains again.

He squatted on the ground next to her. Her leg was swollen, and when he ran a hand down it, the swollen part was hot to the touch. She flinched away from his touch and let out a sharp whinny.

"Shhh, girl. It's alright." He rose to his feet and scratched behind the mare's ear a little. She seemed suspicious of him for a moment, as though she too thought he'd somehow caused the injury.

A horse like her, she lived to run. Had the day before broken her dreams like it had broken his? If he couldn't get that stage fixed . . .

"Just the man I wanted to see."

It was O'Reilly's voice, and for the first time, Jasper could honestly say the reverse was true as well. He rubbed the white diamond on the mare's head while she snuffled her forgiveness; then he turned to O'Reilly.

"You came out to look for me?" he asked.

O'Reilly didn't look like he'd done much drinking of that whiskey he had brought earlier. He got red-faced and loud when he drank, and the man across from Jasper looked as collected as O'Reilly ever did.

Jasper knew what that meant. He wasn't surprised. It was O'Reilly's common practice, after all: he bought up stages and hired them back out to the men who'd sold them in the first place. He always waited until a misfortune hit — either a broken axle or a lame horse or a man who was down on his luck — and then he made his offer. They all knew what he was about, but that hadn't stopped men with no options from taking him up on those offers. Jasper had kept to himself, made his own repairs, tried for two years to keep himself out of this man's sights, but O'Reilly was like any predator — when he smelled blood, he tracked down the source and then struck at the weak. He wanted to have his own Overland or Wells, Fargo, Jasper thought. Maybe the name O'Reilly would be just as famous one day.

"It truly is a shame about that horse. She's a good one. Don't know that she'll ever lead a team again," O'Reilly said.

She was a good one. Clever. Jasper had run horses on these routes for years. He knew stage horses like he knew himself, and liked them a great deal more. Even if she didn't lead a team, he hoped she'd still get to run.

"And the stage too. They're both getting on in years, but a mighty shame to see your property take such a beating." O'Reilly paused for a beat, two. "No matter what it was that caused it."

Jasper wanted to snap at that. But though he didn't want to take whatever offer O'Reilly was about to make, Jasper needed him. He swallowed his words and nodded instead. "A real shame," Jasper said, and managed to keep his voice even. "Especially since I just got a new job."

O'Reilly raised his brows. "A new job?"

"That special run Valdez was talking about. First thing."

"First thing? I thought you *had* a run first thing."

Jasper leveled a look at him. "You got me replaced already. Don't think I don't know it." There were other jehus around there, other stages. O'Reilly wouldn't have had to work that hard to replace him.

O'Reilly looked toward the stage, then down at the broken wheel on the ground, and then back to Jasper. "Can you blame me? Think you can get this thing ready to go by first light?"

"Well, I'm gonna need a new wheel, finish fixing the axle, and a team of horses to get us down the mountain. Thought you might be able to help a friend out."

O'Reilly smiled. "Well, son, I'm sure I

have what you're looking for. It's just a matter of finding a price that works for both of us."

"I'll give you half of the fee they're paying me, on top of the price for the wheel. That's gold for nothing but a loan."

O'Reilly's eyes went sharp just before he averted them, turning to walk around the stage, as though he hadn't already catalogued the damage. "Jasper, I must say I'm not feeling confident. It's a dangerous road, and if JD tells it true, then that there's a dangerous man you'll be transporting."

"Life's dangerous, Mr. O'Reilly, but I'll get him where he needs to be. I will be needing that wheel, though."

"I'll tell you what," O'Reilly began. "I'll give you the wheel. I'll even throw in anything else you need to fix your stage and the use of the company's horses. But not for half."

"What do you want?"

"I want the full payment. You finish the run, deliver the man, and you go on running up and down this mountain."

O'Reilly's voice promised a catch. "And if something goes wrong?" Jasper asked.

"Well, then, I think it's only fair that I'm compensated. I'll take your stage. You can keep running it. You'll have to pay me a small rental fee for the stagecoach, of course." He smiled. "Your decision."

Jasper didn't have to think about it. He'd been ready to sell, after all. For this chance? It was worth it. "Done," he said, and held out his hand.

"Now, you won't mind signing a contract to say we agreed, would you?"

Jasper nodded, and when the man went and wrote up the contract, he signed it. He kept telling himself it didn't matter. All that mattered was finding Alec Casey and making him pay. There were many ways this trip could go, but if it went the way he wanted . . . Well, he wouldn't be needing his stage or his horses if Alec Casey showed up for his brother, would he? Because if that happened, by the end of the day one of them would be dead.

The stage was fixed before dawn. O'Reilly had woken a couple of the hostlers to help. They looked like they'd rather use the tools to bludgeon Jasper than help him with the stagecoach, but they got to work. The three of them, with the parts O'Reilly had handed over, got the stage fixed. It didn't look like the grandest transportation, but it would hold together on this trip down the mountain, maybe its last.

After Jasper finished, he sank down onto a hay bale, staring at his handiwork until his eyes were too heavy to stare anymore. He closed them and drifted. His dreams were full of wry laughter and gunshots, the jangling of metal and a voice trying to convince him to let Alec Casey be. He couldn't do that, wouldn't do that, but he couldn't move and then there was only darkness. And then the creak of the barn door jarred him, blessedly, awake.

He heard the footsteps behind him just as he was splashing water on his face. There was near a dozen folks who could be entering this barn near dawn for cause, but he somehow knew it wasn't any of them. If he ignored her, perhaps she'd leave, he thought, but he knew it was a fool's belief even before she spoke.

"You do what you set out to do?" Charley asked.

She didn't mean fix the stage, but that was how he answered. "Told you I didn't need much. New wheel. Fix the axle." He thought about keeping his back to her. Not speaking. But he couldn't very well do that, could he? Wouldn't be very gentlemanly. He splashed some more water on his face and turned around.

She didn't look like she'd slept much

more than him. "I'm glad O'Reilly was so accommodating. What'd he ask for?"

He didn't answer, but she still didn't leave him be. Instead, she walked closer, pulling something from her pocket.

"I thought since you'll be heading out, I'd give you these. You might not be back to claim them." Charley handed him two envelopes creased from travel, but even in their condition, Jasper recognized the handwriting.

Gentle script, ink slightly blurred as though damp had stolen into the mailbag on its way from the Nebraska Territory. Just plain Nebraska now. He kept forgetting that. The letters were addressed to him, like the others had been. He always took care to let his mother know where he was, even if he never read the letters she sent him. Even if he hadn't so much as opened one in near two years.

His grip on the letters went tight, paper crinkling between his fingers. "This some ploy to try to get me to see things your way?"

"I'm not fool enough to believe I can get you to do anything you don't want to do. This is just a mail delivery, Jasper," Charley said, but *he* wasn't fool enough to believe it.

"Then thank you kindly. Didn't know you were *delivering* the mail these days too." He tucked the letters inside his jacket pocket, then started to walk away. "If you'll excuse me, I have to see a man about some horses."

Jasper had halfway worried O'Reilly was going to stick him with a team of swayback, elderly mares or stallions too frantic to rein in. But no, the hostlers brought out a strong team. O'Reilly must have wanted that fee more than he did his stagecoach, Jasper thought. Either that or he didn't want to be any part of the reason Simmons and Randall lost their man.

The mud wagon was already hitched up, trying to get the earliest start to get over the mountains. Jasper saw two of his passengers from the day before climbing up into the back, and he wondered if they'd have a smoother trip than their last one. Not likely. He didn't see the stagecoach O'Reilly had roped in to replace him. Maybe it would leave a little later, give Jasper some time to get the outlaw farther away from town.

He helped the hostlers hitch up all the horses and lead the stage out of the barn. The sun was just barely peeking over the crest of the mountain, and the sky above the town was indigo blue, like it wanted to show off the town's name to all her residents. There weren't many folks out on the streets, which was what Simmons and Randall would want, after all. Keeping everything quiet.

The last thing Jasper did before he left the stables was check over his rifle.

It had been his father's, and it was one of the only things Jasper had brought west with him. It was a Henry repeating rifle from 1860, a sixteen shooter like the kind the Union Army had used to put fear in the Southerners. His father had taught him to shoot it behind their house. He hadn't hit his growth spurt yet, and his father had joked the rifle was almost as tall as he was. Jasper had felt mortally offended by that. He'd hit the targets his father set up; even then, he'd been a fair shot. When he'd picked it up on the day his father died, blood stained the wood of the stock, and he sometimes thought he could still see the shadow of it. In the dim light of the stables, he was almost sure of it. He kept the rifle clean, always made sure she was ready to fire and in good shape, though despite what the Pinkerton had said about the dangers of driving a stage, he'd only had occasion to shoot it twice since coming to California.

He was sure he'd have cause to shoot it today.

For a moment, when he first set the horses to walking, Jasper worried the repairs wouldn't hold. That the axle would crack again or the wheel would fall off, and he'd lose his chance. He could feel his heart pounding, like it wanted to break out of his chest. He'd never been this close before, even if he had no idea where Alec Casey was. Alec was close to his brother, though, and everyone knew they were never too far apart. Alec Casey had sprung his brother from jail a number of times: once in Denver, right after the Casey brothers brought their brand of lawlessness to Colorado; once down south in California, when Slip Casey had been caught lying around drunk after some sort of parade. There had been a time or ten others too, but those had been the two that stuck out when Jasper heard about them. The parade incident had seemed almost funny until the marshal who was telling him the story got to how many people Casey had hurt pulling off the rescue.

The stage moved forward, smooth as she ever was, and Jasper felt his heart ease up its pounding. This was going to work. He'd fixed the stage, he'd gotten the job, and today was the day he'd kill Alec Casey. He could *feel* it.

The mine was dug into the ground on the easternmost edge of town, but Simmons didn't have Jasper meet them there. Instead, he drove westward, the same direction on his route down the mountain, and met them at another wagon, just past the edge of town. Simmons was waiting beside it, in the shadows the wagon cast. Jasper pulled on the reins to stop the horses, then climbed down from the box. Simmons walked over to meet him.

"What's your usual run?" Simmons asked quietly.

Jasper was certain he already knew it, but he answered anyway. "Indigo to Long Barn, then to Sonora, then Knights Ferry."

"Seventy-some-odd miles, then?"

"All together, sure."

Simmons nodded. "You know that route well. Till the day before yesterday we never had problems with your driving." Jasper held his tongue. Simmons continued. "How well you know the roads around it?"

"I know this land," Jasper said. "You don't spend two years running a stage through this forest and up this mountain without knowing the land."

"Deputy Hatchett knows the land too. Grew up round here. Between the two of

84

you, I figure you know the whole mountain." Simmons glanced around as though making sure there was no one around to eavesdrop on their conversation. "There's more than a chance the Casey Gang tries to stop you, you know."

Jasper knew that. He didn't want to say it, though, in case Simmons could hear the truth in his voice: that he *wanted* them to take that chance.

"If you need to divert from your route, then you divert. Understand?" Simmons' voice didn't give much room for disagreement, so Jasper nodded.

Simmons took a step back, then whistled. A fabric flap on the back of the wagon was pulled back, and they shoved their prisoner out of it.

Distantly, Jasper noticed Hatch and Valdez, and the latter's dog too, come out with the prisoner. But it was only the man in the middle Jasper really saw.

Jasper had never seen Slip Casey in the flesh. He'd seen his face on handbills shouting "WANTED" that lawmen seemed to decorate their jails with. He looked much the same in person as he looked on those flyers — a little older, somehow a little duller than even scratches of ink could make him. In the handbills, he always wore a wide-brimmed hat pushed back from his face, but it was gone now; either he had lost it somewhere, or they'd taken it from him. His clothes were blues and blacks, all faded, and he wore woolen fingerless gloves. His hair stuck up on one side like he'd slept on that side, mouse brown, and his skin was red and wind chafed beneath the smudges of dirt and ash he must have collected sleeping in that abandoned cabin, or maybe in whatever makeshift cell Simmons had tossed him into.

Though he was wanted for murder, robbery, and the like, Slip Casey didn't look so fearsome. Never had, if the stories were true. Jasper had heard him called a clown once, though Jasper wouldn't be forgetting that he was a clown who was wanted dead or alive, just like his brother. But more than anything, the man looked ill, like he'd spent the night drinking and regretted it now. His eyes squinted at even the dim light of the morning, and he reached a hand up to wipe across his eyes. The other one followed suit; he was bound with heavy metal cuffs that Jasper was surprised Randall's men even had up here. Slip Casey let his hands drop in front of him again, and his jaw cracked open in a yawn.

His eyes, which had been cloudy and dim,

seemed to finally focus on Jasper and the stagecoach. "You're gonna take me down the mountain in that thing? 'Dead or alive' isn't supposed to mean you gamble with my life, friends."

"We're not your friends," Valdez snapped, and shoved Slip Casey forward.

"I see you took that fat lip far too personally," Slip muttered.

Valdez and Hatch got Slip into the back of the stage, the outlaw muttering the entire time. Valdez clicked his tongue, and his dog jumped in after him. Hatch climbed up into the driver's box, ready with his rifle.

Randall jerked his head, and Jasper took that to mean he should come closer.

"You get him to Sonora," Randall said, "and you get paid. You lose him halfway there, you get nothing, you hear?"

It was Simmons who was doing the paying, and he'd already given Jasper a version of this talk, but Jasper didn't argue.

"I'll get him where he needs to be," Jasper said.

The numbers man was the last to come out, his ledger tucked up under his arm and a small leather case in his other hand. He'd been sitting in the front of the wagon, and he still looked terribly out of place up in this country. Sam Westin might have been the one passenger to speak for Jasper about their first run, but Jasper didn't miss the look on his face when he caught sight of the stage. Even compared to two days before, the stage looked rough, and Westin hadn't liked the look of it *then.* He looked like he was regretting his words. But he composed himself quickly.

"Where's your Pinkerton friend?" Jasper asked him.

"He decided he'd rather wait for the next available transportation," Westin said.

Jasper wondered if he'd liked to have done the same. Westin nodded briefly to Simmons before heading for the stage and disappearing within.

"Looks like all aboard," Simmons said dryly. "See you when you get back, Duncan."

Jasper gave him a nod, then swung himself up into his seat. The morning chill was leaving the air already. The breeze was light and sweet in his lungs. It was a good day for going down the mountain.

It was a good day to get revenge.

CHAPTER SEVEN

The posse found Alec Casey in a saloon.

Casey and his gang had been holed up there since the night before, spending their pilfered money on booze and painted ladies. The sheriff and Jasper's father both thought that now was as fine a time as any to go in and bring the Casey Gang out.

The sheriff had brought seven men in total. Jasper was told to watch the front, and another deputy was posted round back, which was where the sheriff thought it more likely they'd run. Closer to the stables, he'd said after Jasper's father had done a brief reconnaissance. That left five to go inside.

Jasper was stationed behind a wagon, which gave him cover but a good view of the front door. "Stop anyone who comes out," the sheriff had said. Jasper's stomach felt a little queasy at the idea of killing someone, but he set his jaw and nodded. He could do it. He knew he could.

They'd barely gone in the front door when things started to go wrong.

Jasper heard the angry crack of gunfire and glass shattering. A cry of pain came from inside, and he was almost certain it was his father. Jasper was supposed to stay put; the sheriff had given strict instructions not to leave his position, but he heard the commotion and he had to check. In any case, he was still able to see the door. He wanted to get closer, after all, not farther away.

There were three steps up to the porch that wrapped around the saloon. They creaked, but no way could anyone hear it with the ruckus inside. Another clap of thunder from a rifle came while Jasper was on the top step and he ducked down a little. He'd seen a bullet splinter thin pieces of wood, and realized this saloon was about as sturdy as the little coop they'd made for their chickens. There was glass in the front window, though, a little milky, maybe, but Jasper got up close and peeked inside.

Four men were standing off against the sheriff's posse of five. His father stood next to the sheriff, his rifle trained on the man at the front of the group of outlaws.

That must be Alec Casey.

He looked younger than he did on the wanted bill Jasper had seen that morning. Not much older than Jasper even. His hair was black as a crow's wing. They must have ridden for two days to get here from that train they robbed, but his skin was clean, clear, and pale as though he'd never seen high noon at the height of summer or ridden down dusty roads. Five guns were trained on him, and he didn't even look nervous.

Jasper didn't see what happened next. He had been staring at Alec Casey when another shot rang out, and one of the deputies fell. Jasper ducked down below the windowsill and crept a little closer to the door. He wasn't supposed to go in. But inside folks were still shooting and maybe —

Before he could get any closer, the door burst open and Alec Casey stood above him.

Jasper fell back onto his bottom and started to scuttle away. He'd been closer to the edge of the porch than he thought; the hand he put down to catch himself met only thin air and he toppled off the landing and onto the dusty ground below.

Jasper went for his gun as soon as he landed. He got his hand on the butt of the revolver, but he'd landed awkwardly and it took him a moment to get a good grip. By then Alec Casey had dropped down beside him, and he already had his own revolver out.

The man was smiling. "Why, if it isn't the littlest deputy," he drawled, and leveled his gun at Jasper's chest.

Jasper wondered if it would have made a difference if he'd been standing in position at the bottom of the stairs. Would he have gotten to his revolver in time, called out some slick warning that belonged in a dime novel about lawless San Francisco, and then blown Alec Casey right back into that saloon? Maybe, maybe not.

When the shot rang out, Jasper flinched. But no pain came. Instead, Alec Casey dropped to his knees, revolver tumbling from his hand and the other coming up to clutch his bloody shoulder.

Both Jasper and Alec turned their heads toward the door of the saloon.

"You shot me," Alec said to Jasper's father. His voice held a curious note of laughter. "You're gonna regret that."

Ben Duncan walked down the saloon steps, reached down a hand to Jasper, and hauled him to his feet. "Son," he said, clapping a hand to Jasper's arm, then turning his eyes back to Alec Casey. His eyes had been warm when they landed on Jasper, but the look he gave Alec Casey was anything but. "I think you're wrong, Mr. Casey."

Alec Casey only laughed.

Chapter Eight

"You look like a storm's raging up there."

Jasper turned to Hatch to see him tapping his forehead. "Something have you worried?" Hatch asked.

Jasper shook his head, but Hatch kept watching him. "Casey Gang struck a few days ago," he said, so he'd have something to say. "Why do you think our prisoner wasn't with them?"

Hatch shrugged. "Off on a bender. He was full as a tick when Valdez pulled him out of that cabin. Alec Casey probably don't want the family jester around when he's doing jobs anyway."

Jasper let the exchange die after that. He wasn't too interested in talking anyway; he'd rather ruminate for his own private reasons about what the Casey Gang had been doing a few days ago.

Modesto wasn't far from Sonora.

Jasper wondered if by the time they

reached Sonora, Alec Casey would know they had his brother. Eventually he'd know, and eventually he'd come for him. And Jasper wasn't going to leave Slip Casey's side until that happened, no matter what he had to do to stay there.

They hadn't been traveling long when they started to come up on the place where Jasper had nearly lost his stage two days before. He could see the tracks on the dirt road where the coach had nearly spilled. He could see something else too — marks in the road that he couldn't quite place.

And from the side of the road, a silvery glint of metal.

"What are you doing?" Hatch demanded when he started to slow down. "Answer me, Duncan, or this stagecoach will keep moving without you on it."

Jasper pointed to the road ahead of them. "The other day, that's where my stage got damaged."

"So?" Hatch demanded. But he didn't threaten to steal his stage again when Jasper came to a stop.

Behind him, he could hear Valdez ask what was going on and Hatch answer in a way that was less than flattering toward Jasper. He ignored it and walked forward.

Up the road a ways, Jasper could see

where they'd crashed into the rocks, the splinters of wood the spokes had left behind. He shouldn't still be so angry about that. What did the damage matter when he'd gotten the chance he wanted?

His eyes flickered around the road, looking for that glint of metal he'd seen.

It could have been anything. It could have been, but he knew somehow that it wasn't.

He found the bullet at the edge of the road. Newly fired, clearly. Had this been the bullet that spooked the horse? He remembered thinking the horse had reacted as though someone had fired at her, not just near her.

Maybe someone had.

He scanned the ridge above as though he was expecting to see someone else ready to shoot too near the road, set another team of horses into a panic. But no one was there.

Jasper walked back toward the stage, turning the bullet over in his hand. It didn't mean anything. A shot gone wild? Happened all the time.

"I'll tell you what, though," Hatch called from up in the box as though he'd been saying something before that. His feet were propped up; he looked right comfortable. "Crash or not, you got that damage fixed damn quick. Faster than the damage to that

Pinkerton's eye." He laughed.

Suddenly the stagecoach gave a jolt, pitching Hatch to the side. Jasper stepped forward to reach for the horses' rig, in case they were about to bolt, but no, the motion hadn't come from the horse.

It had come from the coach itself.

The left-side door opened with a shriek, and Slip Casey came flying out.

The jump he made looked awkward; Jasper wasn't sure how the man had been able to land on his feet. But he had, and as soon as they touched down, he was running.

Valdez shouted something from inside the coach, but Jasper couldn't hear what he was saying. He was already running.

Slip made it off the road quickly. Jasper was a few feet behind him, but Slip could run fast. It was those long legs. He pounded down the hill, half tripping the whole way, maybe off-balance because of the cuffs still around his wrists.

Jasper had shorter legs, but he was almost keeping up. There was a stream at the bottom of this hill and, beyond that, a patch of forest. *If Slip makes it in there, does he hope to hide out?* Jasper wondered. *Live off the land until he can find his brother?*

Slip started pulling ahead. He did seem to

be heading for the woods, and fast. Was he going to try to jump the stream?

Even if that was his plan, he didn't make it. A yard from the water, he tripped and went flying. He landed on his belly, hands flying out to catch himself; then he started to holler like he was face-to-face with the Devil himself.

Before Jasper could make it to Slip or Slip could climb back to his feet, a tan-and-brown blur came bolting past Jasper and landed on top of Slip's back. The man started yelling again and thrashing, but the brown thing stayed on him.

It was Valdez's dog.

She must have come running down the hill after Casey, same as Jasper had done. She'd pinned him before Jasper could get his hands on the man, but not before he'd fallen without any aid at all.

Well, maybe a little aid, Jasper thought when he got closer.

He saw that Slip hadn't tripped on nothing. His foot had landed on a skeleton.

That was what made him holler — Slip Casey had come face-to-face with a bear's skull. He was still trying to push himself away from it, but the dog was pinning him to the ground. *Stronger than she looks,* Jasper thought.

He didn't know how to command the dog. What had Valdez done when he told her to do something? Jasper couldn't remember. "Dog," he said sternly. "Move."

The dog looked up at him, brown eyes quizzical.

"Move," he repeated again, his voice still sharp. The dog whined a little. "Come on, girl," he said, and pointed to the space beside him.

He hadn't known a dog could look so reluctant, but she did. She stepped off of Slip's back and strode toward Jasper, her tail between her legs. Had she expected praise? Probably so after catching an outlaw. But Jasper didn't know much about dogs or praise or anything of the sort, so all he did was flip Casey over.

Up close, in the light of the early after-noon, Jasper had figured he'd see more of a resemblance between Slip and Alec Casey. But figuring it wasn't the same as *seeing* it. Those eyes were the same shape and color as the ones that had looked down so calmly and coldly when Alec almost shot him. The mouth was the same, though Slip Casey's was flat. His chest heaved, though Jasper didn't know if that was from the exertion or from the fear.

"I am very glad," Slip Casey gasped, "that

98

we didn't run into that thing when it was still alive."

Jasper looked down at the skull. It was yellowed from age and its teeth were chipped, but they were still larger than anything Jasper would have wanted to see grinning at him, waiting for a meal. Slip was still kicking his leg free. It looked like one of his feet had gone right between two ribs, sending Slip sprawling. *What terrible luck,* Jasper thought, *and right when he was so close to making it into that forest.*

"An angry dog can be just as bad," he said, though he didn't really believe it. Valdez's dog, despite chasing Slip down, didn't really seem like a vicious beast. "Did you really think you could outrun her? And all of us?"

"I ain't much for getting captured," Slip said. "I'd much rather get away."

Jasper wrenched him to his feet. "And I'd much rather you stay captured."

"We'll have to agree to disagree on that, then, brother whip. Seeing that skeleton has certainly made me even more dismayed by the thought of my own mortality."

Jasper shoved Slip forward. "Move."

They trudged up the hill together, Valdez's dog at their side. She gave a bark when they were halfway back, and Jasper saw Valdez and Hatch looking down at them.

"Didn't feel like giving me a hand?" he called up at them.

"You seem to have it under control!" Hatch called back.

Jasper truly did not like the man.

"Good girl," Valdez said, scratching the dog behind the ears when they made it back to the road.

Jasper rolled his eyes and pushed Slip Casey up against the stagecoach, then opened the door.

Westin looked up from his papers, seemingly quite unconcerned about the attempted escape. "Oh," he said, and pulled his briefcase back over beside him. "He was sitting over there." He gestured to the place across from him as though Jasper were highly concerned with the prisoner having the right seat.

Slip shook off Jasper's hand when he tried to shove him into the coach. "I'm no lady needing a hand. I can climb in on my own."

"And out too clearly," Westin said, sending a wry look over his glasses at Slip.

"I had to try," he said with a half-apologetic shrug.

Jasper slammed the door.

Valdez climbed back into the coach after that, but Hatch beckoned Jasper forward.

"Now, friend," he said. There was that word again. Jasper really didn't like Hatch saying they were friends when they weren't. "I can understand dwelling on what happened before. I can't say I blame you, what with the trouble that crash nearly caused. But I am telling you true — you pull something like this again, and I will throw you in irons like Slip Casey and you will be walking back to Indigo. You hear me?"

This threat didn't seem as idle as the last one had been, and Jasper understood why. After all, he wanted to get Slip Casey where they were going as much as anyone. More even.

Jasper nodded. "I hear you. Won't happen again."

"Good," Hatch said seriously. "Now let's get on the road. Alright?"

Jasper swung back up into the driver's box. Once Hatch was settled beside him, he took up the lines and gave the horses a gid-dyup. They headed off again.

It wasn't long before Hatch was talking again, easy as you please. "What'd you have to promise O'Reilly to get your stage fixed so quick?"

"I don't know what you're talking about."

Hatch snorted. "If that's how you want to play it."

"Did you volunteer to be my conductor or did you lose a bet with Valdez?" Jasper asked.

Hatch laughed again. "JD's none too pleased you went right to Randall. If Charley's parlor ain't sacred, what is?"

Jasper thought that might have been the case. He'd have to live with Valdez's displeasure. "I thought you'd know by now that the West is full of outlaws."

"Sure enough," Hatch said. "Never thought we'd get one of the Casey Gang up in Indigo."

Jasper hadn't thought so either. For two years, he'd thought Knights Ferry might attract them or Sonora. Trade flowed through those cities, along with gold and silver and payroll dollars. Prime places for a thief to strike. Sure enough, they'd struck here and there in those parts, but Jasper had never been able to track them down. The best lead he'd gotten had actually been news of that payroll grab north of Modesto. But Slip Casey had been hiding out in that old cabin. Why *was* Slip Casey hiding out up near Indigo? Jasper supposed Hatch was right and the man had just been on a bender, but now that he had asked the question, he found he wanted to know the answer. He told himself it didn't matter. The only thing that mattered was whether or not Slip's brother had heard something of his capture and knew where to come looking for him.

The road down to Long Barn was the longest stretch between stations, and Jasper tried to keep the horses at a slow, steady pace. It wasn't easy ground, but the team handled it well, used to the pace and the land. Jasper had driven this road near a hundred times. It shouldn't have made him this uneasy, but he couldn't stop looking for someone coming for them.

They'd been on the road for a couple of hours when Jasper spotted the rider.

He was off in the distance, wearing muted greens and browns, and though he was on horseback, he wasn't riding at all. He seemed to be watching them.

Jasper's brow furrowed and his hackles went up. There could have been any number of reasons why a man would be out there, but there was something about his stillness that made the back of Jasper's neck prickle.

"You see the man over there?" he asked Hatch, nudging the deputy and gesturing into the distance.

Hatch followed his gaze. "I do. Hold steady now," he said, then stood right up in the driver's box, waving one arm while clutching the roof of the stage with the other. "Heyo, out there!" he called in what must have been his loudest voice. The man put his heels to his horse's side, and they turned and trotted away until they were out of sight.

"Sit down," Jasper hissed.

Hatch did, laughing at whatever expression Jasper wore. "Whoever that man is, now he knows we know he's there. He's not up to no good, well, then, I was just friendly."

Jasper wasn't sure how that had been friendly.

Even after the man faded into the distance, he stayed kicking around Jasper's thoughts. Was he the one who had taken a shot at the road the other day? Just a hunter spending too much time near the road? A rancher trying to bring down a cougar going for goats and nearly shooting up Jasper's team? Was it that simple? But how had the shot gotten that close by accident? Not that Jasper could think of a reason anyone would want to take out his stage.

Well. Not that time anyway. This one? Another story.

The sun was bright and the horses tiring by the time they reached the swing station at Long Barn. The town wasn't much longer than a barn, though it was a mite bigger than Indigo. The road was empty, though. Usually, Jasper saw at least a few people as he approached. As they got closer, Jasper passed the stage horn to Hatch.

"Blow this loud as you can."

"Why?" Hatch asked, staring at the bugle like he'd never seen one.

"To let them know we're coming."

"Let everyone around know we're coming, you mean."

"They don't know we're coming, we're stuck here for longer," Jasper said. "Blow."

Hatch blew, his face turning all red. The sound that came out was pitiful, but better on the second try.

Usually, the hostlers spilled out of the barn, hustling over to the incoming stage, bringing out a fresh relay team to hitch up. But this time, no one had come out of the stables by the time Jasper arrived right outside it.

First the person watching them on the road, then this? He felt his skin prickle. He wasn't sure if it was unease or excitement.

"They always this late getting out?" Hatch asked beside him. Jasper looked over. Hatch's grip shifted on his shotgun.

"No, they are not," Jasper said. He put his hand out for the stage horn, and Hatch passed it to him. Jasper blew a few notes, and Hatch beside him hissed a complaint. But if someone had laid an ambush here, they already knew they'd ridden on up. No use in waiting.

Jasper slowed the horses until they came to a stop in front of the boxy stable. The swing station was half the size of O'Reilly's home station; this wasn't a place people spent the night, even if the town itself was larger than Indigo. Stages just passed through here on their way to Sonora or up the mountains. There was a mine or two nearby, quartz and gravel, Jasper thought, but he hadn't paid much attention to the mining around here, just the outlaws.

He reached for his rifle, but before he could get his hands on it, one of the stable boys stuck his bleary-eyed head out the stable door, waving a hand and then disappearing back inside the barn. The feeling that flickered through Jasper almost felt like disappointment.

"From the looks of it, we caught the hostlers napping," Jasper said.

"You don't sound too happy about that."

"We're on a schedule," he said even though he knew that wasn't what Hatch was implying.

Jasper dropped down from the box. He could hear muffled words coming from inside the coach, from a voice he didn't recognize. The door opened and then the words weren't as muffled anymore.

"— even prisoners should be given that comfort, Deputy," Slip Casey said, and dropped out of the coach. His legs almost buckled as he landed.

Valdez's dog hopped out next, growling at Slip as he staggered back a step. "Easy, easy, Deputy Dog! I ain't trying to run again." He held up his hands. The dog did not stop growling. "Dogs usually like me," the outlaw muttered.

Valdez was next out. "Tabitha has better taste than that." He pointed across the road, where nothing more than a couple of trees stood. "Walk."

"I can't even use the outhouse? Or get some grub?" He looked over at Jasper after he said that. "Not that I'd keep that down, all that rocking and rolling on the road. Is this thing always so rough on your passengers, or did you cook it up something special for me?"

Now Slip was smiling, his lips quirking up in a mocking grin that almost looked like his brother's, though it wasn't as chilly a smile. Jasper felt his stomach turn. He hadn't been ready to see that smile again, for all that it had been six years. He didn't think he could keep anything down either.

"Nothing but the best for you, Mr. Casey," Hatch replied when Jasper didn't answer.

Valdez pushed Slip's shoulder. "Walk," he repeated. This time Slip listened.

"Don't know why Alec Casey would want to get his brother back if he's in this form all the time," Hatch said under his breath.

Jasper wondered that as well, but there was no question that he would want to get him back. This hadn't been the first time Slip Casey had been captured, and he'd never made it to the hangman's noose.

Westin was the last to slide out of the stage and walked to join Jasper and Hatch on clearly unsteady legs.

"You alright?" Hatch asked.

"I don't think I'll ever get used to travel by stagecoach, Deputy Hatchett," Westin said, then turned to Jasper. "I hear these stations usually have somewhere for ablutions?"

Jasper nodded and jerked his head toward the station. "There's a water pump out back." He hoped Westin would feel better once he got the dust off his face.

Slip had stopped complaining by the time they came back, at least. As Valdez opened the door, one of the hostlers finally jogged out to meet them, giving a side-eye at the shackled man beside the stagecoach. Slip gave him a jaunty double-handed salute, then clambered into the coach awkwardly, the dog at his heels.

"Your passengers want coffee?" the boy offered, craning his neck to see into the stage until Valdez shut the door behind himself. "Might have some biscuits too."

Jasper shook his head. He couldn't see Westin drinking down the black sludge Long Barn always had to offer, and Jasper himself wouldn't touch the biscuits.

"I'll take some coffee." Hatch climbed down from the box and slapped his hand against the side of the stage. "Valdez, you keep an eye on that . . . passenger now."

Jasper didn't hear Valdez's reply. He took a few steps from the stage, stretching his arms out, while Hatch headed toward the small building next to the stables that served as a cookhouse for the travelers.

Usually, the hostlers were quick about changing out the teams, but all this one had done was offer coffee and biscuits, and he didn't even run off to get it for them. "Mr. Duncan," he said, noticing Jasper's impatience.

"Shouldn't you be changing out those horses instead of talking to me?"

"Not in a hurry to change out the horses today," the boy said.

Jasper didn't care for his attitude. "*You* may not be in a hurry, kid, but we have somewhere to be."

"There's been a problem on the road up ahead. Can't get through."

Something uneasy swam in Jasper's gut at that. "What sort of problem?"

"A tree fell last night, straight across the road. One of the big ones. We're the only two here; rest of the men in town are out there trying to clear the road. Sounds like it might be a while."

Jasper thought back to the night before. He'd barely slept, working hard with a pair of sleepy stable boys at his side. The wind had barely whistled outside. "You have a storm last night?" he asked even though he knew the answer.

"No storm. Sometimes trees are just like people, I expect. Fall over and die."

Jasper didn't think it was as simple as that. But he nodded along with the boy as he continued on about how big the fallen tree was — or how small really, compared to some of the towering trees that grew up on this mountain — and waited until the stable boy ran quiet before saying, "Well, do me a favor and go ahead and hook up a new team, will you? Want to make sure we're ready." For good measure, he pulled a coin from his pocket and flipped it to the boy without even checking what sort of coin he'd given him.

"Thanks, Mr. Duncan," the boy said, and ran to the other hostler, rushing him to work.

Jasper scanned the horizon, looking for the signs of someone following them. Someone watching them. But he didn't see anything else suspicious, just the road leading east up toward Indigo and the rocks and trees they'd passed by. Even when he didn't see anyone, a feeling still prickled the back of his neck. He'd heard tales of bands of natives who could hide in the brush and you'd never see them coming. Jasper didn't think outlaws would be so good at fading into the background, even a band of outlaws as canny as the Casey Gang. Nevertheless, someone was out there. Two problems on this route in as many trips? That didn't seem like a coincidence.

But no outlaws would have had reason to try to run him off the road two days before, and if someone was going to try now, well, that was what he wanted, wasn't it?

Jasper looked back toward the stables, where the boys were leading the team that had brought them down this stage of the route. Hatch was on his way over, his amble quickened into a purposeful stride. Westin walked behind him, surer on his feet now, his face clean but grave.

"Valdez!" Hatch called when he was a couple of steps from the stage. "Set Tabitha to guard the man and get out here."

Jasper wasn't sure what sort of guard Tabitha would make, but Valdez slipped down from the stagecoach and joined the three of them.

"You hear about that tree?" Hatch asked Jasper, and continued speaking before Jasper could answer. "Blockage on the road ahead. They're clearing it, but the woman inside says we're stuck here for the next few hours. Maybe longer."

Valdez set his eyes to scanning the horizon just as Jasper had. "Think that's on purpose?"

Hatch shrugged his shoulders. "Ain't certain. The townsfolk seem to think it was an accident."

If they stayed here, would the Casey Gang come in force for Slip? Jasper thought of that day in the Nebraska Territory, a day he couldn't remember from end to end, and tried not to shiver. How many men did Casey have, and how many would he risk to take back his brother? Not that it would be a risk. No one would hole up in the swing station ready to die to keep Slip Casey from his brother's clutches. No one, maybe, but him, and he *wanted* them to come.

"We keep standing right here, waiting, they could shoot us like fish in a barrel," Valdez said. "We should at least get inside."

The thing was, it seemed too quick for Alec Casey to have found his brother already. Jasper hadn't expected anyone to come for Slip until they were near Sonora. Maybe the tree really was an accident, fallen, not felled, not a plan put into motion.

But then Hatch started to speak, and Jasper realized he'd been right to begin with.

"There might be another option. When I told the lovely lady inside who served me that concoction — which I will not call coffee, friends — that we were in a hurry to get ourselves to Sonora, she said there was another road that could get us around the fallen tree."

Valdez looked skeptical. "Another road?"

Another road. *That* was the trap. Jasper knew it like he knew the sky was blue.

Hatch went on to explain — there'd been some sort of find in the forest to the south, and the mine had done some work out there. He talked like he remembered it personally, which Jasper could believe; before Hatch had been a deputy, he'd worked for Simmons, and Simmons had been one of the mine's men out here from the beginning.

But it wasn't like outlaws were known to use the main roads. Maybe Alec Casey moved his people along these forgotten, half-made trails, and that was how he hit hard and fast and disappeared with piles of gold. How far away had he been just a week earlier? North of Modesto, the Pinkerton had said two days ago. Enough time to get here, surely, though how Alec Casey had found out about his brother's capture and made it here already was something of a mystery.

"Way she talks, it wouldn't be more than five or so miles before we'd join back up with the main road," Hatch finished.

"Well, then, let's get moving," Jasper said. "I'll rustle up the hostlers, tell them to stop taking their sweet time."

"Hold up," Valdez said, stopping Jasper from heading toward the stable with a hand on his shoulder. "Seems to me we need to make a decision first."

"What's there to decide?" Jasper asked.

"If we take that detour."

"You want to wait here while the road gets cleared?" Jasper asked. "I thought we were meant to *hurry*?"

"Who knows how long it'll be?" Valdez said. "We could ride out, offer a hand."

"You think *we* can clear it?" Jasper asked. If the folks here at Long Barn hadn't cleared the road yet, how could Valdez expect the five of them to do it, even if Slip Casey's hands weren't bound and Westin could lift his fair share?

"You got an ax in the boot?" Hatch asked, jerking his head back toward the stagecoach. Jasper did have an ax in the boot; he'd kept one with him for the better part of a year, along with a coil of rope. But Hatch hadn't asked the question seriously. He continued before waiting for an answer. "You really think it's a good idea to take this other road?"

"You're the one who brought it up," Jasper replied.

Hatch shrugged. "I was just passing word along."

"We don't want to be waiting around with these folks while the road gets cleared," he said.

"How long could it be? Just a tree in the road."

Jasper arched his brows, then turned his

115

head toward the forest behind them, where trees rose up halfway to the sky, it looked like.

"I hardly think a tree like *that* has stood for a hundred years only to fall down in the middle of the night without even a storm brewing," Hatch said.

Jasper'd had the same thought, and he could see the idea form on Valdez's face, his frown more pronounced as he realized that the fallen tree might not have been an act of God. Jasper opened his mouth, though he didn't know what he was going to say, something to take the edge off of his suspicion. But before he could, the stage door gave a shriek.

Then Slip Casey fell out of the stage.

When he hit the ground, a cloud of dust rose up all around him. Before he could move, Valdez's mutt had also leaped out of the stage, landing much more gracefully than Slip himself. Her teeth were bared and a growl was rumbling deep in her chest. As adoringly as she usually looked at her master, she looked now like she was ready to rip Slip's throat out with her sharp canines.

"Call off the dog!" Slip yelped, holding his hands up.

Valdez made some click-clacking sound

with his tongue, and the dog stopped growling, settling back on her haunches but keeping her eyes focused on Slip.

"If you were trying to escape again, why not try the other door? Not the one so close to us," Hatch asked, and Valdez cast a withering look at him as though he would thank Hatch not to give their prisoner any ideas.

"I wasn't going for an escape, honest! I just thought if we were deciding our route, well, then I might try to lend my input."

"Why in the world would we want that?" Westin asked. He looked genuinely perplexed at the idea.

"It's my hanging we'll be late for. I should have some say."

"Back inside," Valdez ordered. When Slip took his time climbing to his feet, Valdez marched over and jerked him the rest of the way up, then shoved him toward the door.

"Can I at least get something to eat?" Slip called as he clambered back into the coach. Valdez didn't reply, instead ordering the dog back inside and shutting the door.

"Troublesome lout," Valdez muttered.

"I think I'm starting to like him," Hatch said.

"You would." Whether because of Hatch or Slip Casey himself, the cloud of suspicion had blown off Valdez's face.

"Are we diverting or not?" Jasper asked.

"There any particular reason you're hankering to take this other way around?" Hatch asked.

Jasper looked up at him. "Say what you want to say, Hatch."

"Just saying you gave in to this diversion real quick. Could it be you don't mind so much if we walk right into a trap?"

Hatch was smarter than he looked, Jasper thought sourly.

Valdez's bushy brows rose. "What do you mean by that?"

"Jasper here has good reason to want a run-in with Alec Casey."

"That true?" Valdez asked. His face looked stormy again, this time pointed in Jasper's direction.

Jasper wondered just who had told Hatch about his history with Casey. Not Charley. But who else knew? "None of this is any of your business. I got hired to do a job. I'm doing it."

Hatch blew out a snort. "Yes, because we all know how good you are at your job."

Jasper took a step forward and didn't realize his fist was balled up tight until Valdez stepped between them. "Don't you go throwing any punches," he said. "I don't want to have to lay out our driver."

Jasper gave a sharp nod and stepped back. "It doesn't matter what reasons I have. *Simmons* gave me orders — don't delay, not for nothing. So we divert."

Westin spoke up, his voice quiet but not inviting argument. "I would also like to get back as soon as I can."

Valdez looked between Hatch and Jasper. "If Simmons said not to delay . . ." He trailed off, but his point was made. The two of them might work for Randall, but everyone knew Simmons was the one in charge in Indigo.

Hatched huffed. "Fine. Looks like I'm outvoted."

Slip Casey poked his head out of the stage window. "Do I get a vote?"

On that, their answer was unanimous. "No."

Chapter Nine

Westin had complained of the rough ride on their way up the mountain, but the way down? It might kill him. Jasper himself had spent the better part of five years on a stagecoach or on the back of a horse, and even he thought this road had something extra to jolt a man out of any comfort. Hatch had mentioned the road was unfinished, but as far as Jasper could tell, this road had barely been started. Whatever mine they'd been looking to start down this way, clearly the idea had sunk faster than they could sink a shaft; wagons with heavy equipment would have had a harder time traversing this road than Jasper's own stage did.

It hadn't taken long to get back on the road. The hostlers had finally gotten the relay team hitched up, and then Jasper and the others had backtracked a mile or so to find this road. Jasper had looked, but there hadn't been any indication that anyone had traveled down it recently. It meandered south a ways before turning southwest, like it was running parallel to the road they should have been on.

At least the natural incline of the land wasn't steep or harsh. The road followed a mostly flat, somewhat winding path, with a small slope down to their left and a steeper incline up on the right. Jasper kept his eyes sweeping the road ahead of them, but all he could see were trees and scrub and stones, and all he could hear was the crunching of the rocky path beneath the wheels of the stage, and the occasional complaint from Slip Casey. Those complaints were usually punctuated by sharp, warning barks from Valdez's dog. Jasper didn't much care for dogs, but he could see why Valdez kept her around if she could make a man like Slip Casey shut his trap.

Hatch and Valdez had switched positions when they'd started off on this diversion. A good thing, in Jasper's mind; he nearly *had* thrown that punch Valdez had accused him of thinking about, even if he hadn't realized he was winding it up. Valdez was as quiet as Hatch was chatty. Silence was fine by Jasper, especially on a route that had his hackles up as much as this one did.

So naturally Valdez chose this moment to break that silence. "You really wanting to run us right into a trap?"

"I said I'd get Slip Casey down to Sonora, and that's what I'm aiming to do."

"That doesn't answer my question."

Jasper was tired of the strange looks he got when he didn't sit at the poker table, tired of the pity in Charley's face when one of his mother's letters came through, tired of people like O'Reilly and Hatch making pronouncements like they knew him. "I ain't trying to get no one killed."

"Running us all right into a trap would get someone killed."

Jasper felt his jaw clench without his permission. "You think you can't take care of yourself if we do run into trouble?"

Valdez kept those steady, dark eyes on him for a long moment, then twisted to the side and thumped on the top of the coach. "Keep awake in there! And keep your eyes up!"

Two sets of loud grumbles sounded from inside: Hatch first, then Slip, then Hatch again, telling their prisoner to keep his mouth shut. There was little chance of that, wasn't there?

The diversion was supposed to be no more than five miles long, and by Jasper's reckoning, they'd reached about the halfway point when the road swung north again, turning around a rocky outcropping about twenty feet high. He could see the road in the distance starting to move uphill, back to join the road he normally took down to Sonora. Jasper had seen the overgrown remains of tracks that headed south, into the seemingly endless stretch of forest, but nothing that would have allowed his stage through with ease, and who knew where they led?

For all he'd been watchful the whole ride down this road, the glint of metal from the outcropping above them took Jasper by surprise.

He nudged Valdez, tried not to look up too obviously. "There's someone up there."

Valdez's shoulder jerked, but he didn't look up either. "Up on the cliff."

So he'd seen it too. "Round that corner is a blind spot. Could be someone waiting there too."

"How good were those repairs you made?"

He wasn't sure about a lot of things, but he was sure about his stage. "Good enough to hold."

Valdez turned to the side again, thumped again on the body of the coach, once, twice, but didn't say anything. "You think we can put on some speed, gallop through?"

"We take this road at a gallop, it could kill us."

"If we don't —"

Jasper would never know what Valdez thought might happen if they didn't take the road at a gallop, because the bang of a rifle cut off whatever he was about to say.

The shot hit the body of the stagecoach and Jasper could feel the stage jolt a little at the impact. They might have been riding right into the trap around that blind corner, but there wasn't much of a choice anymore. He snapped the reins, urging the horses into a gallop.

The team lurched forward, faster, and beside him, Jasper heard Valdez mutter something under his breath in Spanish. The man's legs were shoved down against the floor of the box to keep himself steady and his hands were white knuckled on the rail to his left and the seat to his right.

"You gonna use that shotgun?" Jasper asked, almost shouting over the sound of the crunching earth beneath them, the sound of the horses, and, cracking out again from above, another gunshot.

Valdez steadied himself and brought the shotgun up.

The blast was too loud so near Jasper's head, but he kept his eyes on the road. The bend was coming fast. Taking a turn so sharp with a team of horses wasn't easy at this speed. He'd nearly tipped two days ago doing the same. He pulled on the reins of the leaders first, turning them early slowly, then guided the wheelers to the right. He worried he'd been a beat too late about it, but they made the corner safely.

There were no outlaws waiting there to ambush them, but then, there didn't need to be.

Instead, there was a pile of rocks blasted from the outcropping above.

Valdez let out a shout, but Jasper did his level best to ignore him, instead yanking the reins of the leaders to try to take them around the rocks smoothly. This time he wasn't so lucky with the wheelers, though, and he felt the stagecoach give a lurch as the wheels on the right side rode up against the fallen stones. For a moment, he thought it would tip, wondered if Valdez would survive the crash — he was in the worse seat for it. *Running us all right into a trap would get someone killed,* he'd said. But Jasper remembered what had happened two days before and pulled the reins to the right, like he had then, and with another lurch, the coach settled back onto the correct path.

Right as he felt a small smile tug at the

corner of his lips, another shot cracked through the air. This one wasn't from above.

It was from behind.

"Valdez!" he hollered.

At near the same time, Valdez yelled, "Hatch!"

Jasper was too busy driving the stage to get a good bead on what was going on. Valdez kept shooting at the man above them, and Jasper was fairly certain Hatch was shooting at the ones behind. But Jasper didn't have to be checking behind them to know that the men behind must have been catching up. Riders on horses could outrun a stage. They could flank it and take them out with ease.

Jasper pushed the horses harder.

This road was narrow, at least, and sloped on both sides; it wouldn't allow for easy flanking. Jasper wished he had a hand free to get a grip on his rifle, but all he could do was keep the horses steady, hope that Valdez and Hatch had decent enough aim.

He heard Hatch let out a whoop that he hoped meant the other man had gotten one of them, and dared to glance at his left, where Valdez was reloading.

"Three behind us!" he shouted to Jasper like he knew Jasper would want to know.

"Two now! Hatch just got one. And one above!"

"Three against three!" Jasper shouted back. "Think Westin knows how to shoot?"

Before Valdez could answer, another shot came from above, and one of the leaders of the team gave a shrill scream and fell. The man up there had shot a horse.

Jasper yanked back on the reins, trying to get the other horses to stop, but it was too late. When she fell, the leader had crashed into her partner, pulling the other mare down. She was struggling to get up, and the other two horses kept fighting to move, pulling in different directions, throwing their heads back and letting out nervous neighs into the air. The stage jerked forward and back with their movement.

Another shot sounded from above. Jasper ducked down, the reins still wrapped too tightly around his hand from when he'd been trying to force the horses around the debris and then to stop.

A hand wrapped around his wrist and tugged. Jasper pulled away instinctively, then realized it was Valdez, already out of the box and trying to pull him out too.

"Get down here!" the man ordered.

Jasper let go of the reins, grabbed his father's rifle, and slid down to join him.

They took cover behind the stage, a rocky incline at their backs. They were mostly sheltered from above here, and sheltered the best they could be from below. Jasper crouched beside a wheel. He almost started to laugh — it was the one he had repaired. A part of him, at the back of his mind, was impressed; the repairs they'd done so quickly had held up well. If it hadn't been for the horse getting shot, they might have gotten clear.

Hatch was already half out of the stage, eyes wild and angry and finding Jasper in an instant. "You happy now, you double-crossing —"

Valdez stopped him before he could take a swing at Jasper. "That ain't gonna help, Hatch. Hatch!" he yelled when it didn't seem like the man was going to calm himself. "Let's take care of the men shooting at us before taking care of Jasper, eh?"

"Fine," Hatch snapped. He yanked a second revolver from his gun belt, then spun and shoved it into the coach into Westin's hands. "You watch him," Hatch said, jabbing a finger at Slip. "He starts to get out, shoot him."

Westin's eyes went wide. "No, I —"

Hatch slammed the stage door on Westin, cutting off the objection. "Let's take care of them, then."

Jasper cocked his rifle, ready to do the same.

Valdez had counted two on the road, one above. Jasper peeked over the top of the driver's box, but before he could get a bead on the man above, another shot rang out and he had to take cover again. There might be two up there; he couldn't tell. They didn't come close to hitting him, though.

Jasper felt unease prickling down his spine, a different feeling from whatever was coursing through his body when the guns started firing. It was Alec Casey's way to shoot folks down — that was true enough — but he usually didn't do it like this, from a distance. Even the riders behind them hadn't come charging up to rescue their prisoner. No, there was a reason the Casey Gang had been easy to track, from Nebraska Territory, to Southern California, up to gold country here. Alec Casey liked to be *known.* And if he was coming for his brother . . .

One of the men who'd come from behind rode by, taking one shot, two, and both hit the side of the stagecoach, the wood splintering.

And Jasper realized this wasn't Alec Casey coming for his brother. Whoever was doing the shooting wasn't avoiding shooting at the coach; they were aiming *for* it.

"This ain't Casey," he said, so quiet he was surprised Valdez heard him.

But he did, and the man looked over. "Who is it if it's not Casey?"

Jasper didn't answer. He didn't know, but for every shot that came close to hitting one of the three of them, two had hit the body of the coach, splintering the wood. Jasper couldn't see the other side, but he expected that by now it looked just like someone had taken an ax to it.

"Your accountant is shot!" Slip hollered from inside the coach.

Jasper and Valdez exchanged a look.

"Best get them both out of there," Hatch said, then fired again, "or else they'll *both* end up shot." He was trying to find their shooters, aim and fire back, but there wasn't much of a chance to do so. Each time one of them popped up to shoot at the horsemen, the sharpshooter above took his shot. "Well, do it," Hatch said when neither Valdez nor Jasper moved.

They both did as he said. Jasper pulled the door open and Valdez leaned inside.

Slip Casey was huddled in the corner of the stage on the floor, Westin beside him. "Shouldn't you be shooting those things at them?" Slip asked, gesturing to the gun in

Valdez's hand and then flailing his arms, presumably in the directions of their shooters.

"Get out of there," Valdez said, yanking Slip Casey up by the collar of his coat and pulling him toward the door. Slip hit the ground with a thud and a yelp.

It was Jasper who went in for Westin.

The man *was* shot, and he wasn't looking very good. Slip had been using his bandanna to try to stop the bleeding, and the faded material was darker now with blood. Westin's eyes were glassy when he looked up at Jasper. "Your stagecoach is much too exciting for me," he said, and let out a cough. Specks of blood spurted onto his lips and chin.

Jasper swallowed hard. "Most exciting run of the West," he muttered. He couldn't tell if the gurgle that came from Westin was a laugh or a cough.

Jasper slid his arms beneath Westin's, dragging him out of the stage as easy as he could. Still, the landing onto the dirt was harder than he'd have liked. He looked down to apologize, only to find Westin's eyes closed. He was still breathing, though. Jasper wasn't sure they could keep him that way, but he sure wanted to try.

"Hey," Valdez said, grabbing Jasper's

shoulder. "You have to get out of here."

"What?" That didn't make a lick of sense. They were outgunned with the three of them; Jasper leaving wouldn't help matters.

"We were told to get these two down the mountain," Valdez said, jerking his head toward Slip and Westin, both on the ground. Slip had crawled back to Westin's side and was putting pressure on the wound again. "Hatch and I will cover you, find you when we can. Head into the forest."

"I don't —"

"I'm not asking, Duncan. Go."

Jasper grabbed the rifle he'd left propped up against the stage, slung it over his shoulder, then went for Westin. He muscled Slip aside, then got Westin to his feet.

"We running?" Slip asked, climbing to his feet as well, though staying hunched.

"To the trees," Jasper said. Before he got the words out, Slip was off.

Even with bullets striking down around them and a wounded man at his side, Jasper couldn't help feel sour about that. Slip had been his best chance to get to Alec Casey. His best chance to find the man and kill him. And now that chance was scampering like a jackrabbit toward the forest.

"Stop dawdling and get clear!" Valdez shouted, then turned his attention back to the men trying to kill them.

For such a small man, Westin was heavy. *Deadweight,* Jasper thought, then wished he hadn't. The man wasn't dead yet, he told himself. A bullet hit the ground right near Westin's feet, and Jasper pushed himself to move quicker, and almost lost his balance when Westin's weight lightened against his shoulder.

Slip Casey had come up on the other side, taking half the man's weight. Jasper's surprise must have shown on his face, because Slip grimaced and said, "I'm gonna need some help with these cuffs. Can't have you dying out here."

The road dropped off, and then they were stumbling down a hill of grass and scrub. Jasper could hardly keep his balance and Westin's, even with the outlaw's help on the other side. They were close to the trees — big, sturdy things that could shield them from the bullets that kept coming.

Finally, the three of them staggered into the shade of the trees. Slip let go his hold on Westin, but Jasper wasn't ready for it; the man fell to the ground with a low moan. Jasper stumbled at the loss of weight and dropped his rifle too.

"He's not dead yet; you want to help him get there?" Jasper snapped, looking up at

Slip properly for the first time since he'd noticed him on Westin's other side.

Slip wasn't paying attention to him. His hands had come up to his left arm, left hand dangling awkwardly while the right was wrapped around his biceps. Jasper could see blood slithering out through the cracks between his fingers. "Lousy shots," Slip finally said. "They only winged me."

Jasper yanked off his coat, then his vest, and thrust the blue material at Slip. "Here. Bind your arm."

Slip let the vest fall to the forest floor. "What, myself? In these?" He shook his hand enough that the handcuffs rattled.

"Fine, don't. But you want to get those off, watch Westin." Jasper reached for the rifle he'd let fall, but before he could reach it, Slip's bloody hand was wrapped around his wrist.

Jasper jerked away, grabbing the rifle and aiming it at Slip. What sort of fool attacked a man when he was bound and injured?

But Slip raised his bound hands. "Easy now," he said. "You can't go back there."

Jasper could hear the volleys of gunfire back and forth, then heard a yell he thought might have been Hatch's. "I'm going to help them."

"Don't be a fool. You'll only help yourself

get dead. That what you want?"

"What do you care?"

"Me?" Slip asked. A laugh escaped him, and Jasper wondered if blood loss could drive a man mad this quick. "I don't care if you want yourself dead, but I sure don't want to be up against whoever is up there *alone* without a gun, a dying man at my feet, and these lovely iron bracelets around my wrists."

Jasper looked back toward the road. Hatch and Valdez weren't his friends, true, but they were good men, both of them, and he didn't want to leave them to die. But Slip was right — if Jasper left Westin and Slip there and things didn't go his way, then Westin would probably die and Slip might too. Jasper wasn't sure he cared much about Slip ending up dead, but that sour feeling in his gut came again — could he really let Slip Casey go for what might end up being a fool's errand?

Slip's voice broke through Jasper's thoughts. "Listen. No more gunshots."

Jasper took a step forward, ignoring the exasperated sigh Slip let out behind him, and tried to see what he could of the scene on the road.

What he could see didn't bode well for Hatch or Valdez — or for Jasper. He couldn't see either of the deputies, but he could see one of their attackers, dressed in brown and green, like as not so that he might blend in with the hill he was shooting from. This ambush *had been* planned, just like Jasper thought, even if not by whom he thought. The man shouted something back to someone Jasper couldn't see, then scanned the edge of the forest. He was looking for them. Jasper took a step back and the man's eyes shot right to him. Eyes like a hawk's or ears like a bat's. Jasper wasn't sure which had given them away, but the man took a step forward and opened his mouth.

But before he could speak, a blur of tawny fur slammed into his legs from the side. The man let out a yelp and tumbled over, clearly not expecting an angry mutt to attach herself to his leg with those shiny, sharp teeth Jasper had noted when she'd been growling at Slip earlier in the day.

CHAPTER TEN

Tabitha had the man down, and Jasper thought he could hear her snarls even from a distance. He wanted to go help her. Pull Hatch and Valdez out from whatever cover they'd taken and drag them along with them.

He couldn't.

"We have to go," Jasper said, turning around to face Slip Casey. "Help me." Slip bent down to help him shoulder Westin's weight without arguing. As they hoisted him up, the man gave another groan, but this time opened his eyes a little.

"Mr. Westin, we gotta run."

"I do not think running is —" From the road, Jasper heard a dog's pained yelp and a gunshot. Westin bit back whatever he was going to say, and the three of them started to move.

Calling it running was generous. They stumbled across clumps of dirt and between tall trees, and Jasper lost all sense of direction. The sun seemed to flare and wane as they went, but Jasper knew that was only because they were passing in and out of the cover of trees. They hadn't been running long enough to lose the light, had they? What he did know was they hadn't heard gunshots since they started running. Jasper cautiously hoped that meant they'd lost any pursuers they might have had.

"Stop," Slip said when they reached a craggy spot in the forest, boulders rising up like squat stony trees among the taller pines. A cliff rose up on one side of them, the slope steep enough that climbing wasn't an option either for them or for those hunting them. "Stop. We have to stop."

Slip slid out from under Westin's arm. This time Jasper was ready for it, took the rest of the man's weight, and lowered him to the ground. Slip staggered forward to press his uninjured arm against a boulder. His breathing came hard and uneven. Jasper wondered if that wound on his shoulder was worse than he'd said.

"I ain't cut out for running," Slip wheezed.

"Then you shouldn't have become an outlaw," Jasper said, and turned his attention to Westin. He'd propped the other man against a smaller boulder, and his head lolled to the side.

Slip chuckled breathlessly. "I've been an outlaw a dozen years, and I never ran so much as I have today. Besides, don't pretend you don't know *that* ain't about me."

Jasper couldn't pretend not to know that. Those men hadn't been after Slip. But he did ask, "Then what is it about?"

"Hell if I know," Slip replied. He took a step toward Jasper. "How is he?"

Jasper didn't reply. Slip could see for himself the answer wasn't good. Westin was still breathing, but shallowly. Jasper didn't know when he'd fallen back into unconsciousness, but he hadn't even let out a groan when he was placed on the ground this time.

Jasper took a deep breath and took stock of the situation. He hadn't had time to grab anything from the stage; his bag was still at the driver's box, and most of his supplies had been in the boot anyway. He had his father's rifle, of course, and he had his knife, its holster strapped to his belt. He had a flint for starting fires, and his canteen, a little more than half full.

And that was it.

He wished he hadn't left his vest behind when they ran. *Slip Casey's fault,* he thought angrily. It always came back to a Casey.

139

"We need to find shelter," he said instead.

If Slip noticed the heat in his voice, he didn't say anything about it. "Probably could find a cave," Slip replied, gesturing to the rocks all around them. "Hear tell these mountains are full of them."

These mountains would be full of mine shafts before the century was over, but sometimes nature gave them a head start with a small cave of her own.

"Let's go, then." Getting to his feet was a task Jasper didn't relish, but better to move now before the fatigue set in.

"You want the three of us to go stumbling around, looking for shelter? Wouldn't it be better to send me to scout for one?"

Jasper was shaking his head before Slip finished the sentence. "I might trust you not to run off alone when armed men are in sight, but certainly not when they're nowhere to be seen."

"A suspicious one." Slip snorted. "Sure you're not also a lawman?"

For one day, long ago, he had been. Jasper didn't share that bit of information. Instead he said, "We'll leave Westin here, come back once we find shelter."

Slip looked like he might argue that too, but swallowed down whatever protest he might have, and nodded.

Jasper adjusted his grip on his rifle and gestured forward. "Lead the way."

Slip Casey was blessedly quiet as they searched for shelter, and he'd been right about a cave. They came upon one after very little searching. It was shallow, and they both had to duck down to enter, but there was more than enough room for the three men. It went back far enough that they should be able to light a fire without worrying too much that it might be seen, but not so far that they couldn't be sure it wasn't the home of any sleeping animal.

They made it back to Westin quickly, and Jasper was relieved to find him still breathing and not injured further. Slip made a crack about worrying he'd have been eaten by a bear or wolf that Jasper didn't want to admit had lingered in his mind too. Leaving a bloody, unconscious man in the middle of this wild forest? Jasper wouldn't have done it if he'd seen another way.

But they got Westin back to the cave they'd found quickly, though Slip was panting and complaining about his arm by the time they settled the man down. Jasper stripped off his coat again, this time using it to cover Westin up as best he could. The man felt cold, and that couldn't be a good sign. He was still breathing, Jasper thought. *Focus on that.*

"I'd give him my jacket as a pillow, except . . ." Slip trailed off and raised his hands, his cuffs clanking again.

"I'd give him my vest for one, but you left it on the ground."

Slip shrugged, conceding his point, then winced. "I may be regretting that right now, as I could use the binding."

Jasper ignored that. "Let's make a fire, then see to Westin."

There were enough drying kindling and broken branches on the forest floor for it to be short work to find enough for a fire. Jasper used his flint stone, glad he kept it with him almost always, and soon they had a small, warm fire flaring to life in the cave. And then it was time to see to Westin.

The shot Westin had taken in the chest probably looked worse in the clear light of the sun than it did in their fire's flickering flame, but it was bad enough. Jasper swallowed hard after he moved his coat and the makeshift dressing Slip had put over the wound back at the road. He had to force himself not to look away. Westin had been hit well below the heart, but not in a spot that gave Jasper very much hope to keep him alive.

He didn't have much to help — some water in his canteen, and Westin's own handkerchief he could use for part of a makeshift bandage. He did it as quick and gentle as possible, cleaning the wound as best he could — wincing himself when Westin moaned and flinched in pain, eyes open but not seeming to *see* anything — and doubling up the kerchief and pressing it against the gash. *Not enough,* he thought, and reached for his coat. He stripped out a piece of the lining.

"He's not going to make it," Slip said beside him. His voice was softer than Jasper had expected.

"You don't know that," Jasper said, finishing his bandaging of the wound best he could without making Westin move any more than he already had.

Slip didn't argue, just continued like he hadn't heard Jasper speak at all. "He won't last the night."

"And what? You think we should just leave him here? Let him die alone while we run some more?"

The set of Slip's jaw almost made it look as though that had insulted him. "You know, this is why my brother always bests your lawmen." His voice was still soft. "He doesn't care about leaving people to die."

"Doesn't care about leaving people to die?" Jasper snorted out a laugh that sounded more a snarl even to his own ears. "Don't you mean he *makes sure* to leave them that way?"

Something flickered across Slip's face. Jasper wasn't sure what it was. "Alec Casey leaves a lot of folk dead. You're right about that. Some he makes that way. Some he just doesn't care to save. If Alec were here, he'd take one look at your banker man and walk right away."

If Alec were here, Jasper didn't say, *he'd be dead.*

"Well, let me express my happiness that your brother is not here, Mr. Casey."

Jasper's eyes darted down to Westin. The man's eyes were only half open, but they *were* open and looking up at Slip's face. Jasper hadn't been sure what the man was seeing when he'd cleaned his wound, but he looked better now. No, not better. Clearer.

"I won't argue with that," Slip said, sitting back on his haunches.

"Mr. Duncan, I need you to do something for me," Westin said.

His voice cracked as he spoke, and Jasper grabbed for his canteen. There wasn't much left, but he poured a little into Westin's mouth. Some of it dribbled out of the side,

144

pinkish from the blood still on his lips, but the man swallowed, and when he spoke again, his voice was a little stronger.

"Inside my jacket."

He made to reach for something, but Jasper stilled him with a hand, then reached inside himself. There was a leather folio tucked inside a large pocket on the inside of the jacket. It looked too large for a slim man like Westin to be carrying under his jacket. The leather was finely tooled and a brass latch held it closed. The leather was stained with blood, but the pages inside were not.

"I need you to get this back to my office," Westin said. "The mine office in Sonora."

Jasper paged through the papers: two maps, clearly of the mine and its vicinity; a schedule that looked like it involved payroll; other information penned in the same neat, sloping hand Jasper had seen in Westin's ledger. Jasper didn't take the time to read through it all before he closed the folio.

"Why?" Jasper asked.

"Because I think . . ." Westin swallowed. "I think someone wants that badly enough to kill." He let out a rough-sounding cough. "Kill me, to be precise."

"*That?* Someone wanted *that?*" It was Slip's voice, saying exactly the thought Jasper had just been forming. Slip huffed a

145

laugh. "I'm not even the most important passenger on the very stagecoach bringing me to the executioner. My brother would get a kick out of that."

"Shut up," Jasper snapped. He leaned forward. "Are you sure? This was about you?"

Westin's voice sounded as though a cold had settled in his chest, like he had to force the words out around some sort of water in his lungs. "I know you thought about it. The accident the other day coming into Indigo. Didn't seem like an accident, did it?"

Jasper thought about the bullet he'd found out on the road, right near where that horse had spooked. "It did not. You think someone wanted to stop you from getting there."

Westin's chin dipped in a bare nod. "And now . . ."

"They want to stop you from getting back." Jasper looked down at the leather folio. Because of this? What meaning did any of this have to be worth not just Westin's life but those of anyone else riding along with him?

By the time he brought his attention back to Westin, the man had already fallen asleep again. Or Jasper hoped it was sleep anyway and not something worse.

"You have to admit, it's pretty funny that

the outlaw isn't the one drawing down the danger," Slip said instead of keeping his mouth shut.

Jasper didn't think getting shot at was funny at all. He laid the folio down beside Westin, then realized what he hadn't come upon while digging around inside Westin's jacket.

"You have that pistol?" Jasper asked.

"What pistol?"

"Westin's."

Slip looked over at the unconscious man, then back up to Jasper. "You really believe that man carried a pistol? Pens, maybe, but pistols?"

"The one Hatch gave him," Jasper ground out. "To guard you in the stage."

Slip shook his head. "I don't know what happened to it. The dog did most of the guarding." Jasper clearly didn't look convinced, because Slip lifted his arms and turned in a slow circle. "No pistol. See?"

Jasper still wasn't convinced. He shuffled forward, his head bumping against the cave's roof a couple of times on his way to Slip's side; then he patted down the man as best he could. He found nothing.

Slip snorted and said, "I told you."

Jasper gave him a shove away and Slip's breath hissed out. His arm. Jasper had

147

forgotten he was wounded too.

"Sit down," Jasper ordered. If he jerked Slip's sleeve down his arm rougher than necessary, well, there was no one to tell him he was being a lousy doctor, was there?

The wound really was just a graze. It seemed to have bled quite a bit, dribbling down Slip's arm and staining the gray of his shirt, but it wasn't deep. They didn't have much to bind it, so Jasper stripped out another piece of his coat lining. It was awkward to tie with Slip's hands bound. Jasper was more than a little surprised that he didn't make another plea to have his hands uncuffed. But Slip stayed mostly silent while Jasper did his doctoring.

When Jasper was done, Slip said a quiet "My thanks."

Jasper didn't reply and retreated to the other side of the cave. He checked Westin's breathing again — just as even as it had been, though still rattling a little in his lungs. The bleeding seemed to have slowed, at least. Jasper wondered if it would be enough to save him, or if Slip was right and he wouldn't last the night. He tucked his jacket around Westin and tried not to think of Valdez's quiet voice. *Running us all right into a trap would get someone killed.*

"Can I have some of that water?"

Jasper looked down at the canteen at Westin's side, then lifted it to his lips, and took a drink. Then he corked it right back up again and tucked it down at his side.

Slip snorted, then lay down on the hard dirt floor of the cave. "What'd I ever do to you?" he muttered.

Jasper swirled the warm, tinny-tasting water around his mouth and swallowed. Despite the water, his mouth was dry.

CHAPTER ELEVEN

Alec Casey was an easy captive.

Jasper hadn't expected that, not from the way he'd looked at Jasper when he was getting ready to shoot him. He'd expected the man to rail, to run, to do any number of things he didn't do. He was bound with strong rope, and they'd led him the miles back to their town on foot. He was too dangerous to allow to ride, no matter how easygoing he seemed.

"Did we get them all?" Jasper asked his father.

Ben shook his head. "One of them got out the back."

They'd captured two: Casey himself and a member of his gang. Of the other three men, one had managed to escape, and two had gotten shot and died on the saloon's sticky floor. The deputy who'd let the outlaw get by him had a bruise the size of the meaty fist that must have punched him, and said something about the man being burly as a moose.

The sheriff didn't look like he believed that story, and didn't seem too happy about the escapee.

He hadn't been too happy about Jasper nearly getting himself shot either.

"You were supposed to stay out of the action, kid," the sheriff said. But he was smiling, at least.

Ben Duncan's face was not as forgiving. When they were leading Casey and his boys back toward town, Jasper's father pulled him aside. "What was that out there?"

"He got the drop on me," Jasper said. "Won't happen again."

"You should have seen him coming. He shouldn't have been able to."

"I stopped him, didn't I? Delayed him, at least? You got him, Pa."

"And you almost got yourself killed in the process."

"I didn't mean to —"

"I don't care that he almost got away," his father said, then paused. "No, I do care about that. But I care more about you. That something almost happened to you."

"It won't happen again," Jasper repeated. Shame burned under his skin, but he made himself hold his pa's gaze. He couldn't flinch away, not if he didn't want to be sent on home.

His father squeezed his shoulder. "Alright,

then." Jasper didn't quite believe the smile Pa gave him, but it was close enough to true. Jasper returned it.

They made it back to the town as the sun was just beginning its slow slide toward the horizon, casting squat shadows on the hard-packed dirt road. The jail had two cells, and each prisoner was tossed in their own.

Alec Casey craned his neck, which let out a pop, and looked around the small cell like he was evaluating some fancy digs. "A private room. Why, thank you for the accommodations."

"Even this is too good for the likes of you," Jasper spat.

Casey grinned, showing off straight pearly teeth, and looked over at Jasper's father. "Your son is quite the do-gooder already. Must be proud, Deputy." Ben Duncan's mouth flattened into a thin line, but he didn't reply. Alec's smile soured. "You don't have to say anything. I like to get to know the men I kill, but it isn't necessary. I can kill a stranger just as well."

Jasper bristled at the threat and opened his mouth to reply, but his father's hand landed on his shoulder. "Jasper," he said.

Casey rolled his eyes and sank onto the floor at the back of the cell, looking bored, of all things. He pulled at the shirt covering his wound and seemed to evaluate it with calm, unfeeling eyes.

"You two," the sheriff said, gesturing Jasper and his father toward his desk.

All seven of them crowded around, elbows knocking. The sheriff had a map spread open on his desk, and he'd marked two places lightly in pencil, explaining quietly where he thought the last member of the gang might go.

"We need to hunt that last one down," the sheriff said.

"Four out of five ain't bad," his other deputy said, then blanched at the withering look he received.

"These are murderers, boys. We can't let murderers roam our territory."

The deputy with the black eye said, "I'm going with you."

The rest of the posse volunteered as well.

"Someone has to stay here," the sheriff said. "Jasper?"

Jasper started to object, but his father gave him a sharp look and Jasper relented. If this was how he proved to his father he could be trusted, then this was what he'd do.

"I'll stay," he said.

They packed up and were off. Jasper looked over to the cell where Alec Casey was. The man was on the floor, sitting primly against

the wall, eyes toward the door as though waiting for something.

CHAPTER TWELVE

Jasper jerked awake at the feel of someone hovering above him.

His hand was on the rifle already; it took only a moment to lift it and point it right at the shadow looming above him. A few blinks and his eyes adjusted. Slip Casey, of course, cuffed hands raised in surrender.

"Going for my gun?" Jasper rasped, his voice sleep rough. How had he fallen asleep so close to Slip Casey? And how long had it been before the outlaw came toward him?

The fire had died down to glowing pieces of wood, still giving off a little warmth, but not enough to have heated Jasper's cold, tight muscles. He had no idea what time it was — early morning? Still night? Jasper glanced outside. It was still dark out there, but *less* dark than inside, even with the glow of the fire. Morning, then, just barely dawn.

"Going for the water," Slip replied. He

sounded as hoarse as Jasper did.

Jasper lowered his rifle slowly, then passed Slip the canteen. He couldn't have the man dying of thirst. Not if he wanted to draw out his brother.

Slip took a long drink, then handed the canteen back to Jasper, almost empty. They'd have to find water, more wood for the fire, maybe something else to bind Westin's wounds. . . .

As though Slip could read Jasper's thought in the gaze that wandered to Westin's still form, Slip said, "Your friend's dead."

Jasper scrambled to his feet and over to Westin's side, but Slip was right. Westin was dead. Cold already too. Men strained for breath when they died, in Jasper's experience. He hadn't heard a thing like that, hadn't heard a moan of pain or . . .

He looked over at Slip Casey. "You do something to him?"

Slip drew back, affronted. "No. 'Course I didn't. I woke up and found him like that. I wouldn't have had to do anything anyway. I told you he wouldn't last the night."

"Maybe you made sure of it," Jasper said, his eyes narrowed.

"Why would I do a thing like that?"

"Since I wouldn't just leave him here, like you wanted."

Slip rolled his eyes. "I didn't say I wanted to leave him here. I might have a bounty on my head for a great many crimes, but I'm not my brother. I'm an outlaw, but no murderer."

"You expect me to believe that when you run with that same brother?"

"What do you know about my brother?" Slip demanded. But he didn't sound insulted, like he had when Jasper had accused him of wanting Westin dead. He sounded suspicious, and the look he leveled at Jasper was sharp. "You have a certain tone of voice when you talk about him. I recognize it. Heard it leveled at me a good many times. You *hate* him. Why?"

"Alec Casey is a thief and a murderer, and good men ought to hate that, shouldn't they?"

"Maybe so. No one ever explained to me what good men ought to do. But I don't think that's all it is. No, I think your hate is a special kind." He dropped his pointed stare. "Also I overheard your deputy friend say you wanted him dead."

Jasper didn't know why he answered. He had avoided questions leveled at him for years. "Were you with him in Nebraska Territory?" he asked. He knew the answer; he'd studied Slip Casey's wanted bill just like

157

he'd studied Alec's, if not with the same dedication.

"We spent some time there, yes. That where you had your run-in?"

"He robbed and killed there."

"He usually does."

Jasper thought of the question lawmen sometimes asked about Alec Casey: had he robbed more banks and stages or killed more men? No one could come to a decision on that. The handbill that had been circulating lately said he was wanted for robbery, for murder, but not how many; the number of crimes was most evident from the amount of the reward, and Alec Casey's had been steadily going up since that fateful day in Nebraska Territory.

"And then he got caught," Jasper said. "But he didn't stay that way."

"He never does." Slip's face was all in shadow, so Jasper couldn't tell if the flash of teeth was a smile or a grimace. Probably the former. Proud of his little brother, maybe, for getting himself out of trouble, the way Slip himself never did, if the stories were true.

"He killed my father."

"My brother has killed lots of fathers."

It was the *way* he said it that made Jasper take a swing. As unfeeling as he'd sounded when he said that Westin wasn't going to last the night, as though he wasn't talking about men's lives. Alec Casey had been cheerful about killing. This callousness almost felt worse.

His punch connected poorly. Here in this low, tight cavern, he couldn't have expected anything else, not if he'd planned to do some hitting. But Slip hadn't expected the hit any more than Jasper had expected to do the hitting, and he tumbled backward, causing the dirt and stone wall of the cave to send clumps of earth raining down.

"What the Devil was that for?"

Jasper had half a mind to take the fight further, but Slip raised a hand to his face, and the other came up with it. Handcuffed. Jasper couldn't be beating on a man who was tied up and couldn't properly defend himself.

He was still mighty tempted.

But instead he put his anger into his words. "Maybe you ain't a killer, but I doubt the reason's got much to do with morality. No, you're just too lazy to do more than follow your brother around. Maybe you did kill Westin — a sleeping man's gotta be real easy to kill."

Slip let out a hoarse laugh, but before Jasper could find out what exactly was so funny, the sound of boots crunching over rocks came from the entrance to the cave.

Jasper dove for his rifle as the man came into view. He got a hand on it, but he couldn't raise and aim it before the man had his own pistol aimed right at Jasper's head.

"I'd put that right down," the man said.

Jasper had never seen him before. He wasn't the one who had aimed at them at the edge of the woods, but he wore similar clothes — earthy tones, easy to blend in. He was covered all over in dust, like the wind had swept the earth all over him to help him keep his cover. Jasper would have preferred not to have any man level a gun at him, but especially not this sort: he looked a little twitchy, and a twitchy trigger finger was a dangerous thing.

Jasper didn't listen to his command to put the rifle down, even if there was no way he could aim and shoot before the other man. Throwing his gun away would like as not bring about his death. At least when the rifle was in his hands, he could choose to try.

The man gave a high-pitched little laugh. "Have it your way." The man swept his gaze from Jasper, to Slip, and then back to Westin in the middle, still and cold. "I wondered if this one made it." He leaned down a little, said the next part quietly, like he was imparting a secret. "The others didn't, you know."

Jasper had guessed that — known it really from the moment he'd looked out of the forest and seen that the dog was the only one fighting back. He still felt the punch of that confirmation in his gut.

"Were they all your friends, jehu? Too bad on that count."

They hadn't been his friends. He'd known Hatch and Valdez for more than a year, but he hadn't counted either of them among his friends. That didn't mean he'd wanted them dead.

What had Valdez said? That walking them into a trap meant someone could die?

Jasper swallowed hard. He'd been right.

The man jerked his head toward Westin's body. "Check your dead friend for papers, jehu."

Where had he put the folio Westin had told him to take? He'd tucked it beside the man. Jasper didn't dare look over to see if it was still there. Was Westin right, that that was what this man was after, the papers he was carrying?

Jasper shook his head slowly. "Think I'll stay just where I am."

"I think you'll do as I say," the man said,

cocking the hammer back.

"Hey, hey, no need for that," Slip said. He lifted his hands a little higher when the man's focus slid over to him. "My hands might be bound but I have two of them, and I'm more than happy to help you find what you need from dear dead Mr. Westin's cooling corpse."

The man scowled. "Fine."

"Thank you," Slip said, shuffling forward. The man darted his eyes between the shuffling Slip and Jasper, who was still holding his rifle. "I'm sure a gunshot in here would be loud as a clap of thunder and I do not think my ears will take kindly to it." Slip sank to his knees beside Westin's body. Jasper wondered whether or not he could raise the rifle in time, and his finger twitched; the man must have caught the movement in the corner of his eye, because he focused on Jasper again, his eyes narrowed.

"Now what'd you say I was looking for?" Slip asked.

The man looked back to Slip, and what looked like tiny stars glowing bright red and orange sailed through the air. Before Jasper could tell what had happened, the man and Slip were both shouting.

Jasper didn't hesitate. He raised his gun,

took aim at the man, and fired.

The shot was so loud in the small cave, it rang so painfully through his ears, that for a moment he thought he'd taken aim at his own head. Either that or the man had gotten his own shot off first. But no, after a long moment, the ringing in his ears died down a little, and he could hear Slip cursing up a storm and shaking out his hands.

It took a little longer even before Jasper could understand what he was saying.

"What a fool's plan that was. I should have just let you shoot each other!"

"What did you . . ." Jasper trailed off and wished he hadn't spoken. Slip, as much as he hated to admit it, had been right; his ears had not taken kindly to a gunshot inside this cave. His own voice sounded cloudy. He pressed his fingers against his ears, then shook his head like he could clear it that way.

"Where's that canteen?" Slip demanded. Jasper wasn't sure why Slip didn't seem as affected by the blast. He was still waving his hands around as though he'd burned himself.

And then Jasper realized what it was that had flown into the gunman's face.

Slip had flung the remnants of their fire up at the gunman. That was why they'd both started yelling. Jasper looked from Slip's hands to the floor of the cave; sure enough, while the firepit wasn't smoldering anymore, the woolen gloves Slip had been wearing were.

Slip had found the canteen himself, up-ended it over his hands, only to find that it was almost empty. "Just as well I was wearing those," he grumbled, "though I liked those gloves."

"Why'd you do that?" Slip cocked his head and raised his eyebrows, clearly confused. "Why'd you distract him?"

"Do you think it was likely he'd have let me go? He'd probably have killed us both, buried all three of us in this cave. Maybe a hundred years from now, someone might have found us, wondered how we got plugged up with lead and left with only a single canteen between us, and me still in these cuffs." He raised his arms and shook them again, as though Jasper had forgotten he'd wanted them off the day before. "No, Jasper jehu, I think our best chance to get out of this is to work together."

Jasper looked down at the man he'd shot. "You think more of them are coming?"

Slip snorted. "You're no fool. You knew taking that short cut was a bad idea, even when you agreed to do it. You knew sooner than anyone that my brother wasn't the one shooting at us."

Jasper remembered Slip cowering in the corner of the stage, demanding to know why they weren't shooting back. He said, "You knew before I did."

"Well." Slip shrugged. "*Almost* anyone, then."

Jasper thought back to the men on the road. How many of them had there been? At least three, no more than four. But that didn't account for everyone involved. Someone had felled that tree to divert the stage. Someone knew exactly who was on the stagecoach and the best place to stop them. And they knew good and well who would be blamed for the assault on their party: Alec Casey, rescuing his good-for-nothing older brother from a hanging.

"What's in them papers that those men are willing to kill for?" Jasper asked.

"I don't think we should stick around long enough to find out. I bet this man's friends are out there looking for our Mr. Westin."

Jasper hated to admit it, but Slip was right. That gunshot had been loud enough to be heard quite a ways away. He only hoped that sound bounced around too much in the forest to track it properly.

Jasper looked down at Westin and thought

of what Slip had said — maybe they wouldn't have been found for a hundred years. He promised himself if he made it through the next few days, he'd make sure someone came back for Westin's body, get him a proper burial, let his family, if he had one, know what had happened.

But if they left him here, the animals would get him sooner than that.

"Help me find some rocks," he told Slip.

It didn't take them long, not with the cave they were in. Soon, Jasper had built up a cairn around Westin. He hoped it would keep him safe from any animals that wanted a quick meal.

"Should we say a prayer?" Slip Casey asked.

Jasper almost punched him again.

Instead, he picked up the folio and opened it again. The papers looked the same as yesterday, but this time Jasper noticed the inside. The folio was lined with white and green fabric, unstained except for a single drop of what might have been coffee in the corner. Careful handwriting sloped across the page: Samuel Theodore Westin, San Francisco, California.

Jasper took the pages, folded them up and tucked them inside his coat, next to the letters he'd almost forgotten about. He laid the leather folio on Westin's chest, then added the last of the rocks to the cairn. If he didn't make it back here, maybe someone would find the folio with the body and know who'd died.

Jasper straightened. "Let's get a move on, then."

"Hold up!" Slip stepped in front of him before he could make it closer to the entrance of the cave. "I'm hoping we can come to an understanding."

"We have one. You got caught, fair and square, and I'm bringing you to Sonora."

"Right now you can't *bring* me anywhere. We're alone up here, and folks are coming for us. I'm not asking you to trust me. Just for . . . a détente. Once we're clear of whoever's doing the hunting, maybe we can renegotiate."

Jasper hated that he was considering it. But despite his words a few moments ago, he truly didn't think Slip had done anything to Westin. Jasper might have died without him. He thought about what Slip had said, about their bodies lying in this cave for a hundred years. What would Jasper's family think if he disappeared and word never came to them of his death?

But then he thought of *Slip's* family, and whatever softening he'd done was gone in an instant.

Slip was Alec Casey's brother. Jasper couldn't trust anyone with that man's blood in his veins.

"An understanding, you said?" Jasper asked. Slip nodded once. Jasper continued. "I think we could arrive at one of those." Slip looked hopeful, though the look faded away as Jasper spoke again. "I understand that the bounty on your head is dead or alive, and you understand that I have the gun."

Slip Casey gave a heavy sigh, as though he'd expected something of the sort to come out of Jasper's mouth, and it deeply disappointed him. "I suppose I do understand at that."

Jasper gave a jerk of his head toward the entrance. "Let's get going."

CHAPTER THIRTEEN

"Am I mistaken, or are you leading us west toward Sonora?"

Jasper didn't reply to that — though the answer was yes — and he kept walking. Perhaps disappointment had stilled Slip's tongue, because he wasn't half so chatty this morning as he'd been before. Most of the noise came from the clank of his cuffs, which Jasper was surer than ever was deliberate.

Jasper hadn't found any reason to believe they were being followed. Could it be that all of the men who'd ambushed them on the road were dead? The man at the cave had said that Hatch and Valdez were dead; could it be that the deputies had taken out the other attackers and the one from the cave had set out on his own to find them? If so, the next step in this journey would be much easier.

But Jasper couldn't quite believe it would

be that easy.

"Now, why would you lead us west toward Sonora when Long Barn's more than half the distance closer? I've done enough thieving to know that most men don't hold the thieves against the town, even if they happen to be close by when the thieving's done."

Jasper wished he would have known the silence wouldn't last. He'd have appreciated it more when he had it.

"So it's more than just some thieves after a map or some scribbled numbers or whatever else is in Mr. Westin's papers. You'd have no reason to avoid an entire direction just because of some robbers on the road."

He was right again about that. Jasper had had too long to think about it, falling asleep the night before, after Westin gave him those papers, and then today after leaving the dead men inside the cave. He'd gone over it again in his head. Those men had been waiting for them. Jasper had expected some attack, felt it coming, when he and the others found out about the blockage on the road at Long Barn. Alec Casey rescuing his brother again, he'd believed. But that was not the case.

No, someone else had been waiting for them. Someone else had been waiting for

Westin, and no highway bandit would have known the value of that man's papers. What robber would even know Westin existed, much less that he'd be on Jasper's stagecoach? No, someone had known exactly who they were and exactly where they'd be. There weren't many souls who could fit that description, and each one of them hailed from Indigo.

And each one of them could be waiting at Long Barn with a rifle.

"I reckon you're right about all this," Slip Casey said as though he'd followed Jasper's thoughts without Jasper speaking a single one of them. "No ordinary robbers. And with all this land to search? Assuming there are any of them left, there's a clearer path to Sonora in this whole mess of trees than there would be on that road."

"Glad you approve," Jasper muttered.

"I approve of your thinking, but I would once again like to say that I do not relish the thought of being hanged."

Jasper's eyes narrowed against the glare of the sun, and he pushed his hat lower on his head. "Noted."

They trudged through the forest westward throughout the day. They passed a stream just after noon, and before Jasper could stop him, Slip Casey fell to his knees beside it and dunked his head right in. He pulled his head out and shook it, his hair dripping water all over his clothes and the sandy bank of the stream. His ears and the back of his neck were red; he didn't have his hat anymore, after all, and they'd spent the morning with the sun at their backs. Now it was directly overhead, and Jasper winced, thinking about the burn Slip might end up with on his face. Not that it mattered. A few more days and he'd either be turned in to the authorities at the county seat, or he'd be free. A sunburn would barely have time to fade before then.

Jasper filled his canteen in the stream and entertained the thought of doing some fishing. Before he could think through how he might do that, Slip said, "I wish there were some fish in this stream. I could use a fish fry for lunch. But I don't see any." He cupped his hands and drank straight from the stream. "Maybe I scared them away with this ugly mug."

Jasper fastened the lid onto his canteen. "Time to go."

A couple of hours later, and Jasper wished he'd thought longer and harder about how to catch those fish. That had been a closer brush with food than anything else all day. Once, he saw a rabbit in the distance; he might have made the shot, but with some-one possibly hunting them down? No, Jasper didn't want to risk the noise.

Jasper walked for most of the day, trying to keep a few steps behind Slip. But even though his legs were shorter, his stride was quicker, and he kept ending up beside the man.

The crunching of ground beside him sud-denly stopped, and Jasper whipped around, ready to see Slip Casey getting ready to run. Instead, he was standing stock-still, staring at the sky.

"Why are you stopping?"

Slip threw an arm out, dragging the other with it, and flapped a hand at the sky. "Would you look at that?"

The sunset. Slip Casey, outlaw, had stopped to look at the sunset.

Jasper followed his gaze. The sky was striped in colors, oranges and pinks and golds, and the trees below looked like they were standing at attention to see the sunset just like Slip Casey was, their green boughs bright even in this dying light. The clouds rolled toward the horizon, a lighter shade of blue than the darkening sky.

In the years since his father died, Jasper hadn't had much time for wonder. His mother had been the sort to see the hand of

God in every sunset and every flower. Jasper had been a little like that too once; he'd found heroes to look up to at every turn, and couldn't wait to climb every tree and learn the stories that went with each bright star in the sky. But since coming to California — since his father was killed, truly — Jasper had kept his head down, watching the miles of road his stagecoach ground over and the mountains and hills he was heading toward, not the stars or the trees. And when it came to stories, instead of thinking about heroes, he thought about villains and how he wanted to put one of them in the ground.

"Not one to admire a sunset, then," Slip Casey muttered.

"Not much to admire. Once that sun's down, we can't travel," Jasper said. "We'll have to make camp."

They found a small clearing in a ring of trees, somewhat sheltered from view in case they were being followed. Jasper wouldn't let Slip out of sight, so the two of them didn't go far to collect twigs and sticks for a fire.

Slip kept talking while they collected the firewood. "You know, where you're taking me, I won't get to appreciate sunsets."

"I'm taking you to hang," Jasper said evenly.

"All the more reason to appreciate them now."

Jasper didn't reply, and Slip fell silent. Jasper dug out a small pit for a fire, built it up, and struck his knife on his flint stone. The fire caught quickly, and even though Jasper wasn't sure about signaling their whereabouts if someone was looking for them, once the sun had sank a little farther, he was glad to have the extra warmth.

If only he had something to cook over it.

Jasper always kept jerky and dried fruit in the driver's box of his stage, as well as some for the passengers in the boot. Usually, passengers brought their own meals — he'd found bits of old sausage and crumbs from stale bread back there many times — but he'd rarely been caught without a few biscuits to pass off for a penny or two. But those biscuits, his jerky, and even his spare canteen of water were all back in his stagecoach. The last time he'd eaten had been back in Indigo. They'd have to do something about that if they were going to make their way out of the forest on foot.

"I wish we'd killed that rabbit we saw earlier," Slip said. Jasper pursed his lips, annoyed that their thoughts had followed the exact same trail once again. "Bet I could have found some sweet onions to roast with it."

"That's not helping," Jasper snapped.

"I'm giving you ideas for tomorrow. You kill a rabbit; I'll find some sweet onions."

"Fine." He felt like he was forcing the words out through his clenched jaw. "If we see another rabbit tomorrow, I'll kill it with my rifle, wasting ammunition and helping the men trying to kill us find us even easier than they can now with this *fire.*"

"The fire was your idea," Slip muttered. "Here."

Something was flying at him, and Jasper flinched as it hit his chest and bounced down to his lap.

Jerky.

He picked up the hunk of dried meat, stared down at it, then looked back over at Slip, who was already chewing on an identical piece of jerky. "Where'd you get this?"

"Long Barn. Well, that's when, as a matter of fact. Where is the boot of your stage. Deputy Valdez was good enough to feed me while you were having your altercation, and I helped myself to extra."

Jasper took a bite. It was old and hard and too salty, but for a moment he was sure he wouldn't have traded it even for a fresh roasted rabbit with those sweet onions.

"Tell me something," Slip said.

"No."

Slip went on like he hadn't heard Jasper speak at all. "If you knew we were going to be ambushed on that road, why'd you convince them we needed to go down it?"

Jasper's eyes shot to Slip's face. The man seemed to be paying more attention to the jerky in his hand than to what he'd just said.

"Why do you say that?"

"What, that you knew? Seemed fairly obvious. Why don't you want to answer?"

"I didn't know," Jasper answered. "How would I have known?"

Slip shrugged and licked the salt from his fingers. "I don't know the answer to that one either, but that wasn't what I asked about."

"We had a job to do. One I still have to do. I just want to get it done as quick as possible."

He didn't think Slip believed that, but Jasper didn't much care what Slip Casey believed. Regardless of what he thought of Jasper's motivations, all he said next was "Do you think wolves are going to eat us in our sleep?"

Jasper laughed without thinking. "I think if wolves come to eat us, we surely won't sleep through it."

177

"Well, if they do, at least someone will get supper," Slip said, then stretched out by the fire, closer than Jasper himself would have gotten, as though he didn't mind the chance of being burned.

Jasper took another bite of the jerky. They had something for supper because of Slip's filching from his boot, at least, but even as Slip's face smoothed out in sleep, Jasper wondered why it was he'd stashed food away in his pockets in the first place, as though he knew he might need it soon.

CHAPTER FOURTEEN

Much to his surprise, Jasper discovered the next morning that Slip hadn't been joking about finding onions. They had to backtrack a little ways to find them.

"I'd have mentioned it last night, but you spent this part of our journey scowling, and I was afraid to interrupt the dark thoughts in your head."

That made Jasper scowl again, but he didn't respond.

The plants Slip had found looked more like wildflowers than vegetables, but the man dug a couple up and swung them toward Jasper's face. Sure enough, at the ends of the purplish wildflower stems were small bulbs. Wild onions. Jasper gathered some, wishing he'd grabbed his bag from the driver's box when he'd slipped down, but Slip produced another bandanna and used that as a makeshift satchel instead.

"Keep an eye out for mushrooms," Slip

said after they'd plucked up most of the onion weeds. "Or little white flowers. Might find some carrots to go with the onions." He looked down at the onions he carried, smiling almost proudly, then looked back up at Jasper. "And you owe me a rabbit."

Slip led the way back to where they'd camped the night before. Jasper had fed the fire that morning. He'd woken just before the sun rose, cold seeping into his bones, but there hadn't been enough light to travel by. He'd have smothered it before they left, but Slip had stopped him. Jasper was glad they hadn't. He stepped back — out of ember-pitching range — and let Slip fuss with the onions and hot stones, happy as Missy Banks ever was in the home station kitchen.

"Where'd you learn to forage yourself a meal?" Jasper asked.

Slip looked over his shoulder at Jasper. He looked surprised that Jasper had asked. Jasper was surprised he'd asked and almost wanted to take the question back.

Before he could decide whether or not to do so, Slip said, "A man ought to know how to survive out here. What do you think I was living on in that cabin where they found me?" He looked back down at the onions on the fire. "Well, better grub than this, surely, but this isn't the first time I've found myself in need of a meal."

"What were you doing in that cabin?" Another question. But this one Jasper had wondered about before when he'd first learned they'd caught Slip there, after the rush of blood that came with the realization that he was so close to a way to finally find Alec Casey.

Slip didn't look back up at him. He poked at the onions on the fire, then reached out and grabbed one by the stem. "Think this is cooked," he said. He blew on it, then sank his teeth into the tiny bulb. "Hot!" he said around a mouthful of onion, then laughed, sounding almost joyful. "Come have one; it's good."

The onions weren't much of a meal, but after nothing but a strip of jerky for dinner, they *were* good.

After breakfasting on the onions, Jasper smothered the fire with dirt and started west, Slip to his side and slightly in front of him.

"Don't want your back to the outlaw," Slip said after Jasper had stopped for a second time when Slip fell behind. "Insulting really. I thought we had an *understanding.*"

"Our understanding is that I'll shoot you

181

if I have to," Jasper snapped back.

"Which is why you should trust me a little more. I don't want to be shot far more than you don't want to shoot me."

But aside from that exchange, Slip didn't complain much as they walked. He talked, rambling on, but he didn't seem to require or even want Jasper's participation. For a while, it set Jasper's teeth on edge, the chatter, but soon it became like the roar of a river — background noise, always there in your ears but not demanding your attention.

Instead, he turned his attention to the question of who'd set up that ambush. He knew it had to be someone from Indigo; who else would have known they were heading down the mountain with Westin? Was it a coincidence that Slip Casey had set up shop in that cabin? Could Slip be working with whoever had wanted Westin dead? But Slip could have died just as easily in the ambush as Westin. There had to be something there, though. Too many coincidences, including the shot that spooked his horses a few days ago. *That* could have killed Westin too.

"Are you trying to work out who wanted the accountant dead?" Slip asked, jolting Jasper from his thoughts. Slip was still walking forward but his head was craned around, and almost immediately after Jasper looked at him, he tripped over a fallen branch and almost fell to the ground. Jasper stood back and let him catch and stabilize himself. Never a good idea to put yourself too close to a man you're leading around; that was how you got your gun taken and your prisoner gone.

"The wanted bills never said you flailed about and joked like a circus clown," Jasper said instead of answering.

Slip tripped again — this time on purpose — and turned his almost fall into a bow. "Slip Casey, unlikeliest clown and unluckiest man, here to entertain."

"Unluckiest man?" Jasper asked. He could think of several other candidates for that title, not least of which were men who had stumbled upon Slip's brother and ended up dead for it, or Westin himself, who'd been killed for a bundle of paper.

Slip shrugged. "Unluckiest outlaw, at least."

That seemed true. The lawmen spoke of Alec Casey with a great deal of hate, but almost a little reverence too. Not so the other Casey brother. The wanted bills might not outwardly describe him as a clown, but it seemed like the lawmen might.

"No suspects in that attack, then?" Slip asked after a moment of silence. "We don't know who we're running from?"

"*I* don't," Jasper said pointedly.

"And you think I do? Let me tell you, jehu, that I do not fancy being shot at. It is high on my list of things to avoid. If I were going to set up an ambush, I'd make sure I was far away from the bullets. You might not trust me, but you can surely trust that."

Jasper would have been more skeptical if he hadn't already come to the same conclusion himself.

The walk that day was mostly easy, and Jasper was fairly sure they were going in the right direction. He could navigate well enough by the position of the sun and stars, but he'd never been here before and had no landmarks to go by.

Every once in a while, Slip would call out something about onions, or carrots, or dandelion greens, and push them off the path Jasper was forging to forage for something to eat. Jasper went along with the greens and the onions, but drew the line at the carrots, whose foliage looked far too much like a plant his mother had warned him about.

"Plants look alike," Slip said, biting into a half-cleaned yellow carrot. "But that means more for me."

This stretch of land hadn't been as kind as the one the day before; they ran into some rocky outcroppings and Jasper decided it was smarter to go around than over them, which pushed them farther south than he wanted. Slip didn't seem happy with the decision, and Jasper wondered if he had thought about trying to knock Jasper down the rocky hill or off a cliff.

"Do you even know where we're going?" Slip questioned as they trudged in the shade of a rocky outcropping.

Jasper's stage normally made only four stops, but he'd had occasion to spend time in a couple of the other towns along his route — though for some of them, "town" was a generous word. If they could get down closer to those and then join up with the main road, he thought he could get them a horse and wagon for the last leg to Sonora. Or even, if he was lucky, a sheriff's deputy to come along with them. But he wouldn't just turn Slip over; if Alec Casey hadn't planned an ambush on the road, it meant he would try to bust his brother out some other way, and Jasper wasn't going to leave Slip's side until the other Casey showed himself. *Soulsbyville,* Jasper finally decided. That was far enough away from Long Barn that he didn't think they'd be looped into whatever had happened there, and he knew a person or two among the townsfolk well enough that he could probably borrow a horse.

"Sure do," Jasper replied, and thought it was probably true.

"I don't think you do. I think you're going to get us lost and dead instead of to Sonora."

Jasper stopped. "What does it matter to you if we're lost and dead? Would you prefer found and dead? Or get to Sonora and dead, because that's what ultimately is going to happen."

Slip tried to cross his arms, but the handcuffs didn't allow it. Instead he dropped his hands down in front of him. "Fine. Lead on, jehu Jasper. It's no wonder you found yourself driving a stagecoach. Hard to get lost on the same route every day."

It was the last thing he said for a while, and Jasper enjoyed the silence.

He started back up again once they'd stopped for the night.

"Nebraska, huh?" Slip asked.

Jasper looked over at Slip. He was shifting back and forth, like he couldn't get comfortable, and Jasper didn't blame him. The rocky ground would make for an uncomfortable sleep, but at least they were shielded a bit from the wind. "What about it?"

"You're from Nebraska."

Jasper had as good as told him that the day before, after Westin had taken his last breaths and before Jasper had ended a man's life. It had almost slipped his mind. "I am."

"Why'd you come to California?"

Jasper couldn't tell him he'd come to California to kill his brother. "Why does anyone come to California?"

"To get rich?" Slip crunched on some dandelion greens. "I came to California because people kept trying to kill me. Should have known going west wouldn't change that."

Jasper didn't have much sympathy for him. "That happens when your gang robs and kills."

"Ain't my gang," Slip said easily. "My brother calls the shots."

"And then you take them."

"I wasn't lying," Slip said, his voice more serious than it had been a moment before. "I'm no killer."

He sounded like he was being honest, but it wasn't the first time someone had tried to convince him they were innocent of association with Alec Casey's crimes. Just like then,

Jasper didn't believe a word of it now.

"The one thing you can't outrun's yourself," Jasper said. "You can run all you want, but there you are wherever you go."

"Then why'd you come to California?" Slip asked again like he hadn't believed Jasper's nonanswer any more than Jasper believed he wasn't a killer.

"I wasn't running away," he said. "I was running toward."

CHAPTER FIFTEEN

Alec Casey was keeping to his word about being fine with them staying strangers. He hadn't said a word since the sheriff had left with the posse, just sitting in his corner watching the room with bright dark eyes. The doctor had come to bandage him up, but even then he'd been quiet. Not sullen. Placid. Like none of this bothered him one bit.

His companion wasn't as calm.

"Look, kid —"

"Deputy," Jasper snapped in the man's direction.

"Deputy," he repeated, stressing the title hard as it could be stressed. "You gotta let me explain."

This wasn't the first time he'd tried it. His way of telling it was that it was all a mistake. He'd just been drinking in the saloon, minding his own business, when the sheriff's posse appeared. He'd never run with an outlaw like Casey. The outlaw in question didn't seem to appreciate that claim, but Jasper was just guessing at that. Alec Casey was hard to read when he wasn't flapping his lips.

"This is a misunderstanding. If you let me out, I can prove it."

Jasper folded his arms across his chest.

The man tipped his head backward and let out a groan. "Kid, I can make it worth your while if you'll —"

"You should stop that whining, Jacks. The kid here probably doesn't even know where the keys are," Casey said, his first statement since the sheriff had left.

Almost of their own volition, Jasper's eyes fluttered toward the desk, where the sheriff had put the keys. Just an instant, but Casey saw. Jasper told himself it didn't matter. He couldn't get the keys from the other side of the bars, now, could he?

It wasn't long after that that the other man seemed to realize that Jasper wasn't gonna let him out. He fell silent.

The posse might not be back tonight. Jasper knew that. If they were going to be gone all night, the sheriff had said one or two of the men would come back, relieve Jasper, and then they'd meet up again the next day. If they hadn't caught the last one by then . . . Well, the sheriff didn't seem to leave that as an option.

Not long after, Jasper heard a creak outside the window over the sheriff's desk. He shot to his feet like he'd heard the hammer click back on a revolver. There was nothing there when he peeked his head out, just dusky light. Should the sheriff be back by now? What if something had gone wrong? That was nonsense, though — one man against six had little chance in a shoot-out, or any sort of fight for that matter.

"Getting scared of every creak and moan of this rickety place, Deputy?" Casey asked. "Next thing you know, you'll draw on the sheriff's dog or one of those birds nesting in the roof." He whistled some sort of birdcall with a hint of a laugh at the end. "You have to be a little more brave if you want to be a real deputy, kid."

Jasper took a step toward the cell. "I'm not scared of you."

"I'm in a cage with a hole in my arm," Casey said with another flash of his pearly whites, "and you should still be scared of me."

The creak Jasper heard after that was closer, louder, and he spun around. A man stood in the doorway of the jail, hat tipped low on his head, and a black kerchief tied around his neck. The sun streamed in behind him, and Jasper couldn't quite make out his face. Jasper went to draw his gun, but before he could, strong hands grabbed his upper arms and yanked him back against the cell.

"Told you so," Alec Casey's voice sneered in his ear, and then everything went black.

CHAPTER SIXTEEN

No matter that Jasper had come to California all those years ago with a plan, driving a stage and scanning the wilderness around him in the meantime, the next day he was starting to think Slip might be right, and he'd lost the way back to the road entirely.

Not that he would admit it to Slip.

"You *don't* know where we're going," Slip said for the third time that day.

"The road's northwest. We're going northwest."

That much was true, more or less. But there wasn't a path to follow, and when they came upon rocky stretches or impassable thickets of brush and brambles, they had to go around them, and they were still not going the direction Jasper wanted them to go.

They'd wandered into hilly country, grass and trees, and no water to be seen. They'd been walking most of the day without seeing a creek or a pond, and Jasper's mouth had moved beyond parched into whatever unpleasant feeling came next.

"Ho, there, jehu, I think I see a well."

He'd said something similar earlier. He saw a creek that ended up being a rocky ravine, as empty of water as Jasper's canteen. But as much as Slip Casey's voice was starting to grate on Jasper's nerves, they sorely needed a well. Or a creek. Some water would have been nice about now.

But this time he wasn't wrong. There *was* a well, at the bottom of a hill. But once they got there, they ran into a problem — a tree had fallen onto the well, crushing in half its little wooden roof and blocking the mouth of the well. This tree looked to have actually fallen; Jasper could see where it had been uprooted and sent sprawling across the well.

"Think maybe we can get around it?" Slip asked. "Send down your canteen, maybe?"

Jasper ignored the question. A well like this wasn't just something you stumbled on. Someone had made it. They were miles from a road, even more miles away from anything resembling a settlement or town. But someone had dug this well, and kept it up, from the looks of things, until that tree had crashed down.

Sure enough, he heard a twig snap behind him. He spun, rifle at the ready.

Only to come face-to-face with a child.

A child holding a shotgun, but nevertheless a child, no more than twelve. She looked too small to be holding the gun, skinny, with a pale, pinched face, and bone-colored hair drawn back into two braids. "Get off our land," she said, her voice surprisingly strong.

"We're not after your land, just after some water," Slip said.

"It's *our* water," she replied.

"Not that you can get to it," he shot back.

For a moment, Jasper was afraid she was going to actually shoot back — with her shotgun. He held up what he hoped was a calming hand. "We won't take anything we're not given. I promise you that."

"We ain't giving nothing," she said.

"I fear we've got ourselves lost. Think you might be able to help us get going the right way?"

She threw a hand out and pointed. "That's north." She'd done it carelessly, but she was right.

Jasper looked at the tree. He wondered if this child — and whoever else made up the "we" she'd spoken of — had tried already to move it. He wondered if they had any more water. "Alright," he said gently as he could. "We'll move out."

The girl nodded, but before he could actually move, a little boy darted out from behind one of the trees and ran up to the girl. "Ada, maybe they can help!"

"We don't need help," she said. Slip snorted loudly, and the girl turned her shotgun on him. "We *don't*." She seemed to notice the cuffs on his wrists then, and looked back and forth between Jasper and Slip, alarmed. "Why's he wearing those?" she asked Jasper.

"I'm taking him down to Sonora. He's a wanted man."

"You're a lawman?" Her eyes were narrowed.

"I was doing a job for the lawmen up in Indigo. You know where that is?"

The girl nodded shortly. The little boy tugged on her arm. "He's a lawman, Ada. We should ask for help."

"Help with the well?" Jasper asked.

"Tree fell last week," she said shortly. "Been walking to the stream to get water."

"But it's not more than a trickle once the rains stop," the boy said.

"We can't lift it off," Ada said. "Bet you can't either."

Jasper looked over at the tree. He thought she might be right. Could take the tree apart, maybe, but that might take days. He

196

cast his eyes over at Slip. He didn't have days. He opened his mouth to tell them so, but before he could, Slip spoke up.

"Ain't all that difficult. You have some rope?" At the boy's nod, Slip gestured to a nearby tree. "Could rig a pulley, lift it off the well. Easy enough for the four of us to do." He pointed at the boy. "You'd have to supervise. Very important job."

The boy laughed. "And I can get the rope! Ada, please?"

"We can offer supper for your help, but nothing else," Ada said, her jaw set.

Slip started to speak again, but Jasper cut him off. "Supper and a night on your land. In a barn or stable, not the house."

She frowned at him, clearly trying to work out if he had ill intentions for wanting to stay the night, then gave a tight little nod. "But you also have to help us clear up the mess."

Jasper thought that over himself, then agreed. "Deal."

It was the work of the next few hours to collect the supplies, rig up a makeshift pulley, and string the ropes. Jasper half expected Slip's makeshift machine to fail completely, but to his surprise, it didn't. It wasn't easy work, and Slip *supervised* almost as much as the boy did. But the girl, Adaline, was handy with the rope and her brother, Thom, was a fair climber, and between the four of them, they'd cleared the well before the afternoon died. The four of them perched on the felled tree they'd moved and drank from the bucket of water Jasper had pulled up.

Jasper thought back to Hatch arguing that they could break up the tree on the road at Long Barn with the three of them and an ax. Jasper wondered if the man would have still been alive if they'd listened.

"Watch out for splinters," Slip muttered but took as long a drink as any of them.

Adaline pulled her coat around her tighter. Was she cold? The wind had only the hint of a chill. Jasper looked back toward the house. If their firewood store was only what was stacked up beside the house, it certainly wouldn't last them long.

"Can't just waste the tree. If you chop it, you'll have firewood soon as it dries out. We can get it started. Since you'll be using some of your own to make dinner."

Adaline looked skeptical but gave a nod.

Jasper jerked his head toward the log. "Gimme a hand, Slip."

Slip grumbled but did it, helping him

cleave part of the tree off with a wedge and an ax.

He let Jasper do most of the chopping, though, once they'd dragged the piece of trunk over to the chopping block, planting himself in the grass while Jasper split the trunk into pieces with the ax.

The cabin where the children lived was small but well-made, with a Mudcat chimney stretching up the side. There were flowers in a bed right next to the door, and Jasper wondered if one of the children had planted them or perhaps one of the parents neither child had yet mentioned. The barn where Jasper had negotiated their stay was only a stone's throw from the cabin and almost as large. What had once been a paddock was only half fenced in; two-thirds of the boards were on the ground, but there didn't look to be an animal to keep in anyway. The chopping block was next to the part of the fence that still stood, and Thom clambered up, seeming without a care that it might fall like the rest of it.

"So he's your prisoner?" Thom asked, hooking his arms over the top of the fence and staring at Slip with wide eyes. Ada had gone inside to start dinner, and Jasper was almost surprised at the mark of trust, leaving her brother out here with them.

"He is at that," Jasper said.

"What did he do?"

Slip started to talk before Jasper could and he winced, thinking of the things the man might recall from his colorful past as an outlaw. "Why, I am innocent of all the crimes I am accused of. I was taken into this man's custody by mistake, surely."

Jasper rolled his eyes. "He's a bank robber."

Thom looked back to Slip, his eyes wider than ever. Slip shrugged. "I'm a bank robber."

Jasper kept chopping while Thom peppered Slip with questions, he assumed about bank robbing. If Adaline heard this, she'd probably get her gun again, but Jasper let Slip talk. At least for once he wasn't talking at Jasper.

Ada had baked potatoes for all four of them, small and shriveled though they were, and made a salad of the same greens that Slip and Jasper had foraged from the woods the day before, along with some mushrooms and pickled beets that Thom started to complain about until he saw the look on his sister's face when he opened his mouth. Jasper thought of the stash of jerky and dried fruit in the boot of his stage again, left on the roadside, wasted.

The children explained that their pa had left them before the winter, going off to do something he claimed was for their own good, leaving Ada and Thom to take care of the land. *And take care of themselves,* Jasper thought. He'd promised them he'd be back before the weather got bad, but never came.

"He'll be back soon," Ada said confidently, and Thom nodded along.

Jasper half expected Slip to say something about that — he always had something to say — but he stayed quiet.

As though she wanted to make sure they both stayed that way, Ada hopped to her feet, collecting plates and sending Thom to fetch the map. The boy spread the battered map on the equally battered table. "We're here," she said, pressing her finger on a spot on the map that looked stained in the shape of a fingerprint. Jasper wondered how many times she'd traced various routes with that finger, trying to work out where their father had gone or maybe trying to work out where they should go if he didn't come back. "Where you say you're going?"

He pointed down to the bend in the road where Soulsbyville would be. "Here."

"If you get down to this creek, you can almost follow it to the road," she said, tracing her way through forest and rocks and down a squiggle that must have been a waterway. "You gotta go northwest from here."

Northwest, then follow the water to the road. Jasper nodded. "Thank you."

Ada sent her brother off to the bed in the corner of the room, then showed Jasper and Slip out to the barn. There were no animals inside, though there was some tack that had belonged to a horse. Ada didn't explain where theirs had gone, and Jasper didn't ask.

"You can sleep here," Adaline said, handing him two folded blankets. She still watched him like she'd rather have a gun on him than not, but she'd left it inside the house. He wondered if that would have been folly, had he been someone else, or Slip had.

"Thank you very much, Adaline."

He must have made his voice too soft, because she gave him a narrow-eyed look and then strode away. He remembered after his father died, when he thought anyone who spoke to him softly was trying to get him to go back to how things used to be, to let go of his anger or some other nonsense. He should have kept his tone businesslike, the way he'd have talked to O'Reilly on a good day.

"I don't know why you're still making me wear these cuffs."

Jasper shoved one of the blankets at Slip. "Didn't you hear your own stories today?" Jasper asked. "You're a bank robber."

"I'm the one who got us dinner and water from that well."

"It was my idea to help them."

"Your idea to help them, my idea that actually did help them." But Slip didn't seem too angry or surprised at Jasper's refusal. He settled himself down on the ground across from Jasper, a good distance away.

Jasper laid his rifle across his lap, set about cleaning it with the rag he'd gotten from Adaline. He'd shot it more in the last few days than he had ever before, and not once had that been at the man he'd intended to kill. Life was a funny thing, Jasper thought. He'd spent years thinking on killing, and when he finally did take a man's life, it was someone whose name he was never going to know.

Slip was quiet so long, Jasper almost thought he'd fallen asleep. "I can't believe you let those children feed us. You realize they're not much more than skin and bones?"

"If we didn't take their food, they wouldn't have taken our help."

"They're kids. Someone should be looking out for them." He folded his arms across his chest, and Jasper realized he'd never heard anything about any other member of the Casey family, aside from the two brothers. He carefully put the thought away. "You're really going to just leave these children here alone?"

"They say their pa will be back soon."

"Who's to say if he is? Gone all winter? He's probably dead. I thought for sure a man like you —"

Jasper cut him off, his voice sharp. "You don't know anything about me."

Slip sat back against the wall of the barn, which gave a groan. He sat forward again. "True enough. But you hate my brother. You said that's what good men do, right? Wouldn't think a good man would leave these children here by themselves."

"They'll be fine. Better off here than with me dragging them away from where their pa can find them."

"Surely you know some nice soul who would take them in?"

Jasper thought of Charley, who'd set them both to work but make sure they never had that lean, hungry look they both had now.

"We ain't taking them with us," he said. He had more reason than just one to avoid that. He wouldn't just be dragging them through the woods. He'd be dragging them into a shoot-out if he had his way about it. He didn't need any more kids coming up against Alec Casey.

But the next day it was a harder decision to stand by. They were ready to leave shortly after dawn. Jasper folded up the two thin blankets they'd been allowed to use and handed them back. Ada looked surprised, like she'd expected the men to try to take them. Thom looked like he wanted to throw his twiglike arms around both of them, and Ada even looked sad — or Jasper thought she did anyway; the girl would have a good poker face when she got older. If she got older.

That thought made him approach her.

"Listen," Jasper said, lowering his voice so Thom wouldn't hear, "are you sure your pa's coming back? I know you want to stay but —"

She had the shotgun in her hands and pointed at him before he could say another word. "Thank you for your help, Mr. Duncan. But I think you and your friend should be leaving now."

He nodded and stepped away. "Good luck," he said, and he and Slip headed northwest.

CHAPTER SEVENTEEN

Heading northwest — to get back on track to make it back to the main road and Soulsbyville — meant they had to ford their way through thick brush and trees. Slip stomped through ahead of Jasper, grumbling about thorny branches grabbing at his clothes. Jasper did his best to ignore him and found some tiny plums on one of the branches in his way. He pocketed the ones that looked the ripest and caught up to Slip before he'd even realized Jasper had paused in their trek.

Slip stopped complaining midmorning, only to start again when he heard rustling in the brush ahead of them.

"Could be a cougar," Slip said, but at least his voice was pitched low.

"But it ain't," Jasper whispered back, but he stopped moving, eyes scanning the different shades of green and brown around them for something that didn't quite belong. In the distance, he saw a flash of tan. He swallowed. *Could be a cougar,* he thought, then shook off the feeling.

"Did you see that?" Slip hissed, grabbing Jasper's arm.

Jasper reacted immediately, grabbing Slip's arm and twisting it until he forced Slip down. The other man let out a pained grunt when he hit the ground.

"I wasn't trying anything!" Slip cried, seeming to forget his worry about the cougar.

Jasper looked over where he'd seen the flash of tan. Nothing. Whatever it was, it seemed to have run away. He hauled Slip to his feet and pushed him forward. "Keep your distance," he ordered.

Slip brought his hand up to his shoulder. "I'm wounded, you know. Might have a little more consideration."

"Don't put your hands on me, and maybe I will," Jasper said, but the truth was, he wasn't inclined to be considerate when it came to a Casey.

The next time Jasper heard a noise in the distance, it wasn't leaves rustling. It was the sound of water. Not rushing but burbling. Just in time, because Jasper's canteen wasn't going to last them more than a day. It was also good to know they were heading the right way. They could follow the water toward the road, then head right down to Soulsbyville.

"You hear that?" Slip asked. "Much better than a cougar."

"It wasn't a cougar," Jasper replied, but jerked his head forward for Slip to walk toward the sound.

"I've never been so excited to get to a squiggle on a map," Slip said.

The creek was bigger than it had looked on the map. Bigger than the last one they'd come to also and looked deep enough in the middle that Jasper wasn't sure whether or not a man could cross without swimming. The bank wasn't steep, and they walked down to the water's edge easily. There was a sandy bank where the shallows lapped up onto the earth, but Jasper walked a ways down where the current ran a little quicker over a line of smooth stones before settling down into a placid little pool. One of the trees had grown up crooked and close to the earth, and some of its branches dipped low into the water.

The water was cold and sweet, and Jasper drank down almost a full canteen of it, kneeling right there at the river's edge. Slip, who'd kept his distance just as Jasper wanted, clearly had the same idea, drinking from his cupped hands like he was as parched as Jasper was. Jasper silently thanked Ada. They couldn't have kept going without knowing where the next water would come from, and Jasper's canteen wouldn't have lasted one man more than a day, much less two. He looked upstream and smiled. Fresh water for sure on the daily until they got back on the road. That was a relief.

Jasper filled his canteen and hooked it back onto his belt. A fish darted through the small pool below, silvery in the sunlight, and then disappeared under the leaves.

"I think we'll stop here for a while," Jasper said.

Slip looked up from where he'd been splashing water on his face. "Why?" he asked.

"I think I'll catch me some fish."

"When you said 'catch me some fish,' you actually meant 'us,' right?"

Jasper didn't answer Slip, keeping his eyes on the stick he held and the knife he was using to sharpen it.

Jasper had been fishing before with his father on the pond near their farm and since leaving home on the rivers and streams of California. He'd always fished with a pole, of course; spear fishing seemed like something from an adventure story he might have read in a dime novel. But how hard could it be to spear a fish? He'd found a long, thin branch, the straightest and strongest he could find, and broken it off. The tree had speared him with a long, thin splinter in revenge, but Jasper worked it out without bleeding much, and got to work whittling the end to a point with his knife. When he thought it looked sharp enough, he tested the point against his finger, then carved off a little more. With enough force, he could spear a fish with that; he was sure of it.

Jasper walked to the edge of the creek. He couldn't get a good enough angle from the shore, but if he walked out a little on those rocks . . .

He glanced back at Slip. The man had settled onto a branch of the tree that grew out over the water, his back against the trunk. His balance looked precarious, especially for a clumsy man like him, and Jasper wondered if he would fall off if he tried to stand. He didn't look like he was readying himself to shove Jasper in the water, try to steal the rifle slung across Jasper's back, or take Jasper's boots if he took them off to wade into the water. He didn't much care for walking in wet boots all day.

Jasper pulled off his boots and put them where he thought he could still grab at them if needed, and waded into the creek. The rocks were slippery beneath his feet, but his toes could grip like the soles of a boot couldn't, so he kept his balance fairly well until he was finally situated to see some fish.

The only problem was from his position in the creek, Slip was out of his field of view. Jasper kept imagining what he could be doing behind his back — moving closer, finding a branch to hit Jasper upside the head with, getting ready to run. Jasper couldn't very well run after him into the woods without his boots on. No, this would be the ideal time for Slip to run. Jasper should have made him do the fishing.

There were a few fish in the pool, most fairly small, but there was a good-sized one swimming leisurely what looked to be a foot or so into the water. Jasper gripped his spear and aimed, then stabbed it into the water. He didn't even get close, and the fish all darted away.

Jasper glanced up at Slip, assuring himself the man hadn't moved, and tried again.

He wasn't sure how long he'd been at it — long enough to lose three or four likely candidates for dinner — when Slip said, "You can't stab fish with your makeshift spear there if you're spending all your time watching me."

Not for the first time, Jasper wished he had the rope from the boot of the stage. Wished he had some more cloth too to make a gag so the man would *shut up.*

As though Slip could read Jasper's thoughts, he raised his bound hands. "I'm only saying, Mr. Duncan."

He was right, a fact that Jasper wasn't too fond of. Jasper couldn't get a bead on the fish's rhythm, or what was making his aim so off, when he kept looking back and forth. Jasper let out a sigh. "Just don't move."

"I won't do," Slip said, kicking his feet up on a rock. At least the clinking of his cuffs would mean Jasper could hear it if he started to come toward him.

But even giving it his full attention didn't help much. Fish would swim by leisurely, but whenever he'd strike at them, he'd end up with the spearpoint sunk in the earth at the bottom of the pool, clouding the water so it was hard to see the next fish coming. After a while the fish got wise, swimming to hide under the leaves of Slip's shady tree, where Jasper couldn't try to get at them.

Jasper would have stomped back out of the creek, if the rocks would have been a little easier on his feet and he could be sure he wouldn't fall and stab himself with his spear. As it was, when he returned to shore, Slip Casey was watching him, laughter in his eyes.

"Shut up," Jasper said, yanking on a boot.

"I did not say a word," Slip replied.

They followed the creek upstream, like Ada's map had directed them to. Slip didn't seem to have any compunction about following the water, even if it was leading them where he'd likely be hanged. He'd tried to run back on the road before the stagecoach ambush. Why not now? If he were his brother, Jasper was sure he'd have tried to escape by now. If *Jasper* had been the one captured, he'd have tried to escape. But Slip walked along easily enough. He'd stopped darting off their path, drawing Jasper away to grab at wild onions, and Jasper wondered if it was because he wasn't seeing any or because he was so hungry, he didn't even feel it anymore. Jasper felt a little like that. Or maybe Slip was still worried about the phantom cougar he thought they'd seen back a few miles. Jasper didn't ask.

They found a small clearing toward the end of the afternoon. Jasper had kept his makeshift spear with him, thought he'd give fishing another try in the morning, though a part of him just wanted to throw it in the small fire he built up. There was nothing to cook over it, but at least it was warm as the air started to chill.

"I think we should have brought those kids with us."

Jasper looked over at Slip. The man had his hands held out over the fire, and Jasper thought for a moment to warn him that the metal around his wrists would get heated too. But he stopped short of saying anything. "They didn't want to come."

"Think that should have mattered?"

"When one of them has a gun on me, yes, it matters," Jasper said. He thought of Ada's thin face. The girl was definitely foraging better meals than they had today, but how long would that last? "They're waiting for their father," he said finally.

"Their father's not coming."

"You don't know that," Jasper said even though he did. They both did. Sometimes people never came home. Jasper thought of his mother and the look on her face when he came home that terrible day, sheriff beside him, his father laid out at the under-taker's. Then he stopped thinking about it. He scrubbed his hand over the top of his head. "They live out so far. Wonder how far it is to the next farm. Why'd their father bring them there?" Why'd he *leave* them there?

"Some folks like peace and quiet," Slip said, and when Jasper laughed, he seemed genuinely offended. "You don't think I like some quiet?"

"I think if you ever met quiet, you'd talk at it," Jasper said.

Slip stared at him for a moment, face blank, then started to laugh. As though to prove a point, he stayed quiet while the fire danced in the breeze.

The first rustle Jasper heard, he put down to the wind, but across from him, Slip's shoulders tensed. Jasper was about to roll his eyes at the man when he heard another one, something moving through the brush, something bigger than a squirrel or a rabbit.

"It *ain't* a cougar," Jasper whispered before Slip could say a word.

But something was moving toward them, and the glimpse Jasper got of it certainly looked like it could have been the sandy color of a cougar. He reached for his rifle, raised it to his shoulder, and watched the brush.

Whatever it was got closer, and Slip scooted backward, away from the thing coming toward them. Jasper's finger slid to

216

the trigger, ready to shoot.

And then the creature came bounding out of the woods, and Jasper's breath left him with a whoosh.

It was a dog. Medium-sized, a tan-and-brown mutt with floppy ears and bright eyes, and Jasper *knew* that dog.

She barked once, as if to say hello.

"Deputy Dog!" Slip cried, reaching for her.

The dog let out a growl and backed away from him. She bared her teeth, her ears back and fur bristling.

"Fine, then," Slip said, dropping his hands back to his lap. "Don't be friendly. Lone survivors of an ambush — you'd think she'd want to band together, but no."

Jasper clicked his tongue quietly, like he'd heard Valdez do, and the dog quieted down. She looked over at him, her brown eyes trusting. "Come here, girl," Jasper said.

The dog padded over to him. She looked a mess, brambles and leaves tangled in her fur. Jasper remembered how she'd sat at Valdez's side, her chin on his knee. He'd doted on the dog, and she'd looked at him like he had hung the moon. But Valdez was dead, and Jasper was part of the reason.

Tabitha, he remembered. Valdez had named her Tabitha.

He reached a hand toward Tabitha. She let him. Her fur was surprisingly soft, even with the tangles. He combed the worst of it out the best he could, though a couple times she whined when he pulled her hair too rough. He'd heard a shot and her yelp, and he'd been sure the man had put her down. Jasper brushed through her fur, looking for a wound. He found blood on her side and a wound beneath it that almost matched Slip's. She'd been winged, but it hadn't stopped her from trekking through the woods and finding them.

"How'd you do that, girl?" he asked quietly. "How'd you find us?"

"A fair tracker, this girl. Think she can hunt?" Slip asked, perking up.

Jasper looked over at the dog. She didn't look too muscular. A strange sort of dog for a lawman to have, much less a hunter. "I certainly hope she can find her own food, at least. I ain't got any for her."

Her ears perked up, like she knew what "food" meant and thought them talking about it might get her some. Jasper frowned at her. If only getting food was so easy.

"Well, go on," Jasper said, pointing off into the woods. "Go get yourself some food."

He didn't think she could possibly understand all the words he was saying, but she stood up, shook herself off, and bounded out into the woods, moving like she certainly had some sort of purpose.

Jasper pulled the little plums he'd picked out of his jacket pocket and tossed one of them to Slip.

Slip caught it. "This ain't ripe," he said, and then took a bite.

"I'll keep the rest, then," Jasper said, but tossed him another when Slip held up his hands.

"It would have been better to be caught out here in the summer," Slip said, his voice almost wistful. "Sweet berries, some stone fruit maybe, and those onions might make a better meal too."

"You should have thought of that before getting yourself caught in April," Jasper muttered.

"Come summer, I wouldn't have been around to be caught," Slip retorted, then popped another sour little plum in his mouth, grimacing when he bit down.

Jasper wondered again why Slip had been holed up in that cabin. He'd come around to believing Slip wasn't a part of the ambush up on the road; if nothing else, he didn't seem like the type to risk his own neck for seemingly little gain. But that didn't explain why a member of the Casey Gang had been hiding so close to Indigo. Was Alec Casey planning something that had to do with the town? That would have been Jasper's luck, wouldn't it? Getting himself all the way out here in the middle of this mess when all he really had to do was wait in town for Alec Casey to show himself.

As the sun was setting, a rustling in the brush had Jasper sitting up straight, but it was the dog coming back. She ran right up to Jasper, holding something in her mouth. She dropped it in front of him, tail wagging, looking up at him with what almost looked like a smile.

Slip leaned forward. "What's that she brought you?"

Jasper looked down and let out a laugh. A fish. Small, not even the size of his hand, and ripped open from her teeth. But still — she'd brought him a fish. Jasper picked it up by the tail and held it up for Slip to see.

Slip looked from the fish to the dog, then back up to Jasper. "I don't think that's going to feed all three of us."

CHAPTER EIGHTEEN

The next morning Jasper decided to try fishing again. This time, he had more luck. The sun was just starting to come out, just showing itself on the water. Maybe even fish liked to enjoy the sunshine, because they were closer to the surface than they had been the day before. Jasper watched them swim, dark scales flashing silvery in the light, and got his spear ready.

He lost more fish than he managed to spear, but by the end of it, he'd gotten three fish. Trout by the looks of them. Two of the three were small, but they'd certainly make a better meal than the plums and the bits of fish from Tab's catch the night before. Jasper gutted the fish, then fried them on a hot stone, something like Slip had done with the onions.

"We got ourselves that fish fry," Slip said, licking his fingers.

Jasper felt better with something other

than wild greens in his stomach too. His spirits didn't seem as high as Slip's, but it felt good to walk that day, Tabitha trailing beside him. Her dislike of Slip didn't seem to fade. Maybe Valdez had trained her not to trust men in cuffs, or maybe Slip just wasn't the sort dogs took to. He seemed put out by it, grumbling whenever the dog would growl at him. Jasper certainly didn't mind it; he didn't have to watch Slip as careful with Tabitha beside him.

The land around the creek got rockier as the day went on, and Jasper decided to lead them up the embankment. Before they left the water's edge, he tried his hand at fishing again; this time, he speared three good-sized fish. That would do for dinner, at least. Tabitha hadn't caught so much as a minnow this time, though she seemed to have a good time swimming in one of the deeper parts of the creek.

Jasper made Slip carry the fish as they walked. He seemed in good spirits; maybe the promise of supper did that. He'd sometimes drift away from Jasper, but each time he did it, Tabitha would run up beside him and herd him back to the path they were supposed to be treading.

"I see why Valdez liked that dog," Jasper said, then felt another pang of guilt. He buried it. He wasn't the one who had ambushed the stage. Valdez would have died with or without his desires. He refused to feel guilty for them.

"Only because she's the greatest," Slip said. He tried to pet her after declaring her the greatest, and she nipped at his hand in warning. He'd apparently decided not to hold her dislike against her and didn't seem to mind being herded by the mutt.

The bank of the creek wasn't the only thing that was rocky in this part of the forest. Fewer trees sprang up here, more rocks, and Jasper wondered if the way they were walking might become impassable.

Slip didn't seem concerned about it, though that almost made Jasper *more* concerned.

The light started to die, and clouds had moved in. "We need to find a place to sleep," Jasper said. There would be no moonlight to see by if those clouds stuck around.

"Let's split up, cover more ground," Slip said with a cheeky grin.

Jasper was unimpressed with the joke. He pointed toward a rise a little ways off. "That way."

He hoped he'd find a nice alcove in the stone, sheltered from the wind that sometimes swept through here, but what he found was better. He found another cave.

"Well, look at that," Jasper said, ducking down and poking his head inside.

Tabitha had been right by his side, but she shied away from the cave opening. She gave a small whine when he dropped to his knees to see if he'd fit inside, and pawed at his arm, like she was telling him not to go.

"She doesn't like it," Slip said, his tone wary.

Jasper looked over his shoulder at Slip. His face looked wary as well. Jasper rolled his eyes. "She doesn't like you either."

That didn't lift the wariness from Slip's face, though Jasper hadn't expected it to.

"Stay here," Jasper ordered. "Right there."

Slip sat down on the ground where he'd been directed. "Trust me not to run now?"

He didn't answer that question. Instead he said, "Tabitha, watch him," in the same tone Valdez had used back on the stage. Her focus shifted, bright eyes on Slip, and he knew she'd at least bark if Slip tried to run.

Not that Jasper thought he would.

The cave opening was fairly small and didn't look particularly natural. Someone had widened it, probably with pickaxes. Miners most likely. He wondered if they'd found anything. Probably not. If they had, there wouldn't be just rocks and trees and water here; there'd be men. There were always men where gold was.

Once he'd gotten through the opening, the cave widened. It was tall too; Jasper could stand up in full, though if he raised his hand, it brushed the ceiling. Big enough for two, certainly, plus the dog. There wasn't any light in the cave, so he couldn't see how far back it went. He'd have to get wood to make a fire if they were going to stay the night in here and cook those fish. If the cave was too small, they might have to do that outside or risk choking on smoke. Jasper took a deep breath. The air smelled fresh enough, like it was flowing through the cave to somewhere else from here. Jasper had no intention to find out where that somewhere was, and he hoped no creatures were coming from the other side. He didn't relish bats or bears waking him up out of a deep sleep, though if he had to choose, he'd have taken the bats.

Jasper crawled back out. "We got ourselves a place to sleep."

"Whatever we do, we can eat first, right?" Slip stood and started to walk toward the closest trees. Tabitha gave two sharp barks. "You'll get some fish too, Deputy Dog. Stop your barking."

She sat back on her haunches and regarded him skeptically, and Jasper ducked his head, trying to hide his smile. "Let's go. Get some firewood."

It didn't take long to collect enough wood for a fire and some dried leaves for kindling. Before heading back inside, Jasper made a makeshift torch with a solid piece of wood and another piece of fabric torn from the lining of his coat. Soon, he'd barely have a coat if he kept it up.

He got the torch burning, then gestured to Slip. "You first."

Slip did not look pleased with that, but he did as Jasper said, grumbling something insulting under his breath. Slip was taller than Jasper, lanky, and he had to crouch down, even on his knees, to fit inside the small opening.

Inside, Jasper could see the cave went back farther than he could see with the light the torch gave off. It seemed to be less a cavern than a crack deep in the rock; it stretched up higher the farther back it went, but never seemed to get wider than it was where they stood. Against the stone wall lay a broken pickax and a lantern with its glass all shattered. *That might come in handy,* Jasper thought, and set about figuring out if he could light it.

Tabitha had crawled in after Jasper, though she still didn't seem fond of the cave. Her tail was tucked between her legs, and though she wasn't whining or growling, her fur was bristling and her muscles seemed coiled, like she was ready to pounce on any threat that emerged from the dark.

Slip stacked the firewood they'd brought in a few feet off from the entrance, then gestured down the cave passageway. "I'm going to find some stones to go round the fire. Unless you think I'm gonna run off into the dark."

Jasper didn't dignify that with an answer. The lantern seemed to be in fine condition aside from the broken glass, and it had some oil left in the bottom, though he had no clue how old it was. He decided to take the chance and lit the wick. The lantern flared to life and the cave got the smallest bit brighter.

"Are you planning on roasting those fish on a spit? Because I tell you, though I am hungry, I like some vari—" Slip's words cut off and suddenly became a scream.

Jasper grabbed the torch and the half of the broken pickax with the blade and ran toward him.

For a moment, Jasper thought he'd just disappeared. Or maybe he had run, after all. Or the ground had opened up and swallowed him whole.

At that thought, Jasper's steps stuttered to a stop. The ground had opened up alright, sometime hundreds of years before, leaving a gaping hole in the rock that had half swallowed Slip Casey.

He was holding on to the side closest to Jasper, one forearm pressed against the dirt, the other hand clutching the edge. His body looked twisted, like he'd been half turned around when he fell. He had turned back to ask about the fish, Jasper realized, and walked right into a hole. He really *was* the unluckiest outlaw.

Before Jasper could give him a hand and haul him up, Slip started to drop deeper into the hole. "Help!" He tried to heave himself up but then immediately dipped back down. "I think my foot's caught. I can't pull myself up."

Jasper crouched down, looked inside the crack in the earth. Closer to one of the walls, it was narrower, and it was there that Slip's foot was caught. The other side was wider, perfectly wide enough to swallow up a man. Jasper brought his torch closer. Even with the light, he couldn't see a bottom.

"Stop exploring and pull me up!" Slip cried. He tried to push himself up as he said it, then gave an anguished yell when his foot still wouldn't move.

"Stop your hollering!" Jasper yelled back. His voice echoed down the tunnel, like a dozen Jaspers were telling Slip Casey to be quiet.

But even a dozen wasn't enough because Slip just kept talking. "I don't want to die in a cave. You'll just leave me here like we left Westin, and I don't want to rot and get eaten by bats."

"Bats don't eat people," Jasper snapped back, though honestly he wasn't sure that was true. True enough, he supposed, if it would stop Slip from rambling. "And you ain't gonna die here. Just be calm for a second and we'll get you out."

This time Slip listened and quieted down. His breathing was still sharp and fast and loud, but other than that, all Jasper could hear was the slight whistle of the wind and the occasional whine from Tab, who clearly didn't like what she saw and smelled.

Jasper lay down by the edge and stared down at the rocks that held Slip's foot captive. He wasn't sure how the man's foot — large to begin with and then covered with a big leather boot — had fit through them. There was room enough to slide it to the side and get it out, Jasper thought, but he couldn't see properly in the dark and with Slip's lanky, shaking limbs in the way. It would have been better if he had some rope, he thought for what felt like the dozenth time since leaving his stage behind. If he had rope to tie around Slip's torso, he could make sure pulling his leg loose wouldn't send all of him tumbling down into the deep.

Jasper wondered how deep it went, and fought the urge to toss a rock down to see if he could hear it land at the bottom. He didn't think that would help the already panicking Slip keep his calm.

"Alright," Jasper said. "Here's what we're going to do."

Jasper put his torch to the side, then looped one of his own arms between Slip's; the chain between the handcuffs at least wouldn't break as easily as a hand's grip. He made sure he was planted as firmly as he could be on the ground, and grabbed ahold of Slip's shoulder with his other hand.

"Alright," Jasper said, his voice as calm as he could make it. Slip wasn't going to like what he had to say. "I want you to drop down a little."

"Drop down?" Slip's voice went shrill with disbelief. "You want me to drop down?"

"A little, yes! Your boot is caught. You have

skinny chicken legs, so you get it down a little farther. Then you can swing your leg right out."

"I drop down farther, I'm gonna *fall.*"

Jasper gripped Slip's shoulder tighter. "I'm not going to let you fall."

Slip's panic was as clear in the firelight as it would have been at the brightest part of the day. He must have been at least five years older than Jasper, but for a moment he looked like a child, his eyes wide and afraid. Then he nodded. "Drop down a little, then pull my leg out."

"Just so," Jasper said, and braced himself.

If Slip had tried it on his own, he probably would have fallen. As it was, when he lowered himself, he nearly lost his purchase on the edge. Jasper felt Slip's weight dragging him closer to the edge, and pulled backward as hard as he could, his arm straining against the metal of the chain.

Then Slip caught a firmer hold on the edge, though he still felt heavier than before. "You gotta pull me up," he said. "I'm just dangling here."

"Kick off the edge," Jasper said. Slip was heavier than he looked, and even though Jasper had tried to get the best angle he could, it was certainly not ideal. For the first time, he wished he'd taken off the man's cuffs.

"And get my foot stuck again?" Slip demanded.

But Jasper felt his body swinging a little and he must have kicked off against something, because it gave Jasper the added leverage to help haul Slip out of the crack and back onto the solid ground of the cave floor.

Jasper untangled their arms and Slip lay there, panting, staring at the endless black above them.

"Your foot okay?" Jasper asked.

Slip looked over at him, his eyes a little hazy, before they sharpened and he scrambled into a sitting position. He brought his hand to his boot, feeling along his leg until he seemed satisfied nothing was broken, bone or leather.

"I'm fine," he said, then let out a breath. "You saved my life."

Jasper climbed to his feet, brushing the cave dust off his shirt and pants, even though he was just going to sit back down in it. "Well, I couldn't very well let you fall down a hole."

"Dead or alive, remember?"

"In this case, 'dead' implies that I have a body to deliver."

Slip snorted. "Can we get out of this place now?"

Jasper looked around. "We got four walls and a roof here. Best shelter we've had since day one."

Slip looked back toward the crack he'd almost died in. "It's a death trap."

"Just don't fall down the hole," Jasper said. He walked back to their firewood and set about spitting and cooking the fish.

Slip pressed himself against the cave wall and grumbled to himself unhappily until the smell of sizzling fish seemed to pull him back toward the fire.

"You just like things that almost kill me," he said as he settled across from Jasper.

"Eat your fish."

Slip looked over at Tab. "He doesn't even deny it!"

She narrowed her eyes at him and let out a low growl. Slip threw his hands up, exasperated, and Jasper had to resist the urge to smile. He did give Tab a scratch behind the ear when he gave her her portion of the fish, though.

CHAPTER NINETEEN

The next day, the land got less rocky, and they started heading toward the water again. Jasper wanted to keep on the right track, not get them turned around again, but something was spooking Tabitha as they went. Her fur would bristle, and every once in a while, she'd sniff at something and let out a low growl. The first couple of times, Slip seemed poised to fight whatever it was she was smelling, and even Jasper tensed, but after the first hour, neither of them thought much of it.

The burbling noise that let them know they'd made their way to the water was a welcome sound. When they broke through the trees and saw it, Jasper realized the bank here was higher; the water was a good ten feet below, narrower here than it was downstream, rushing faster. They could still follow from up here.

Beside them, Tabitha started to growl again.

"What is that dog growling at now?" Jasper asked.

She shot forward into the brush and Slip followed close behind. "Do you think she can hunt better than she can fish? We can send her out into the woods for our dinner. Get us some rabbits or a goose."

Jasper's laugh caught in his throat when he heard the growl. Not Tabitha this time. No, this time it *was* a cougar.

Tabitha came crashing back out of the brush, teeth bared, barking. The cougar came with her, the growl in the back of her throat becoming a scream. Slip threw himself backward, slamming into Jasper. They both ended up in a tangle on the ground while Tabitha and the cougar faced off.

The cat was full-grown, rangy, and *mad* by the looks of her. Her teeth and claws were sharp, built for tearing meat apart. She lunged toward Tab, front paws open like she was going to tear into the dog from both sides. Tab backed up and the cougar landed on the ground, a cloud of dust rising up around her. Tab advanced, snarling, and the cat sidestepped, growling low in her throat.

Jasper had lost his grip on his rifle when he fell, and he scrambled to get it while Slip got to his feet. But the rifle had fallen down the creek embankment, and before Jasper could decide whether to climb down and get it, Slip grabbed a rock and pitched it at the cougar's head.

The cougar jerked her head toward him and let out another scream. The sound of it — Jasper wanted to throw himself down the embankment and run as fast as he could to get away. But the cougar swiped a paw at Tabitha and the dog yelped in pain and slammed to the ground, and Slip picked up another rock. This one connected, and the cougar stalked toward him, the scream simmering down to a rumble in her throat.

Slip Casey — the fool — really was going to be eaten by a cougar.

Jasper started to back up toward the embankment without the cougar noticing. Maybe he could get to the rifle. Maybe —

Slip fell to the ground and curled up, like maybe if he made himself small, the cougar would leave him be. But then he seemed to be pulling at his shoe, and did the fool really think he could use his boot as a weapon against —

Before Jasper could finish the thought, Slip uncurled himself, and in his hand was a gun.

Jasper froze.

Slip didn't hesitate before shooting. One shot, two, and the cougar backed away quickly, her fur still bristled, her throat still growling, but like she knew whatever made that noise could kill her, she disappeared back into the brush.

Slip lowered his arms, then started to crawl toward Tabitha. "Aw, Tab, why'd you go and find a cougar?" he asked quietly.

Jasper had reached Slip's side before he realized he was moving, grabbing the hand that still held the gun and forcing its fingers to let go their hold.

"Ow!" Slip said as Jasper wrested control of the revolver. "You ain't gotta do that."

Jasper surely did gotta, but he didn't say that. Instead he stared down at the revolver in his hand.

He recognized this pistol. It was the one Hatch had shoved at Westin in the stage. He'd asked Slip about it, even searched him, but clearly he hadn't done a good enough job.

"You had this the whole time?"

"I did," Slip said. "Wasn't about to give it up. And it's a good thing I didn't since we almost got eaten by a cougar."

"*You* almost got eaten," Jasper said without out even really meaning to. He'd gotten comfortable with Slip over the last few days, found himself retorting without thinking about it, even sharing his thoughts when he did think about it. And the whole time, Slip had had a gun, waiting for the right moment to shoot. Jasper didn't know what to think about that.

"I'm getting my gun," he said, and then tucked the revolver into his belt. "And I'm keeping this one."

"Then you'd better get better at taking on mountain lions," Slip snapped back at him, petting Tabitha again.

Jasper wanted to ask if she was alright. Wanted to sink down next to her himself. But he'd let himself get too comfortable around Slip as it was. They didn't need to both be worrying about the dog.

"You're miserable with this thing anyway," Jasper muttered. "Not sure how you missed that cat."

"I wasn't trying to *shoot* it." His eyes were wide and horrified. "I just wanted it gone. Big, beautiful cat like that, why would I want to shoot it?"

Why indeed? Jasper didn't say anything else, just retrieved his rifle from where it had fallen. He brushed the sandy soil from it and climbed back up again. Slip was where he'd left him, but Tabitha had climbed to her feet. She didn't seem to be injured any worse than before. She seemed to be tolerating Slip poking at her, though when she saw Jasper, she walked over and stared up at him with those big brown eyes. She looked like a child asking her pa if he was mad at for her getting into a fight. He gave in and scratched behind her ears.

"The cat was probably headed for water," he said. "Let's get away from the creek for the night."

"You could have shot me," Jasper said later. Tabitha's head was on his knee, and she looked up at him, eyes quizzical. Slip, across their small fire, looked over at him with much the same look. "You had that revolver for days, and you could have shot me anytime."

Slip shrugged his shoulders. "Not anytime. You were watching me pretty careful like."

"Not that careful." Jasper wondered if Slip had thought about doing it at the creek. He would have presented the perfect target then, standing on those slippery rocks, his back to Slip like he trusted him. One shot and he'd have ended up in the water. It wouldn't even have had to be a fatal shot. He could have drowned as easily as bled to death.

"I told you before, I ain't a killer. I don't

239

want to die, sure, but I don't want to have to kill anyone else either."

At last, Jasper believed him.

CHAPTER TWENTY

Jasper remembered only bits of what happened next. A few words — *"The keys, slip 'em here"* — and the jangle of metal, followed by a clang. Boots on wood close to his ears. A voice, muffled. *"He's just a kid. Leave him be."* Gunshots. One, two, three. He felt like someone had shoved his head underwater and he couldn't make it to the surface.

And then finally, his eyes opened.

It couldn't have been too long, because when he came to, it was still afternoon. It took him a long moment to remember what had happened. Alec Casey in the cell. Alec Casey grabbing him through the bars.

Alec Casey.

Jasper scrambled to his knees, even though it made his head swim to do it. The cell that had been Casey's was open and empty. The cell beside it was still occupied — but this time by a corpse. It looked like someone had slashed Jacks' throat from end to end. The cell was painted with red, and bloody boot prints led from the cell to the door.

Jasper forced himself to his feet and followed them.

The boot prints led down the steps onto the street, and then the blood mixed with the dirt. Jasper didn't follow them, instead stopping at the top of the steps and looking down the road.

There were as many people on the street as there had been when they'd ridden in earlier that day. But instead of looking proud, they looked panicked. Two women huddled together in front of the general store, crying. Jasper wondered dimly who had died, because someone had to be dead for everyone to be acting like this.

The sheriff was suddenly in front of him, a hand on Jasper's shoulder, steadying him. Jasper hadn't realized he needed to be steadied.

"Son," the sheriff said, "you don't want to go down there."

But he needed to go down there, Jasper thought hazily. He needed to follow the boot prints. He'd let Alec Casey get away. He'd —

"He got out," Jasper said, then repeated it again, his voice stronger. "He got out."

The sheriff took a deep breath. "I know."

If he knew, why wasn't he doing anything?

Why wasn't he following the boot prints? Jasper tried to follow them with his eyes and saw that there were people clustered on the road itself, all standing around something, over something.

Who died? Jasper wondered again and started down the steps.

The people standing in the middle of the road parted as he got closer, and instead of looking down, they watched him as though he were more interesting than whatever — who-ever — was in the middle of the road. *The man who died,* Jasper thought as he looked down. No, that couldn't be right, because the man in the middle of the road was his father.

Jasper remembered the gunshots he'd heard. One, two, three. Only two had hit his father. Did that mean the third had hit Alec Casey? Jasper looked around wildly, like by finding another body that would make his father less still on the road in front of him.

But Alec Casey was nowhere to be seen, alive or dead.

And his father was. But not alive.

Jasper didn't remember dropping to his knees beside his father, but suddenly his vision was clouding from the dust his knees kicked up. That and from tears.

His father's eyes were already closed. Jasper realized that he'd never see them open again, that his father's mouth would never speak words, that his hand, so strong, would never clap Jasper on the back again. *You're gonna regret that,* Alec Casey had said, but Jasper's father was dead: he wouldn't regret anything ever again.

CHAPTER TWENTY-ONE

Jasper finally realized they were being tracked the next morning.

He'd woken up with a dry mouth and a full bladder and had left Slip — still asleep — under Tab's watchful eye to relieve himself and find water. They'd left the creek only the afternoon before, but they'd run through their water quickly, what with Slip insisting Tab drink her fair share instead of finding her own. It couldn't be too far off.

After he'd relieved himself, Jasper backtracked a ways to the rocky incline they'd seen, then climbed up. Get enough height and he figured he should be able to see the creek. Once they found their way back to it, they could keep following it a ways, at least. Keep their access to fresh water — though preferably without any more cougars. The squiggly line had led almost all the way to the road on the map, after all. They would be in Soulsbyville soon.

By the time he got to the top, Jasper could feel the burn in his legs. It had been steeper than he thought, but the view at the top was just what he'd wanted. He could see for miles. He thought of Slip admiring the sunset and wondered what he'd say about this, watching the sunlight spread toward the west, the last vestiges of dark at the edge of the horizon. Would he be as much a fool for a sunrise as he had been for the sunset? He didn't have many more of either once Jasper got him to Sonora.

Jasper put sunrises and sunsets out of his mind and started scanning the forest for the creek they'd left behind. It didn't take him long to see the glint of the morning sun off the water. He started to trace its path northwest, toward them and toward their destination, when he caught sight of something else.

A fire.

A low fire, to be sure, just like the one Jasper had made the night before. The smoke wasn't wafting upward in curls; it billowed. Whoever had made the fire had just put it out. How long had they been tracking him and Slip? Had they heard the shots the day before and started to close in?

Jasper was about to scramble back down the rocks, then stopped. Jasper's hand went to the papers tucked inside his coat. They wanted those papers. If they found him and Slip, they'd kill them both once they had those papers in their hands. But without them . . . Would they risk killing them if they didn't have what they were looking for? Could that be enough to keep them alive, at least long enough to *do* something?

He had to hope it was.

By the time Jasper made it back to the makeshift camp, Slip was awake and Tabitha was growling at him.

"Pretty girl, when are you going to stop acting like I'm the enemy? We were fine yesterday. Now you know ol' Slip wouldn't —"

"Stop talking to the dog," Jasper said. He strode over to the mostly dead fire, kicking the dirt and stones he'd dug out from the pit over the embers. The smoke made his eyes burn. "We gotta go."

"I think you got some of the dirt in my eyes, Duncan," Slip said, squinting.

"We have to leave now, or the both of us are gonna catch a bullet."

That got Slip moving. He staggered to his feet, and Tab let out a low growl in warning. Jasper clicked his tongue like Valdez had and Tabitha stopped growling, but only after looking over at Jasper. If a dog could look droll, then she definitely did.

"What'd you see out there?" Slip asked.

"Someone's tracking us. They're about a mile off, maybe, but I think they're already moving."

"What's the plan?" Slip asked.

Run and hope the man tracking them wasn't as good as all that, Jasper thought. Run and hope that the mountain lion Tab had tangled with the day before might end up right in the man's path. But beyond hope? The plan was just to run.

Jasper pushed Slip forward. "The creek's that way," he said as they started through the brush. "If we can get to the water, maybe we can walk upstream a while, get him to lose our trail."

Jasper wished he would have gotten a closer look at the person — or people — after them. How long before he had seen the remains of that fire had the man chasing them smothered it? They could have a head start of nearly an hour, or they could have five minutes. He wasn't betting it was on the longer side.

From above, Jasper had thought the creek looked fairly close. That was wrong. They ran, Slip huffing loudly beside him, and Jasper started to wonder if he'd somehow gotten turned around. The creek had been this direction, surely? But the trees grew denser here, sugar pines and oaks, and Jasper wondered whether or not he'd made up that glint off the water, or whether it had just been a trick of the light.

Just when he was about to suggest they take a sharp turn west, run full out as hard as they could, he heard the rush of water from up ahead.

He nudged Slip, who seemed to hear it too, and they both went hard for the river.

The embankment was an easier incline here. Part of it looked like the ground had suddenly fallen away, leaving a small cliff of crumbling earth. But beside that was a sandy slope. Easy to descend, if easy also to leave tracks.

Tabitha bounded down the slope. She stopped at the water, then turned around, ears back suddenly, growling.

"You sure she was Valdez's dog?" Slip muttered, starting to amble down the bank. "She sure seems to read your mind. 'Keep moving, fool of an outlaw. Get on down here.' "

Jasper almost laughed, and then he realized Tabitha wasn't looking at Slip.

He spun, and he had his rifle almost up to his shoulder when it was knocked out of his hands with a swift blow.

"Hands up. Both of you."

A revolver was pointed at Jasper's chest. The man in the cave had been twitchy, as though keeping an eye on both Jasper and Slip made him nervous, and that split focus had cost him his life. *This* man didn't seem twitchy *or* nervous. His eyes were calm and cool and leveled right at Jasper, just like his revolver.

And Jasper recognized him. This was the man who'd stood by his stagecoach, who had raised a rifle at him and would have taken the shot, had Tabitha not gone for him. Jasper's eyes darted to the other man's leg. Sure enough, there were tears in his heavy trousers, and Jasper could see traces of blood at the edges of the rips.

But it wasn't just that. Something about his face — wide, plain, middle-aged — tickled the back of Jasper's mind. Someone from Indigo? The station at Sonora?

"Come on up here, Casey," the man called down to Slip. When he hesitated, the man said, "You ain't far enough away to think I can't hit you if you run."

That seemed to convince him. Slip climbed up the slope, bound hands raised, feet sliding a little on the sand.

"Stand over that way," the man directed,

and Slip took a few steps to the side, too far away to go for Jasper's rifle. "I think you know what I'm after," the man said.

Jasper nodded. "The accountant's papers."

He nodded once. "Hand 'em over. No need for your death to be painful."

"And if I don't?"

"Then there will be a need, won't there?"

"I don't have them," Jasper said. Out of the corner of his eye, he could see Slip's head turn sharply toward him.

"Then there's no use for me to keep you alive, is there?" the man asked, and cocked the gun.

"Considering I'm the only one who knows where they are, I'd surely say there is."

The man smirked. "You hid them."

"When I realized you were tracking us. Think you can search the whole forest? Really think you'll find them?"

"Take the coat off and toss it here," the man said.

Jasper did as he said. The man shook the coat out, but all that fell to the ground were the little leaves and twigs that had been caught on his coat as he ran. The man dug into the pockets, and Jasper heard the fabric tear, but it wasn't as though his jacket hadn't already been ruined. After a minute, the man grinned and jerked his hand out of a pocket, papers crushed in his hand. But when he looked at them, his smile faded. He'd pulled out Jasper's mother's letters, not the papers Westin had written about the mine.

"I told you I didn't have them."

The man threw the letters on the ground and Jasper felt a pang of sorrow for his mother's words. He hadn't read them anyway, Jasper thought bitterly.

"You, turn," he said to Jasper.

He turned in a circle, arms out, then watched as the man repeated the routine with Slip, patting him down quickly. He didn't find the papers on Slip either. Jasper and Slip didn't have any bags, and there was nowhere else to hide the papers on either of their persons.

"You *did* hide them," the man said. "Smarter than you look."

"I'll take you to them," Jasper said. "Hand them over easy as can be."

"You aiming to trade them for your life?"

"Why not? The papers is what you want. And I ain't got no use for them. You get those, there's no cause to shoot us, is there?"

The man looked like he was considering it. "True," he said. He lowered the revolver.

And then before Jasper even realized what he meant to do, the man shoved Slip off the embankment.

A strangled cry and then a splash came from below, and Tabitha lunged at the man, growling. The man brought the gun back up, but instead of shooting the dog, he hit her across the head with it and she crashed to the ground, whimpering.

"Leave the dog be," Jasper said, "and let me take you to what you want."

"The mutt ain't even yours and you've got a soft spot," the man said with a smirk. "Next thing you know you'll be wanting me to check on the outlaw."

"The outlaw's as good as dead down there." Jasper wasn't sure if it was true. The fall wasn't too bad, but how deep was the water? And Slip in those metal cuffs . . . Jasper didn't turn his head to check, only kept his eyes on the man in front of him.

"Alright, then," the man said. "Lead the way."

CHAPTER TWENTY-TWO

Jasper marched through the woods, a gun at his back.

The sky had lightened and it should have been easier to walk, the dimness of dawn not hiding roots and rocks to trip over. But instead each step felt heavier than the last. He'd hidden the papers, he had a plan, but there were too many things that could go wrong. Jasper didn't think, not for an instant, that this man would let him live. No, he might string him along with that promise until Westin's papers were in his hands, but the moment that was done, he'd be dead. He'd bought some time with the hidden papers, but now that he'd made his purchase, he wasn't sure his plan would work. The man had Jasper's own rifle pointed at his back, and another revolver tucked away. Jasper couldn't outrun him, and the man kept enough distance between them that he wouldn't be able to pull a move like the man had pulled on Slip back at the creek.

Unless he could get him to close that distance. Make him mad. Jasper thought of Slip, who'd made Jasper want to slap him upside the head a dozen times in the last few days.

"How'd you know she's not my dog?" he asked.

"What?"

"You said the mutt wasn't mine. How'd you know that? You from Indigo?"

He didn't answer. So Jasper did what Slip always did and kept talking. "You one of the miners that got laid off? Heard about that trouble. That why you went into the outlaw business? Less opportunity to be fired?"

"Quiet," the man ordered.

"Fired from the mine," Jasper mused, and then it clicked. Something Jack had said back at the saloon, one of the bosses being fired. Jasper snapped his fingers. "Tough luck, Brady."

When he spoke, Brady didn't sound angry. Not yet anyway. "Why, I didn't think you'd remember me. You never show much interest in what goes on up in town, do you? But then your deputy friends didn't seem to recognize me either."

"Well, your face was covered. Makes identifying folks a little harder, even when they're shooting at you."

"Just being cautious. I didn't ever really think your stage could outrun us but didn't want word getting back if one of you did make it out."

"Who's this 'us'? And is there a reason you don't want to fire that gun?" Jasper asked. "Someone else out here?"

"Bullets don't come cheap. Maybe I didn't think he was worth one."

Jasper didn't think that was all there was. Maybe someone else was out here — maybe close. "You're not wrong about that, though he was marked for the noose, not for drownin'."

"Dead's dead, Duncan. Not sure it matters how you get there."

Jasper thought of his father lying on the ground, his blood pooling in the dirt, and Westin's blue lips, still forever in the dark of that cave. He'd rather die here under the open sky than in a cave. His father would rather not have died at all.

It seemed to take less time to get back to the camp and Jasper's smothered fire than it had to get to the river.

"This your camp?" Brady asked like he didn't know it was. "Where's the papers?"

"They're not here," Jasper said.

"Then where?"

Jasper looked up the rocky incline toward where he'd watched the sunrise. "Up there."

Brady clearly realized the climb up was more precarious for him than walking through the forest had been. A sharp shove could send him toppling, just like he'd sent Slip. The rocks would probably be less forgiving than the water had; Jasper laid even odds that Slip had made that fall just fine, but he didn't think Brady would make this one, if Jasper managed to get his hands on him to push. But the man still kept his distance as they climbed.

When they reached the top, Jasper's lungs were burning. After his morning climb and then the run, all following four days of trudging through these woods, he'd already felt tired. Now, at the top, he bent at the middle, hands on his knees. His breath came faster than those fish he'd speared the day before.

"You've had enough of a rest," Brady said.

"Can't talk if I haven't caught my breath," Jasper wheezed.

That, it seemed, was what made Brady lose his temper. "Where are they?" The man smacked Jasper across the face with the revolver, just like he'd done to the dog. Like

257

Tab, Jasper dropped to the ground. "Tell me where you hid them."

Jasper looked up at him, smirking. "Maybe we used them for kindling. Burned them right up."

"If I believed you did that, I'd put a bullet through that brain of yours."

Jasper swiped his hand across his lower lip. His thumb came back bloody. "You're going to kill me no matter what I give you."

Brady shrugged his shoulders. "I told you, it doesn't have to be painful."

"I thought it doesn't matter how a man dies."

"Well," he said with a bit of a smile, "I suppose it matters to him."

Jasper snorted. "Fine. Clean shot. You swear it?"

Brady nodded. His word didn't mean much to Jasper.

He wasn't far from where he'd left the papers. He could have shuffled closer on his knees, but instead he got to his feet and staggered closer.

There was a crack in the stone, one layer jutting out over another, leaving a small hollow that Jasper's head wouldn't have fit inside. His hand did, though, and he reached it inside. His fingers brushed the creased paper of Westin's notes.

And then the metal beside it.

Jasper's fingers closed around the grip of Hatch's revolver. He'd get only one chance.

"Are they in there or not —" Brady began.

And Jasper pulled the gun and shot.

Brady staggered back, Jasper's rifle falling from his hand. But *he* didn't fall. Jasper had caught him in the shoulder, not the chest like he'd been aiming to. Jasper didn't have enough time to fire again before Brady let out a roar and lunged at him.

Jasper's back slammed against stone. Brady got one of his hands around Jasper's arm, slammed it against the ground once, twice, trying to get him to let go of the revolver. Jasper held on as best he could and raised his left arm, slugging Brady in the head.

They grappled on the ground. Each hit from Brady drove Jasper against rock and he eventually lost his grip on the revolver. Brady pulled away to grab for it, but Jasper pushed his knee upward into the other man's stomach. The breath whooshed out of Brady and Jasper shoved him off. Before he could get to the gun, Brady grabbed Jasper's hair, tried to slam his head back against the stone like he did his hand. Jasper grabbed onto Brady's arm and rolled.

They were close to the edge. Jasper heard

rocks start to slide down the cliff. Could he roll Brady closer, send him toppling? He didn't think he could, not without maybe going over himself.

Instead, Jasper tried to free himself from Brady's grip. He managed to get in another good hit to his temple, get enough space that he could scramble away — only to realize he'd gone in the opposite direction from the revolver.

Brady realized it at the same time he did. He let out a laugh, pushing up to his knees, and pulled his own revolver from his holster. "Nice try," he said, revolver trained on Jasper. He reached into the crevice in the stone where Jasper had tucked the papers and the gun. Brady pulled out Westin's papers. "Thanks for these," he said, then folded the papers in two and tucked them under his belt.

He cocked the hammer, and his mouth opened again, as though he were going to send Jasper off to his death with some sort of pithy remark. But before he could say a word, a shot rang out. Jasper flinched at the noise, though Brady's finger hadn't pulled the trigger.

Slip's had.

Brady's revolver slid from his grasp, and then he slumped over, face pressed against the stone, the eye Jasper could see still open. Slip stood behind him, Jasper's rifle in his hands, the butt of it still pressed against his shoulder, as though he was ready to take another shot if Brady tried to get up.

Brady didn't get up.

Slip still hadn't lowered the rifle. He was wet from head to toe. His pants were muddy from wading out of the creek or trudging through the forest after them.

Jasper climbed to his feet, shaky. "You want to point that somewhere else?" Jasper asked, but there wasn't any bite to the question.

Slip lowered the rifle until it hung loosely at his side. "Want this thing back?" he asked.

Jasper did, but first he retrieved Westin's papers from Brady's body. He also picked up the man's revolver. He'd used the last bullets in Hatch's gun; maybe this one would come in handy. Then he made it to Slip's side.

Jasper took the rifle back. The last shot his father had fired from this rifle had been at Alec Casey. Odd that the man's brother had used it to save him.

He didn't say any of that. He just looked Slip over. His cheeks were red and his eyes looked a little cloudy. "You hurt yourself in that fall?"

Slip shook his head slowly. "I got a harder head than that."

But Jasper wasn't sure that was true, especially when Slip started to climb down and Jasper saw the wound at the back of his head, the dark hair around it matted with blood.

When Slip sank to his knees at the bottom of the slope, Jasper thought for a moment that the outlaw had keeled over. But then Jasper realized he was on the ground beside Tabitha, whose face was pressed into Slip's chest as Slip scratched her ears.

When Slip let her go, Tabitha trotted to Jasper's side as well, her tail wagging despite the beating she'd taken. He ran a hand along her head. Where *had* Valdez gotten this dog of his?

"We need to go," Jasper said. "I think he was alone, but we can't be too careful."

"No," Slip said, his face solemn for once, "especially not with all those gunshots. Lead all sorts right to us."

They hadn't gone far when Slip started to lag behind. When Jasper turned to face him, Slip held up his shackled hands and laughed. "I know. You don't want the outlaw behind you." His words ran together slightly and his shoulders were slumping.

"Let's take a rest," Jasper said, gesturing to a log a little way off.

Slip sank down when they reached it, stretching out his neck, then wincing at the movement of his head. He looked pale and clammy, and Jasper busied himself with pulling his knife out from its sheath on his belt so he wouldn't keep looking at Slip and wondering if he was getting worse.

"Now, you didn't stop us here so you could use that on me?" Slip asked, shrinking back a little when he saw the knife. "I know the handbill says dead or alive, but I would honestly rather it be alive."

Jasper couldn't tell if he was joking or not. He crouched down on the ground in front of him and gestured to Slip's hands. "Lift 'em up."

Slip's brows rose sharply, and he did as Jasper said. "If I knew all I had to do was show you how much these weighed me down, I'd have made sure to be obvious about it from the beginning."

It wasn't hard to force the locks on the cuffs with his knife. Jasper wondered if they were old or badly made or if this sort of cuffs was always so easy to force.

When they fell away from his wrists, Slip rubbed each of them in turn. His skin was red and raw from the metal. "I never much liked being chained up," he said.

"You picked a lousy career if you don't like being cuffed."

"Well, I just have to get better at it," Slip said with a laugh. "You know how many times Alec's been caught by the law?"

"Once," Jasper said without even pausing.

Slip didn't look surprised that he knew. "Once. I suppose it helps to shoot first instead of giving deputies a fat lip. But you know, I always wondered why Alec liked shooting people so much. Still don't understand. I have decided that I myself don't care for it."

Jasper thought of Brady falling to the ground, and of his father's body lifeless in the road.

"You said you'd never killed anyone."

Slip nodded. "I hadn't."

It didn't seem like something Jasper should thank him for, not when he clearly found Brady's death unpleasant. "You saved my life."

Slip rose to his feet again, still looking shaky, and stretched out his arms. He didn't look back at Jasper when he spoke. "Let's call it returning the favor. Say what you want about the Casey brothers, but one thing we have in common is that we always repay a debt."

Jasper had thought that Slip might improve as the day went on. Shake off the cloudiness in his eyes like he'd shaken off the gunshot wound on his arm. But though his spirits seemed better since Jasper had taken off the cuffs, Slip seemed to be getting worse. He tripped over rocks and branches that he wouldn't have the day before, no matter that he was a clumsy fool.

Jasper knew this happened with head injuries. Someone could get a conk on the head, and it would set his head to swimming for a few days. Someone could even get a conk on the head and die in his sleep that night. Jasper stopped their walking earlier than he might have another day, when he hadn't been smacked in the face with a gun and Slip wasn't bleeding onto the collar of his shirt.

They stopped in a clearing with a few stones in the middle, like seats waiting for them to sit in. The moon shone bright in the sky. Tabitha settled between them, curling up in a little ball, her head resting on her paws, prim as a lady.

Slip started to stand. His legs were trembling, and his face was pale.

"What do you think you're doing?" Jasper asked.

Slip looked at him as though it should have been obvious what he was doing. "I'm going to get firewood."

"No," Jasper said.

"No?"

"Someone could be following us. You know that."

Slip sat down heavily, as though his legs had just decided to follow Jasper's command and give out on him. "I don't think I would have gotten very far anyway."

That was certainly true. Jasper could have gotten the firewood, but a fire seemed like too much of a risk when neither of them was at their best for fighting. They didn't have any food to cook anyway.

But it sure would have been nice to have a fire.

After a few long moments of sitting together in silence — something Jasper had almost gotten used to going without — Slip spoke up. "Found something of yours." He dug around inside his coat, then pulled something out and passed it over to Jasper.

The letters. The ones Charley had given him, the ones from his mother. He'd kept an eye on the ground as they went, but he hadn't wanted to stop and look. He hadn't wanted to tell Slip why. But Slip had found them without him saying a word. Jasper took them back the same way.

"You didn't open them," Slip said.

"I did not."

Slip didn't ask why.

Jasper turned the letters over in his hand, then tucked them inside his coat with Westin's papers. The night was as cold as it was clear, and Jasper pulled his coat around him tighter. Soon, the nights would be warmer. Hopefully they'd live to see them.

"How far you think we are to that road?" Slip asked.

Jasper had no idea. They'd spent a couple of days all turned around, after all. He knew they were traveling in the right direction to get to Soulsbyville, but he'd completely lost track of how far they'd traveled.

"Can't be too far, I don't think."

Slip looked around, like he might be able to tell from the rocks and the trees where exactly in the middle of nowhere they were. "We should go hard north. Maybe that'll get us there sooner."

"Sure, Slip," Jasper said. "First thing."

"Don't be so agreeable, Duncan. I'm gonna think I'm dying."

In the morning, Slip barely roused when

Tabitha nudged at his shoulder. She looked back at Jasper and whined as though he could wake the man, fix what was wrong with his head. Jasper felt as at sea as the mutt did. He was no doctor; he didn't know a lick about injuries except to keep them clean and keep the injured man comfortable.

Jasper grabbed his canteen, leaned over Slip, and shook his shoulder, harder than Tab's nose had. Slip's eyes flickered open. They didn't look very focused.

"Here, drink some of this," Jasper said, putting the canteen to his lips.

Slip drank as best he could, though some of the water dribbled out of his mouth. He looked disappointed when the water was gone. "I wasted half that," he complained.

"I'll go get some more," Jasper said, and stood.

"Trust me not to run off?" Slip asked. The smile he gave made his lips look even paler.

"Tabitha'll keep an eye on you," he said, and he could have sworn the dog gave him a solemn nod of her shaggy brown head.

"Better watch out or I'll steal your dog," Slip called. His words sounded slurred, like he'd been drinking more than water. "I grow on folks!"

The thing that stuck in Jasper's craw as he

left the camp was that he *did* grow on folks. Tabitha had been ready to attack without a word from Valdez just days before, and now she looked downright worried for Casey, if dogs could do such a thing. And Jasper . . . Jasper had started on this journey ready to deliver Slip to the hangman's noose if he didn't draw out his brother. Jasper had looked at him and seen Alec Casey's calm, hateful face. But now he found he didn't want Slip to die, and not just because he'd tracked him down and saved his life, and not just because he was still the clearest way to Alec Casey.

Jasper found a slim stream running between two hills, but when he walked down the slope and bent to get water, he realized he could see something in the distance. He stood, craned his neck.

A cabin stood in the distance. Rough-hewn but solid — not a burned-out ruin like the one Slip had been found inside — and smaller than the one Ada and Thom had lived in. He crept closer, in case he ran into more angry children armed with shotguns. But there were none. He saw no sign of livestock or a garden, and no smoke rose from the stubby chimney. There weren't even any flowers growing right outside. Jasper couldn't see any sign of human occupation — at least not recent.

The door resisted when he pushed to open it, but finally let him in. There wasn't much light in the cabin. Early-afternoon sunshine slanted through one window; the other one was shuttered and latched. The cabin was one room, with a fireplace on one side and a rickety-looking bed on the other. There was an iron pot hanging above the empty fireplace. One stool accompanied a banged-up table, and a hatchet and a hoe hung on the wall. Everything was covered in dust and cobwebs.

It wasn't hard north, like Slip had suggested, but a night's sleep in a bed, food cooked in a pot over the fire instead of on a hot rock, and maybe even a proper bandage for his head if Jasper could find some material? That might do Slip a world of good, getting them back to a faster clip and out of these woods before someone else tried to kill them.

When Jasper got back to Slip, Tabitha's head shot up, her ears back. She gave a whine. She'd been curled up next to Slip, and his fingers were buried in her fur. *He* gave a whine when Tabitha stood and moved so Jasper could give him a shake.

"I don't think I want to walk today," he said, not even opening his eyes. "The forest is nicer than the hangman's noose. This is all I wanted, to hide out in the woods."

"You were hiding in a cabin."

Slip's eyelids flickered, like he wanted to open his eyes and argue but couldn't quite manage it. "A cabin in the woods, Jasper."

Jasper got a grip on him and hoisted him to his feet. "Well, let's get you to a cabin, then."

Slip stayed on his feet to Jasper's surprise. He walked haltingly, but of his own power. It took near twice as long to get to the cabin as before, but once it came into sight, Jasper found himself relaxing.

"You didn't take us north," Slip said, his words slurred but accusing. Jasper couldn't believe he could tell which direction they were traveling in his condition, but Slip had proven himself a more able woodsman than Jasper would have thought he was.

"We'll go north tomorrow."

"And what if I don't feel like walking tomorrow either?"

Jasper didn't know what he would do then. He could force him at gunpoint; Valdez and Hatch had done that to get him into the stagecoach and on the road, after all. Jasper hadn't forgotten that Slip was a prisoner, even if in his injured state, Slip himself seemed to forget.

Slip seemed to decide he didn't feel like walking at all; he stopped, swaying back and forth a little on his feet. When Jasper tried to nudge him forward, he pulled his arm back.

"There's no one in the cabin," Jasper said in case that was his worry. "Checked it out. Looks like no one's been inside in months."

Slip swallowed hard but started to walk again. His foot slid on the grassy slope and he almost went careening into the stream. Jasper caught his arm.

"Whoever gave you that nickname sure knew how to pick 'em," Jasper muttered.

"Sure did," Slip said, and Jasper wondered if it had been Alec. He didn't want to know.

Jasper got Slip in the door and over to the bed. Slip all but collapsed down onto it.

"Stay right here," Jasper said. Slip let out a laugh as though him moving was the funniest thing he'd heard in days. Maybe it was. "I'm going to get some water. Some firewood."

Slip's hand caught Jasper's arm before he could move. "Don't know who's around. Best be careful about making a fire."

Slip hadn't had that opinion when he'd asked for a fire the night before. Then it had been Jasper who didn't want a fire. If someone was going to catch up with them, it certainly would have happened today, when Jasper had gone out searching for water and left Slip alone with Tab. Jasper was fairly certain Brady had been the last of the men chasing them from the road ambush. But Slip wasn't *wrong.* He nodded, and Slip moved his hand away.

Jasper took the iron pot from the fireplace and his canteen and headed back to the stream. He filled them both up, then walked upstream, searching for fish to catch, but all he saw were minnows, far too small to eat.

Before heading back inside, Jasper did a loop around the cabin, looking for anything that might be useful. There were the remains of a stack of firewood against one wall, what looked like enough to last two days at the most, and a rusty watering can next to it. Jasper picked it up — it couldn't hurt to have something else to carry water in — only to realize the bottom had rusted out. It wouldn't hold anything anymore. Jasper let it fall to the ground.

There was a thicket just beyond the cabin, and Jasper found a bush of small tart berries, barely ripe but close enough. He picked as many as he could carry, then headed back to the cabin.

When Jasper went inside, Slip was in the same place he'd been when Jasper left him.

Tabitha was lying across his feet, and she watched Jasper as he walked over to the hearth. The fireplace was full of long-cold ashes.

"You want a fire, girl?" Jasper asked.

Tabitha's ears twitched. He took that as a no and hunted around for a spare blanket. He found a ratty one beneath the bed, threw it over his shoulders, and ate his berries before falling asleep.

CHAPTER TWENTY-THREE

He woke to Slip retching.

The cabin was near pitch-dark. Jasper hadn't meant to sleep so long. He hadn't meant to sleep at all, just rest. He sat up, aching and cold from the cabin floor, and walked to the cabin's window. From the look of the sky, he'd been asleep for hours.

Unfortunately for Slip, there was nothing much to come up, and nothing much that Jasper could do, beyond giving him a sip of water when the spell seemed to pass.

"Glad we skipped dinner," Slip muttered after he swallowed the water. He fell back to sleep moments later.

Jasper sat in the dim predawn light, not sure what to do. There wasn't anything he could do, was there? He'd told Slip it didn't matter to him if he brought him down dead instead of alive. Maybe now that was how it was going to be.

But in the morning, Slip seemed a little

better. His eyes focused a little more, at least, and the wound on the back of his head didn't look infected when Jasper wrapped a length of cloth he'd found around it. Jasper headed out to look for food after bringing back some more water from the stream, leaving Tab behind, though she looked more likely to fall asleep with her head on Slip's knee than stop him from running off.

Luckily, he was in no shape to be running off.

Near the stream, Jasper found more wild onions. He'd gathered enough to fill the makeshift sack he'd made out of his ratty blanket when he saw the tufts of fur peek up over the grass.

A rabbit.

Jasper would have laughed if it wouldn't have scared the thing away.

He pulled his rifle around from its strap on his back and took aim. The rabbit seemed to realize it was being hunted, but Jasper shot before it could bolt. The shot sounded like thunder in the quiet of the morning. Jasper hoped he was right and there were no more men hunting them down. If he wasn't . . .

He skinned and gutted the rabbit outside, then brought in a stack of firewood and got a fire going. Slip was asleep again, but Tab seemed mighty interested in what Jasper had brought home.

"You'll get your share," he told the dog. She sat back on her haunches as though she understood what he was saying.

Slip finally woke up when the stew was simmering over the fire. Jasper wasn't anything approaching a cook, but he could cut up some onions and cook them with a rabbit. It could have been his hunger talking, and probably was, but the stew smelled delicious.

"Did you actually cook us up a rabbit?" Slip asked. His voice sounded groggy, but his words were clear enough.

"Tab and I are gonna share," Jasper said, "since you've been sleeping too much to earn your keep."

Slip sat up and stretched. "Hey, if I recall —" He stopped abruptly and looked around. "How'd . . ."

"Found the cabin when I was looking for water yesterday," Jasper said. "It seemed like a good enough place to hole up until your head was on straight enough for you to walk."

Slip's eyes darted around the room like he was looking for threats. There was nowhere in the cabin to hide a threat, though, so Jasper wasn't sure what he expected to find.

"We been here a day?" he asked. Jasper nodded, and Slip seemed to relax. "Clever find."

"Maybe your luck's turning around."

Slip snorted. "I doubt it."

"Whoever lived here only left two plates and I promised one to the dog," Jasper said. "You'll have to eat out of the stewpot."

Slip didn't seem to mind the idea. Jasper had taken the stool, so Slip sat cross-legged in front of the fire. "That fall nearly did me in, I think," he said, staring into the fire.

Jasper nodded. "Thought you might die."

"I've seen it happen before," Slip said. "A man gets knocked in the head, goes to bed like nothing's wrong, then doesn't wake back up again."

"I'm glad you woke up again," Jasper replied. "It would have been a right pain to drag your body all the way to Sonora."

A laugh burst out of Slip's mouth like he hadn't expected that. "See, I knew you'd prefer alive to dead. Took you long enough to admit it."

The stew looked done enough, and Jasper was hungry enough not to care if he was wrong. He dished out some to Slip — on a plate despite his promise to Tabitha — then to himself. He was sure he'd had better meals — he must have — but he wasn't prepared to name one, not when he was so hungry and the rabbit was more filling than anything he'd had since the night before he left Indigo.

For a while they didn't talk, and the only sound was spoons against metal plates and hearty chewing. Until Slip broke the silence. "I came to California to get away from my brother."

Jasper's spoon stopped halfway to his mouth. He had to force himself to keep eating. Each time Slip had spoken about Alec, there'd been something off there. Jasper had thought Slip was proud of him at first, then realized that couldn't have been it. But this?

"I'm the first Casey who robbed a bank. Our pa always said I'd grow up to be no good, and he was right. Got away clean that time, but without much to show for it. But then Alec got wind of what I'd done. Sixteen years old, he was, but it was like he'd been born to crime. The next jobs we pulled, we got a lot to show for them. But then he got a taste for killing."

Slip put down his plate of stew, only half finished, like his brother's taste for killing had taken away his own taste for rabbit.

"Finally, I decided to leave, get myself away from the Casey Gang. But then there he was again, moving west on my tail," Slip said. He watched the fire as he spoke. "Alec makes you listen to him. Not with threats or violence, though he uses those too. No, there's just something powerful about him. He's easy to follow. And I've always liked to do things easy."

He fell silent after that, even though Jasper knew there was more to the story. Why had Alec followed Slip? Or had it been a coincidence, following the gold to California? All Jasper knew was that one day the Casey Gang was gone, and then he'd decided to leave too.

Jasper didn't even realize that he'd started to speak until the words were halfway out of his mouth. "I came to California to kill your brother."

Slip looked over at him. Jasper had no idea what he was thinking. "I know," he said, then picked up his stew and started eating again.

The sun was sinking low when Tabitha started to growl.

Jasper was on his feet just after she was. She padded toward the door, growl low in her throat, as though to alert them to danger, but not alert the danger they were there.

Jasper looked over to the fire dying in the hearth. Tab didn't have to bark to alert anyone to their presence. The smoke would have done that. Or his shot at the rabbit.

"Think it's another cougar?" Slip asked quietly. He'd moved back toward the bed after they ate, still sprawled on the ground, but with his back against the bed frame.

The odds of that were low. Jasper brought his rifle up and creaked the door open. Tabitha ran out the moment he did, and disappeared around the side of the cabin, growling. He didn't call her back. If she wanted to chase after cougars or bears or even the men who might be tracking them, he couldn't do anything to stop her.

Jasper walked outside, more cautiously than Tab had. He didn't see anything outside, didn't hear anything either. He followed Tab's path around the cabin, walking as quiet as he could, then speeding up when he heard the dog's sharp yelp.

Just as he rounded the corner, he saw her scrambling back onto her four legs and then launching herself at a man again.

The man standing there looked vaguely familiar in the same way Brady had before Jasper placed him as a shift boss from the mine. He was tall and rake thin, with red hair and freckles and a scar across his upper lip. Tabitha had her teeth in his leg, and he was shaking it and cursing up a storm.

Jasper had his rifle up before the man clocked that he'd come around the corner. "It's best if you stop moving," he said.

"Why would I want to do that?" the man asked, scarred lip lifting in a sneer.

Jasper looked from his rifle to the man's own gun, a revolver still in its holster at his belt.

"No matter that. I think it's *you* who shouldn't move," the man said, and Jasper felt the barrel of a gun nudge at his back. "Call off the dog." The man shook his leg, but Tabitha held on. Jasper didn't think she was getting much skin through the heavy trousers, but he hoped he was wrong. "Now or we shoot her."

He clicked his tongue like Valdez had. "Tabitha, stop."

She did as he said, but she seemed grudging about it. She kept growling.

"Shoot her anyway," the red-haired man said to the one holding a gun on Jasper.

"He shoots her, I shoot you, no mistake," Jasper snapped quickly.

"Lawmen and their dogs," the man said with a roll of his eyes. Jasper didn't bother to correct him on either count. "Put that thing down, fool."

"I didn't think Brady had so many friends to help him with his dirty work," Jasper said, lowering the rifle slowly.

"Don't know who this man Brady is, but I'm certainly not here to help him with his dirty work."

And then Jasper realized where he'd seen the man's face before.

He had always kept up with the Casey Gang's exploits, but rarely had he paid as much attention to its members. With the exception of Alec and Slip, well, the Casey Gang didn't keep members too long. They had a bad habit of dying. But every few months, Jasper would see a new face on a wanted handbill, members of the Casey Gang wanted for robbery, for indecency, for murder.

Jasper had seen this man's face printed on a handbill in Sonora.

He wasn't working with Brady. He was a member of the Casey Gang.

Jasper almost wanted to laugh. He'd been wanting them to come, and here they were. How had they found them way out here? Was the man at his back Alec Casey? No, Jasper didn't think he was the type to hold his gun to a man's back. Not from any compunction about shooting it. No, he was the type to face a man and kill him with a smile.

"Why don't you put down that gun and

then we take a walk?" the first man was saying. He still hadn't drawn his gun. "There's a nice stand of trees over there. And you can see the sunset. As good a place and time as any to die, right?"

Jasper had no intention of dying next to that bush full of unripe berries, especially not killed by one of Alec Casey's henchmen. These last few days he'd had far too many guns leveled at his back for his taste. He was getting mighty tired of it.

"It's a mercy to get a moment to pray before you die. Truly," the man said. "Now put the rifle down or you and the dog will go right here without a moment to make sure God's expecting you."

"No need to do that." Jasper bent, laying his rifle on the ground next to the remnants of the woodpile. He glanced over his shoulder as he did, catching a glint of metal in the corner of his eye as he did.

"Move," the man behind him said, shoving the barrel of the gun into the small of his back again.

Jasper twisted, moving as fast as he could to get his body away from the revolver and get control of it. The gun went off before he could grab it, the bullet splintering the side of the cabin. "Tab!" he ordered, hoping the dog would do as he wanted. The growl she let out made him hope she had.

He slammed the hand holding the gun down, once, twice, and it came loose from the man's grip. Jasper kicked it away as hard as he could, but it left him off-balance and he toppled over. He groped for his rifle. It must have been close. His hand hit metal — but the wrong shape to be his rifle.

He glanced over at it.

The watering can.

He grabbed it from the bottom, the uneven edge of the rusted-out metal biting into the palm of his hand, and swung as hard as he could.

The metal connected with the gunman's head and he fell back onto his rear, stunned. It lasted only a moment, but that was enough. Jasper grabbed his rifle and fired, then stood and faced the other one.

Tab had him on his back in the grass. The man's right hand was bloody from where he'd clearly tried to grab his revolver and Tabitha had taken a finger or two. He let out a scream and shoved at the dog, throwing her off of him and into the dirt. He reached for his gun with his other hand, got his fingers on the hilt.

Jasper cocked the rifle, ready to fire again — only to realize he was out of ammunition. Jasper strode over, flipping his rifle around, and slammed its butt into the man's head as hard as he could. The man flopped back onto the grass.

What was it they said about the Henry? Load it on Sunday and keep firing through the week? Well, it hadn't quite lasted him seven days, but it had still gotten the job done.

Jasper slung his rifle over his shoulder, then took the gun from the man's holster. He'd never seen one quite like it; there was a different look about the barrel and the cylinder. He'd take it with him anyway. It wasn't as though the man could use it now anyway, not effectively, not with his hand destroyed like that.

Jasper strode back to the cabin door and shoved it open. "Slip, we —"

Jasper's words died in his mouth.

Sitting on the lone stool in the middle of the cabin, revolver held loosely in his right hand, was Alec Casey.

Chapter Twenty-Four

Time had gone easy on Alec Casey.

He looked much the same as he had six years before. His hair was combed and shiny, and he wore a white shirt under a black waistcoat, all neat and trim even in the middle of the woods. He sat the same way he had last time Jasper had seen him, his limbs loose, as though a man bursting through a door with a gun in hand was nothing to worry about.

Jasper brought the revolver up, aimed.

"Don't do that," Alec said, his voice as placid as his face.

Jasper pulled the trigger.

The gun didn't fire. Jasper pulled the trigger again, with the same result. His stomach sank. Had Alec Casey known that somehow? He must have to just sit there, even though he easily might have gotten shot.

Casey stood and walked toward Jasper. "May I?" he said, and took the revolver right out of his hand. "Bell's weapons never do work quite right for anyone but him. Not unless you know their tricks. You should be careful when using someone else's gun." He pointed the revolver off to the side, shifting something near the cylinder with his thumb, and pulled the trigger. The shot burst hot and loud into the wall of the cabin.

Then Alec returned to his chair. He leaned back and crossed his long legs at his ankles. "You kill both my men out there?"

Jasper shook his head. "One. The man who had that gun, Bell? Even alive, he won't be much use to you, though. He's missing some fingers."

"Alec," Slip said, then stopped when they both turned to look at him.

He was sitting up on the bed, his face still pale and a little sweaty. His eyes were clear, though; maybe the sweat came from the confrontation in front of him.

Jasper had noted the similarities in their faces on first meeting Slip. Similar eyes, similar mouths. But seeing them so close together? They looked more different than Jasper could have imagined. Alec could have marched off the pages of a dime novel, a bad guy wearing black, almost unreal. Slip? Slip looked like he was going to keel over at any minute.

"You know, I sent men out to look for you," Alec said to his brother. "No sign. Thought you might have gone off on a tear through Stockton or something till word came that you got picked up in Indigo. What were you doing there?"

"Looking for some peace and quiet."

Alec's brow rose, clearly skeptical of that. "Isn't that what you use this place for?"

Jasper's eyes had drifted to Alec as he spoke, but shot back to Slip when he finished. *Isn't that what you use this place for?* Slip had been to this cabin before.

Everyone knew Alec Casey had a hideout, somewhere close to those stages and banks he kept hitting, but nowhere anyone could find. Jasper thought of all the times Slip had ventured from the path Jasper was making, driving them a little farther east than the route he wanted to take. *Just hunting for onions,* he'd said. No, he'd been trying to get Jasper to venture close to his brother's hideout. A way to get himself out of this bind without drawing a gun. He'd said it himself — he liked the easy way.

Slip's face practically confirmed it without Jasper saying a word. His mouth folded into a frown and his eyes took on that hangdog look. He looked like a sad clown.

Was that why people underestimated him?

A frowny face and the occasional stumble, and people forgot he'd been an outlaw just as long as his brother. That was their game. Oh, how they'd laugh together now.

Slip didn't look like he was going to start laughing, though. He drew himself up so his shoulders weren't so slumped. "Just let him go, okay?"

"Why?" Alec looked as confused as Jasper felt. Why would Slip want Jasper to be let go? Why, when Slip knew all Jasper wanted was his brother dead, when Jasper had led him more than a dozen miles closer to the hangman's noose?

"He's just a jehu. He ain't no lawman. No reason to hurt him. He kept me alive."

"Kept you alive to bring you to hang if I'm not mistaken." Alec looked to Jasper. "Am I mistaken?"

Jasper shook his head. "You ain't mistaken."

Alec nodded once and looked back to Slip. "You saved my life, brother. I'll keep saving yours. The Casey brothers pay their debts. That's what we've always said, isn't it?"

"But what if I owe him? Then will you let him go?"

Alec seemed to be considering, but then he shook his head. "He shot at me — meant to, at least. I can't be letting those things go, Slip."

"Why not? Why not this time? Leave him be."

Something about the way he said that tickled at the back of Jasper's mind. *Leave him be.* Had he said it before?

"You're always trying to get me to spare folks, Slip. It's one of the things I like about you, brother."

"Then why don't you ever listen?"

"I listened once," Alec said, then climbed to his feet. "And then you never stopped asking."

Slip started talking again, saying something about Westin and Indigo, but Jasper wasn't listening anymore. Alec's words . . . He listened once.

He's just a kid. Leave him be.

Jasper hadn't gotten a proper look at the man who'd come to break Alec out of that jail cell back in Nebraska. His face had been all in shadow and then Alec had grabbed him, knocking him clean out. But Jasper thought about the picture on the handbill, the hat Slip hadn't been wearing, the dark bandannas he'd had with him. Where Slip Casey was, Alec Casey was never far away, and the reverse was true as well.

And then he thought back to the voice

291

asking Alec Casey to leave him be.

The voice had been Slip's.

You know how many times Alec's been caught by the law?

Once.

"It was you," Jasper said. "You're the one who broke him out of that cell."

Slip's mouth snapped shut with a loud clack of his teeth.

Jasper started to laugh. "I blamed him, 'cuz he pulled the trigger," he said, gesturing to Alec. "And I blamed me, because I got too close to him. But I should've blamed you too. You let him out."

Alec had taken the revolver, but Jasper still had the rifle, unloaded, useless when it came to bullets. Maybe Jasper didn't need bullets.

He launched himself toward the bed, swinging the rifle into his grasp and then swinging the butt toward Slip's head. One more good hit on that head, and it could finish him off. But Slip darted sideways, and the blow hit his shoulder. Slip let out a pained shout; it was his injured arm Jasper had hit.

He pulled the rifle back again, ready to deliver another hit, but strong hands grabbed his shoulders. He knew those hands, would never forget the feel of them, jerking him backward, the feel of the bars, slamming against his shoulders, against his head. Jasper flung his elbows back, dropping the gun as he did it. He felt his right elbow connect, maybe with Alec's ribs, but the man barely grunted in pain. Alec dropped one of Jasper's arms, spun him around, and landed a punch that sent Jasper crashing to the floor.

Jasper looked up. Alec's hair was mussed and his waistcoat crooked, but as soon as he had his hands free, he tugged the waistcoat down and then smoothed back his hair. His right hand went for his gun again, but he paused, hand hovering just above it.

Something in his eyes sharpened. "You look familiar. We met?"

Jasper looked up at him. He could feel blood trickling down his chin from the split in his lip. He thought back to when he'd first heard about Slip Casey's capture, the split lip he'd given Valdez. They were a matching set now . . . and soon they'd both be dead.

Jasper spat out a mouthful of blood. "You killed my father," he said.

Alec's shoulders slumped a little. He almost looked disappointed. "Oh," he said, "is that all?" He pulled his fist back.

Then everything went black.

CHAPTER TWENTY-FIVE

His father was dead.

It didn't feel real. It couldn't be real.

But his mother's tears, those were real. The pity in the sheriff's face. The feeling Jasper couldn't shake no matter what he tried.

No, it was real. He just didn't want it to be.

The worst part wasn't how it felt when he thought about it. That was bad enough. He'd think about the blood trailing through the dirt; he'd think about the jangle of metal that must have been the keys that let Alec Casey out of his cell. Most of all he'd think of his father when he saw him in the street and how whatever spirit that had made him Ben Duncan was gone.

But the worst parts were the moments when Jasper would almost forget. The first thing in the morning, opening his eyes and thinking for a bare moment that he had to help his father in the barn. Pulling three bowls from the shelf when his mother asked him to dish out their stew, then remembering there were only two to serve.

He couldn't stand it, and there was no way to stop it.

He deserved it, of course. It had all been his fault, hadn't it? If he'd drawn his revolver earlier, he could have taken a shot. If he'd been a little more vigilant while watching Casey, that last member of the gang wouldn't have been able to get the drop on him. He'd thought of so many things he could have done better to fix what had happened, and if he'd died as a result, well, the world would have been better with his father in it than his weakling of a son.

Jasper started hanging around the sheriff, waiting for news on Alec Casey. He kept hoping someone would catch him, hang him, shoot him dead in the street. He deserved to be shot dead in the street. But no one had. And then the news came that he'd hit a train west of Nebraska Territory. That he'd *left.*

And that, Jasper couldn't stand.

He wrote a letter explaining to his mother. He placed it on the table when he knew she wouldn't be in for hours. Too much of a coward to face her properly. His last stop before he left his home was the sheriff's station. If anyone had an idea of just where Alec Casey was going, it was like as not to be him.

There were wanted handbills tacked up on the walls at the sheriff's. Outlaws Jasper didn't recognize, names he'd never remember, and of course, Alec Casey, whom he wouldn't ever forget. "Murder of a lawman" had been added to the most recent of the bills. Jasper supposed "murder of a father" wouldn't have been something they'd think to add. How many of the other men the Casey Gang had killed had been fathers?

"You here for a reason, Jasper?" the sheriff asked. His voice was always easy with Jasper these days. Easy and even, and Jasper thought it would have been better if he'd railed at him.

Jasper asked his questions. Where was Casey last seen? Which direction was he headed? Had he gone west before only to come back?

When he finished, the sheriff was quiet for a long moment. "Son," he finally said, "if you go looking for revenge, you'll find yourself back in front of Alec Casey's gun, and this time no one will stop him from firing."

"Not if I fire first," Jasper replied.

"It's not gonna help." The sheriff's eyes were kind. "You could kill Alec Casey a hundred times and it won't help you feel better about losing your pa."

The sheriff might have had kind eyes and

an even voice, but he had to be wrong. Because if killing Alec Casey didn't make this feeling go away, then nothing would.

Jasper set his hat back on his head and spoke the last words he said before leaving home. "I don't need to kill him a hundred times. I only need to kill him once."

CHAPTER TWENTY-SIX

Jasper woke up in the dark.

He hadn't thought he was going to wake up at all. Alec Casey had been about to kill him, hadn't he? Out in that cabin in the woods.

Slip's cabin.

Jasper really was a fool.

There was something over his face. Jasper tried to bring his hand up to move it and found he couldn't; his hands were bound. He shifted, trying to figure out just where he was. There was wood beneath him. A floor?

"Well, now, look who's awake," a voice said, slightly muffled by whatever was over Jasper's face. Then it was lifted and standing above him was the man whose hand Tab had mangled. His hand was bandaged now, and his face was as red as the blood pouring out of his hand had been. What had Casey called him? Bell?

Bell looked mighty angry.

The thing that had been covering Jasper's face was his own hat, now in Bell's good hand, and the wood beneath him was the bottom of a cart. They'd carted him someplace. Where? How long had it been? It was evening now, but the same evening? The next?

Jasper struggled to sit up despite his bound hands. Bell noticed his struggle and gave an angry laugh. He shoved Jasper's hat back on his head, grabbed a handful of Jasper's shirt, and hauled him to his feet.

"Come on now, friend. Let's get you to your new accommodations."

Bell yanked Jasper forward. As he stumbled along, he looked around the place they'd brought him to.

Alec Casey seemed to have built himself a town.

No, Jasper realized. He had taken one over.

These buildings were more than five years old, built before the Casey Gang set up in California. There weren't more than four or five of them, but one was clearly meant to be some sort of way station. No road he knew had made it this far out, and Jasper wondered if the people who had built this town had wanted to be left alone. He thought of Ada and Thom and their father, who had never come back. Had this place once been filled with peaceful people? He didn't think Alec Casey had let them be. He'd probably killed them all.

This, then, was the hideout where the Casey Gang retreated after a job, the mysterious place that confounded the lawmen out there searching. Some of them had convinced themselves Alec Casey and his men were phantoms, even though the men they buried should have shown them otherwise. But this place, *this* was why. There weren't many people around the camp. Jasper saw only three or four. He wondered just how big the Casey Gang was right now. Was this everyone?

He stumbled and Bell yanked him upright again. "Be more careful. I'm under instructions not to hurt you yet."

He sounded like he relished the idea of that *yet.*

Bell was leading Jasper toward a shed at the end of the makeshift street. "See, we don't have a jail. After all, who would we lock up? You'll be our first prisoner. We don't usually take them."

"You just kill them," Jasper said tightly.

"Exactly." Bell pushed Jasper to his knees in front of the shed, then opened the door.

He pulled him to his feet and shoved him inside. Jasper landed hard on the dirt. "Remember how I said you should let God know you're on your way? Now would be a good time to tell Him."

Bell slammed the door to the shed behind him and left Jasper in the dark again. This time, it wasn't just his hat that kept the light out.

Jasper managed to get to his knees. Rope, at least, was easier to slip than handcuffs. He managed to get a hand free, then unwound the rope. His arms were stiff. How long had he been tied up? How long had it been since the cabin?

He reached up, brushed some dried blood off his chin, then poked at the tender skin of his lip. Alec Casey, unsurprisingly, knew how to throw a solid punch. Then Jasper patted himself down. His knife was gone, and there was no sign of Brady's pistol. His rifle, he assumed, had been taken when he'd dropped it after his unsuccessful attack on Slip.

His rifle. His father's rifle. He'd wanted to confront Alec Casey with it. He'd wanted to hold it up and shoot, taking his revenge with the same gun that had soaked in his father's blood in the road that day.

He'd gotten the chance and he'd wasted it.

He almost wanted to laugh at himself. This was what he wanted, after all; he'd been searching, hoping so desperately that he'd somehow stumble upon Alec Casey, never mind that California was made up of huge tracts of land, never mind that his stagecoach route didn't usually carry much in the way of money for an outlaw like Alec to target. He'd settled for being close to the Casey Gang, in a place where he might be able to find him, if only . . . Well, *if only* had happened; he'd gotten exactly what he wanted.

And it was probably going to kill him.

Jasper stood. Making it out of this camp might not be likely, but maybe he could find a way out of this *room* he was being kept in. If he could get to Casey, then maybe he could still find a way to bring him down. If he could just get to Casey . . .

The shed had only the one door and a small window in the wall to the right of it. The door was latched from the outside, and the window was shuttered and nailed closed. There was nothing in the room that he could find on his circling of it.

And no way out.

What were they waiting for? Why wait to

kill him? Maybe it was Slip's doing. Jasper laughed bitterly. Here he'd been walking around with the brother of the man who'd killed his father and he'd thought what? That they were friends? Or near enough. He'd been worried when it looked like Slip was going to die and had done what he could to keep him alive after that fall into the creek.

He thought back to the moment he figured out it was Slip who had been there the day his father died. Slip had been talking, trying to convince Alec to let Jasper live — which, apparently, he had — and he'd been saying something about Westin and Indigo. . . .

Westin's papers.

Jasper's hands went to the inner pocket of his coat, where he'd folded up the packet of papers and stashed them. They were gone.

He tried to remember what was in them, what good they'd do for Alec Casey. Numbers slashing across paper, the pen probably blurry from the damp of the morning air or Jasper's sweat. And then he remembered. *Payroll.* There was payroll information there, and times and routes of gold transportation. Those numbers were literally worth their weight in gold to a man like Casey, and Jasper was the reason they'd just been handed over.

Maybe he should have just burned the papers.

Jasper shifted and felt something shift with him, something inside his coat. For a moment, he thought they'd done a worse job searching him than he thought, but when he dug his hand into that pocket, he realized it wasn't Westin's papers.

It was his mother's letters.

These were worth nothing to Alec Casey, so they'd left them alone. Jasper let his eyes fall shut, then pulled the letters out. The room he was in was too dark to see even the slope of his mother's writing, but he held the letters close.

He'd meant to read the letters. He'd always meant to read them and to reply. He'd tell her about the mountains, their craggy rises and piney woods and the way the rivers swelled when the snow melted, and they rushed their way to lower ground. He'd tell her about Indigo, Charley's wry humor and kind ear, and the way Missy Banks always kept him fed. His mother would want to know someone did. He'd talk about his stage, how many strange pickles he'd gotten himself into on the road, leaving out the dire ones so she wouldn't worry.

So she wouldn't worry. He scoffed at his own thought. He'd left her six years before, writing only to let her know whereabouts he was and never replying to a single letter, and he didn't want her to worry? He didn't just feel a fool; he was a fool. The worst kind of fool.

He tucked the letters away, this time in the pocket closest to his heart. More foolishness, but at least this was a different kind of foolishness. Jasper couldn't read them now, but he'd read them soon. He thought of Bell back at the cabin offering him sunset and a prayer, and wondered if whoever killed him would let him read the letters before he died.

He'd ended up back by the window, trying to see if he could force part of the shutter open, when he heard the latch at the door.

For a moment, Jasper thought about launching himself at the door, trying to knock down the person coming in, and get out. But that idea went out the shuttered window the moment he saw who it was.

Alec Casey himself. He walked into the room, almost smiling. He was wearing the same clothes as when Jasper had last seen him — with another man, Jasper wouldn't have bet on it meaning anything, but Alec Casey? It seemed a fair enough indication that Jasper hadn't been brought here too long ago.

Alec had two of his men behind him, and for a moment Jasper felt almost flattered that Alec had brought two men to what amounted to his jail cell. Then he realized one was holding a lantern and the second was Bell. He was sneering again. That did not bode well. Jasper was sure he wasn't going to enjoy the next few minutes and was almost equally sure they'd be his last.

"I thought you said he was tied up?" Alec asked Bell, then shook his head as though it didn't matter. He looked at Jasper. "Jasper Duncan, my brother calls you. Your father shot me in the arm, you know. I have a scar." He pulled his shirt down enough to show the pale skin of his shoulder.

Sure enough there was a scar there. It had healed up nicely. Jasper wished it hadn't.

"I don't think I would have recognized you. That look on your face sure was different. You weren't so angry before. Wide-eyed boy staring up at me outside that saloon about to die." His voice was soft, almost fond. "Did you come to California for me?"

Jasper kept his mouth shut. He'd never wanted to talk to Alec Casey. Only to kill him.

Alec shrugged, moving on. "Just wanted to tell you a couple things, since I won't see

306

you again. Thank you for delivering those papers right to me. Slip says some accountant got shot for them. I'd thank him too if he weren't already dead. Gold ore is a little troublesome to steal, but the payroll? Now, that's the kind of gold I'm fond of."

"Why didn't you just kill me?"

"I told you. I have things to say." Alec's voice hardened a bit like he was losing patience with Jasper. "Slip asked to talk to you before we kill you. He's around here somewhere. I reckon he's drinking. But once he's said his piece, Bell here will be the one to kill you. He wanted to kill the dog too, but she ran off somewhere."

Jasper looked down at Bell's bandaged hand, then back up to the man's face. "Can Bell shoot left-handed?"

"I guess we'll find out," Alec said.

Bell sneered. "It might take a few tries to aim properly."

"Let's hope not." It didn't sound like an order, like Alec didn't want Jasper to suffer. No, his tone was matter-of-fact. "I keep you around for your aim, Bell. Best be just as good."

Then he smiled and clapped Bell on the shoulder. Bell let out a half laugh, but Jasper could see he wasn't stupid enough to think Alec was joking.

"Alright, then," Alec said. "You were up by the window. Trying to get out? I don't think you can, but let's be sure. Tie him up again," Alec ordered. "This time try to make sure he doesn't slip them."

The man holding the lantern had a coil of rope looped around his other arm, and he moved toward Jasper. Jasper struggled, but the man had him down on his knees quick enough, coiling the rope around his wrists, then his ankles. Jasper was left lying on the ground, craning his neck up to watch Bell and the man with the rope walk out of the shed, leaving Alec at the door alone.

"Good to see you again, Jasper Duncan." Alec's voice was pleasant. It sounded like he *meant* it. "If there is an afterlife, I hope you join your pa. Be sure to tell him about the scar."

The door closed again, the latch fell, and Jasper was left in in the same dark he'd woken up in.

CHAPTER TWENTY-SEVEN

Jasper didn't sleep much that night. He faded in and out, noise from outside buzzing in the background, and once a sharp crack that sounded like a tree branch breaking close to the shed. He ignored it best he could. Thoughts drifted through his mind. Memories too. He remembered his father telling him to stay clear of trouble unless it came right up to find him. It *had* come right up to find him, striding out of that rickety saloon's double doors and then pointing a gun to his head. But all the trouble since then? Jasper had found that himself. He thought of the sheriff — not surly Pitt Randall, but the one who had been friends with his father. He'd said killing Alec Casey wouldn't make Jasper feel better about losing his father, but he wouldn't ever know now, would he?

He'd searched for Alec Casey. Blundered right into someone else's trap, and Hatch and Valdez — good men, not his friends, but *good* men — had died because of it. All he'd wanted for six years was to face down Alec Casey, pull the trigger, and make him pay, and when he'd gotten the opportunity? He'd failed.

Failed and given him easy directions to a big payday to boot.

He wondered how many men would die when Alec Casey robbed the payroll. Would it be anyone he knew? Probably not. He hadn't let himself get to know many people, had he? He thought of Charley, hands on her hips, or kicking out a chair for him, or telling him she was one of the only people in town who cared whether he lived or died. She probably already thought he was dead.

If he held his hands up close to his chest, he could feel the outline of his mother's letters there. He tried to imagine what they'd say, and found he didn't have a clue. Did she write him about what folks in town were doing? Which of his friends had gotten married, had children, died? Did she write to tell him she'd sold the farm, since he'd run off and she didn't have anyone else to help her run it? He liked to think she just wrote to say she loved him, but he wasn't even sure that was true anymore.

He'd like to see her one last time, but it

didn't seem like that was going to happen.

When the dawn broke, thin beams of light stole in between the shutters of the nailed-up window. Jasper climbed to his knees. He couldn't quite get to the letters, not with his hands tied, so he looked around the shed to see if there was anything to help him get free. He didn't find much, but there was the end of a nail someone hadn't fully pounded into one of the walls. He ran the rope back and forth across it until the rope splintered. He untied his hands, then his feet, then pulled the letters from his pocket.

He sat on the ground, back against the wall, and opened the first letter.

Dearest Jasper, it began, his name in his mother's curving writing almost enough to make him cry.

The letters had been through creeks and misty nights, and pressed close to his body. Like with Westin's numbers, the ink was blurred. Jasper climbed to his feet, angry that he hadn't taken better care of the letters, and hoping better light might make them easier to read. He leaned against the shuttered window, letting the thin beams of light shine down on the letter.

And then stopped when the slats shifted under his weight.

The night before when he'd checked the

shutters, they hadn't been so loose. They'd been nailed tight. He pressed against the wood. It gave a creak and he pulled his hand away. Had Alec assigned someone to watch the shed? Did he warrant a jailer? If he pushed hard enough and the shutters broke, could he climb out and run quick enough to get away, or would he just be captured again?

No, he'd have to wait. He wasn't sure how long he had until Slip came to see him — and then Bell was allowed to kill him. But if he could wait until the folks in whatever camp Alec Casey had going started making some sort of ruckus, then maybe he could break those shutters out without anyone the wiser. Camps like these never stayed quiet for long.

Jasper felt better with a plan. He took stock of himself — no injuries to speak of, aside from the sore mouth and the tightness in his muscles from being tied up all night. A shame they'd taken his knife. More than a shame about the rifle, but Jasper tried not to focus on it. His father would rather him have his life than any gun. He tried to think about that instead.

The only thing left to do was wait. No one brought him food or water, which didn't surprise him much. They'd left him the canteen on his belt, but that had been empty when he was captured, so it didn't do him much good. He tried to keep his muscles limber, waiting for any kind of noise from the camp to erupt.

He wasn't sure how long it was before something happened. Someone gave a shout, there was the sound of a dog barking angrily, and then gunshots. As soon as the commotion started, Jasper was on his feet heading for the window.

It wasn't as quick as he thought, prying the nails loose, pushing the wood from the frame. It was as loud as he thought, though, and he said a small prayer that the gunshots would go on a little longer. He wondered what God thought of that one. Finally, the broken shutter dropped with a dull thud on the hard-packed ground.

The noise outside settled before Jasper could get himself out of the shed. He just had to hope no one was close enough to hear him dropping from the window. He poked his head out, looked around.

The source of the commotion seemed to be down the single packed-dirt street. Jasper caught a glimpse of a fiery head and wondered if it was Bell shooting up a storm with his left hand. Better for Jasper, at least — if Bell was shooting something over there, he wasn't about to come into this shed and shoot *him.*

Jasper pulled his head back into the shed, then tried to figure out the best way to climb out quick and quiet like. He boosted himself up and out of the window and almost crashed down onto the shutters, but caught himself just in time to lower himself out the window more quietly.

He darted around the back of the shed, crouched down, and took a few deep breaths, trying to collect himself.

Where was he? He'd been knocked out for the journey here and had no idea which way they'd taken him. It couldn't have been far; even if they'd been on horseback; he didn't think he'd been out for more than a couple of hours. Farther south, deeper into the forest? Or farther west, closer to Sonora but away from the road people took to get there? He tried to remember which way Slip had been nudging them all those times. *West,* Jasper thought. West until that last day, when he'd told Jasper they should go hard north. What did that say about his location?

"Psst," a voice said, and Jasper rose to his feet, spinning around, ready to hit.

Slip stood there, a bag slung over his shoulder and Tabitha at his side. He flung his hands up, like Jasper was aiming to shoot him, even though Slip was the one with the gun — a revolver holstered on his belt. "You got out," he said, and grinned.

Jasper punched him in the nose.

"Ow!" Slip said loudly, then winced. "Stop punching me if you want to get out of here instead of being shot!"

"You want me to trust you?" Jasper demanded, his voice as low as he could make it while so angry.

"Considering I'm the one who let you out, yes, I do."

"I let myself out," Jasper said, but even as he did, he remembered the sound of wood cracking the night before.

Slip confirmed it a moment later. "I'm the one who loosened the shutter. Needed to get a few things before coming back, and I couldn't very well show myself around here since I'm supposed to *talk* to you before Bell executes you. You're *welcome* for the rescue, by the way."

"Why?" Jasper asked. "Why'd you let me out?"

"I told you. I don't want this. I don't want to follow his orders. And I don't want you dead."

"Because I saved your life?"

"No," Slip answered. "I already paid you

315

back for that. Now you owe me one."

Jasper shook his head. "Pretty sure you'd have died after that fall if I wasn't around. Think we're even." He gave Tabitha's head a scratch. "Lead the way."

Slip led them away from the camp through some trees. After a few minutes, they were apparently far enough away from the gang that Slip felt safe enough to talk.

"I pretended I saw Tab," he said, and Jasper must have given him a confused look, since Tabitha was right there beside them, trotting to keep up with their strides. "Back at the camp. Bell's spitting mad at her." Slip cast an adoring look down at the dog, like biting off a man's fingers had won his affection forever. "Passed it along that I'd just seen her. Knew when he heard it, he'd be trying to use her as target practice. I think he might be chasing down a squirrel."

"A rat, in fact."

Jasper whirled around. Bell stood behind them, the revolver in his left hand. "Looks like I got you nailed to the counter on this one, Slip. What do you think your brother's gonna say about this here ploy?"

"He'll probably be disappointed I got caught again," Slip said, voice desert dry.

"Well, I was just waiting till you said your piece. You've said it. I'll be shooting your

316

friend now and taking you back."

"No, you're not," Slip said.

"What are you going to do? Send your dog after me?" Bell chuckled and pointed his gun at Tabitha. She growled. "Enough of that."

He pulled the trigger just as Slip moved.

The shot went wide as Slip crashed into Bell. The two ended up on the ground. Slip got a hit in, but then Bell punched him and rolled. He brought the gun up, but Slip got a hand on it and the two grappled.

Jasper went to pull Bell away, but before he could get to him, the gun went off. He grabbed the man by the shoulders and jerked him backward. Bell went without a fight, falling to the ground, his shirt bloody, his eyes rolled back.

Jasper looked back to Slip. He held the revolver in his hand, then tossed it aside as quick as he could. "He dead?" Slip asked. Jasper nodded. Slip climbed to his feet a little unsteadily. He looked down at Bell's body. "Still don't like killing. Even when it's someone I detest."

Jasper didn't know what to say to that. So all he said was "Let's go. Before someone comes to see what that shot was all about."

Slip led Jasper to a small clearing where two horses were waiting, saddled and tied to a tree. Strapped to the saddle of one of them was Jasper's rifle. Jasper stopped still when he saw it.

"I didn't recognize you," Slip said. He wasn't looking at Jasper; his eyes were focused on some point beyond them. Maybe he was trying to remember the boy from six years ago. Jasper didn't blame him for that lack of recognition. Sometimes he didn't recognize himself. "Alec's always been better at faces than I am. He put it together much quicker than I did. Look, that day —"

Jasper didn't talk about that day. He'd avoided talking about it ever since it had happened, and he didn't want to talk about it now. But though he let out a choked sound when Slip said it, the sound never formed into a word.

So Slip kept talking. "He's my brother. He was nineteen years old, and I knew they'd kill him. I couldn't let that happen. Not after I'd run away when the shooting started."

It all made a strange sort of sense. Slip Casey running out the back when the posse came to get them; Alec slamming out the front like he didn't have need to run away from anything.

"He was going to kill you, and I stopped

318

him. It's the only time he's ever listened to me. I tried to get him to just leave. But he said a man had shot him, and he'd promised him he'd regret it. I told you, Casey men always pay their debts, and Alec owed him a bullet."

"And I owe Alec one," Jasper said.

Slip nodded and finally looked up at Jasper. His eyes were wet with tears, but he blinked them away. "I know. I ain't gonna stop you. But I did want to say I'm sorry. About your father."

"I am too."

Slip walked to his horse and started fussing with the saddlebags. "Alec's headed to Sonora. He won't hit the stage with the payroll until it's up in the mountains. I told him about our friends and their clever plan to murder us on the road, and he liked it so much he's gonna try it himself. So if you're gonna track him down before he goes for the mine payroll, you got two days."

He pulled out a sheaf of papers, which he pushed at Jasper. *Westin's papers,* Jasper realized.

"You might want to give these back to your friends at the mine when you're done," said Slip. "Alec took the times and dates, but these are the rest. By the way, he thinks someone's skimming off the top. He's probably right. He's the smart brother, after all."

Jasper took the papers and stared down at Westin's neat numbers. He remembered the other man speaking up for him and waiting for a thank-you that never came, and Simmons asking if Westin wanted to take a seat in Jasper's stagecoach.

"I'm not going to Sonora," he said, realizing as he said it what he was going to do. "I'm going back to Indigo."

Slip cocked his head. "I wasn't expecting that. Want some company?"

Chapter Twenty-Eight

They arrived at Indigo after the sun had set.

The horses Slip had stolen — stolen in the first place by his brother, Slip had said, as though stealing stolen property negated the thieving itself — were fast and strong, and they'd managed good time, even keeping off the main road near places like Long Barn, where folks might recognize one or the other of them. The journey back was far quicker than the one that had brought them to Alec Casey's camp. Jasper knew these roads and the land around them. Tabitha had run alongside for part of the journey; she'd clearly been trained to work around horses, and tried to nip only a little. But her legs were much shorter than the horses' legs, and eventually Slip had tied a blanket like a sling, picked her up, and ridden with her like she was a baby held close to her mother's chest.

"You'll ruin that dog," Jasper muttered.

"Not possible," Slip said, and wouldn't hear another word about it.

Jasper didn't fight him on it hard, because Slip had brought bread and cheese in that bag of his, and Jasper was too hungry on their short stop to spend any more time arguing.

When they got to the town, Jasper led them around behind the home station to the back of Charley's saloon. No one was out here, but he could hear people talking inside and a guitar tonight instead of the fiddler. There were lights on upstairs in the parlor; he wondered if there was a game of poker going on, or if he'd catch Charley on her own. Always best to go in having some sort of a plan, and he wasn't sure how well Pitt Randall was going to take what he had to say.

Jasper swung down from the horse, and so did Slip, though dismounting with Tab almost made him lose his balance and fall. Tabitha shook herself all out as soon as she was free from the sling and walked away from Slip as though some distance could save her dignity.

"You ain't gonna hole up in that cabin again, are you?" Jasper asked.

Slip scoffed. "Learned my lesson there. I

also didn't bring any whiskey. Figure I'll wait till I'm somewhere where people aren't trying to kill me before imbibing again."

"And you say Alec's the smart brother."

Slip laughed. He filled his canteen at the water pump, took a long drink, then filled it up again. "Long ride ahead of me. I should get going," Slip said, "before someone sees me and I get arrested again."

Jasper gave a nod of his head. "Travel safe. Take care of Tabitha."

"Good luck," Slip said, though the words caught in his throat. *Good luck killing my brother* was what he meant, and Jasper wasn't sure he'd have been able to say it any easier than Slip did. "See you around."

He walked back to his horse and gave a quick whistle for Tab. She started to return to his side, then froze, her ears and nose both twitching. And then she bolted.

"Tabitha!" Slip left the horse and started to chase after her, despite what he'd just been saying about being arrested.

It was Slip's bad luck that caused what happened next. Jasper couldn't see any other explanation.

Tab went running for the small building that housed the doctor's office and home, right next to the saloon. She made for the alley between the two, faster than Jasper had seen her run this whole time he'd known her. She was whining below a half-open window when Slip caught up to her and knelt down, Jasper close behind.

The light from the window barely shone into the alley, and Jasper started to pull Slip away, when the door to the saloon opened and a group of people spilled out into the street.

Pitt Randall among them.

At the sight of the sheriff, Jasper stepped forward, a hand raised, but Randall already had his gun drawn.

Slip hadn't even noticed anything was amiss. "What is wrong with this dog? Honestly, why —" He straightened up as he muttered, his hands going to his hips. And one of them landed on the butt of his revolver.

"Casey!" Randall hollered, and Slip turned toward him.

It was all the warning he got before Randall shot.

The bullet hit Slip in the chest, and he went flying backward, landing against the doctor's woodpile with a pained grunt.

"Stop!" Jasper yelled. "Sheriff, put your gun away!"

He didn't know if Randall had listened to him or not. He ran to Slip's side.

The wound was on the left side of his chest. Near his heart, Jasper thought, but it was hard to tell in the dark.

"You fool," Jasper said, "running after the dog and getting yourself shot . . . again."

"Ain't so lucky this time, am I?" Slip asked.

Jasper didn't tell him he was right, but lying didn't feel right either, so instead he said nothing. It was clear he was in worse condition this time — much worse — without Jasper saying a thing.

"Make sure to get Westin out of that cave?" Slip asked, and then his eyelids trembled and closed.

Jasper wondered if Slip's bad luck had somehow transferred to him, because the next thing he knew, the sheriff had arrested him.

"What did I do?"

"Consorted with a felon," Randall answered, shoving Jasper into the cell of Indigo's makeshift jail.

Jasper wanted to know if that felon was alive. While he'd been shoved toward the jail, he passed the doctor, in his nightclothes, sure, but with his bag, ready to do his job and save Slip if he could. Hopefully. But Randall had been with Jasper since then, so he didn't know whether Slip was alive or dead, and asking Randall the question wouldn't make him any more likely to believe Jasper.

"You don't understand what happened."

"Then tell me," Randall said.

Before Jasper could, in walked the mine boss.

Simmons didn't look surprised to see Jasper alive. He wasn't sure if that was because he'd already assumed Jasper had survived when Brady and his men didn't come back, or if all surprise was hidden away behind the layer of ice in his eyes. His lips were set in a frown.

"Your friend out there kill Mr. Westin?"

"No," Jasper said. "Your man Brady killed Westin." That might not have been true; it was impossible to know who had fired the bullet that killed him. But Jasper wanted to see the look on Simmons face when he said it, see if it changed at all.

A twitch of an eyebrow. That was all. "Brady?"

Randall looked at Simmons. "That the man you told me about? One who got fired last week?"

"That would be the one," Simmons said. "I didn't know you two were friends."

"We're not," Jasper said. "He's dead."

Simmons took that in stride as well. "I'll have to send word to the company," he told Randall. "They'll want to know about Westin."

Randall clapped Simmons on the shoulder. Giving the comforting gesture looked strange on the man and receiving it even stranger on Simmons. "My sympathy on your man. Mr. Westin seemed like a fine sort."

"He was," agreed Simmons, who had paid one of his employees to shoot another. Jasper managed to hold his tongue as the mine boss left the room, but he was hard-pressed to keep it that way when the man stopped and turned back.

"Were you with him when he died? Did he give you anything?"

"No," Jasper said.

Simmons turned around and left after that. Randall looked like he was leaving with him. The fool wasn't much of a sheriff, couldn't even tell when he was working with a criminal.

Jasper kicked the bars of the cell. "I need you to listen to me!"

Randall turned around. "Why? Why should I listen to you? We paid you to convey an outlaw to jail, and instead you end up helping him escape. And I lost a good man that day!"

Jasper was about to tell him again that he'd had nothing to do with the ambush that had cost the deputies their lives when he realized exactly what he'd said. "*A* good man?" Jasper asked. "One?"

"Isn't one enough for you?" Randall demanded.

"I already told you what happened! Now tell me who lived?" He thought back to Tabitha running straight to the doctor's window. "Valdez. He's alive?"

Randall confirmed it with a nod.

"Well, what did he say happened? He wouldn't have said I was involved, because he knows I wasn't. He *told* me to run. Take Slip and Westin and run."

"JD hasn't woken up for more than a minute or two. It's a miracle he's alive."

"I had nothing to do with that ambush," Jasper said.

"So you escaped and Westin died. Then you and Slip Casey borrowed some horses and came back here?"

"It's not that simple. I need to show you something," he said. Randall looked wary, so Jasper opened his coat as careful as he could and pulled out what remained of Westin's papers. "The accountant gave me these before he died."

328

"You just said —"

"I lied. Listen, and you'll understand why."

Randall folded his arms across his chest. "I'm listening. But I'm not going to listen for long."

Jasper did his best to explain. The attack on the stage, Westin giving him the papers, Jasper trying to outrun Brady and get to Soulsbyville with Slip Casey still in custody, and then the run-in with Alec at his hideout.

"You know where the Casey Gang's camped out?"

Jasper wasn't sure Randall believed him but at least now he had his attention. "Better than that. I know where the Casey Gang is going to hit in two days' time."

Even if Randall didn't believe him, it was too good a chance to pass up. Jasper knew the sheriff would have to bite. "Where?"

"He's gonna hit the payroll stage coming up from Sonora. He knows when it's scheduled to come through because he took pages out of these. He's probably going to hit it out near Long Barn, just like my stage got hit." He held up Westin's papers but kept them back when Randall reached for them.

"Thought it wasn't Alec Casey who did that."

"It wasn't. This time it will be."

"So why are you telling me this, but you won't tell Simmons?"

"Casey took only the pages with the timetables. Slip got the rest back and gave them to me. He's how I know what his brother's planning."

"Slip Casey helping us catch his brother. That don't seem too likely."

"Slip's not a killer. He saved my life. Couple of times."

"What does any of that have to do with why you don't trust Simmons?"

Jasper held up the papers again, shook them for good measure. "These are why I don't trust Simmons. Someone's skimming. I heard at Charley's a few days back that the mine laid off a bunch of workers. Said the mine was slowing down, but they just hit a solid vein of quartz. Lots of gold in there."

"Just because some miners think —"

"Who do you trust to know this land better, a miner or some company man from the city?"

Randall closed his mouth. "So where does Westin come in?"

"That ambush wasn't meant for Slip Casey. It was meant for Westin. To shut him up before he could let the company men in Sonora know that someone up here was skimming the gold."

Randall grabbed for the papers, and this time Jasper let him take them. "You think it was Simmons."

"I know it was Simmons."

Randall's face looked surlier than ever in the dim light of the cell. "Am I supposed to just believe you?" he demanded. "You come on back here with an outlaw in tow and then tell me a man I've known for a decade got folks killed for some gold, and I'm supposed to trust you? Based on some numbers?"

"Don't believe me, then. Go talk to Valdez. If he wakes up, he'll tell you. You'll see."

Randall folded Westin's papers and tucked them carefully into his pocket — an inside pocket, so Jasper felt confident he wasn't just going to run out to Simmons and hand them over. "We'll see."

Jasper stopped him with a call of his name, and then asked, "While you're with the doctor . . . will you see if Slip Casey's made it? I'd like to know."

If the way Randall slammed the door behind him was any indication, Jasper had been right: asking about Slip surely didn't help his cause.

One thing the jail in Indigo had over Alec Casey's shed, aside from the fact that Jasper didn't have to sit on the floor, was that he got fed.

It was Charley who brought his meal in before the dawn had broken. Oatmeal with dried berries and some sugar on top.

"Missy Banks believes I'm innocent?" he asked, taking the bowl through the gap in the bars.

"Missy Banks thinks everyone should eat, even if O'Reilly doesn't agree."

"He must be fit to be tied," Jasper said. "He bought my stage off me and then I crashed it."

"He made his money back," she said. Jasper raised a brow. "I bought it from him to repair. Thought I might get back in the life."

She was lying. She'd bought it for Jasper. "I'll work off that debt," he said.

"You certainly will, Jasper Duncan. Barman Jack is ready to train you up to throw these fools out on their rear ends when they're too drunk as soon as you've come out the other side of this mess."

"You sure I will come out the other side?"

"I know your thoughts on Alec Casey. You weren't with his brother out of friendship."

Jasper nodded. He wondered, though, if she was wrong. Maybe he and Slip were some sort of friends now. They'd saved each other enough times to be called that, surely. He took a bite of his oatmeal and wondered if anyone would be feeding Slip Casey. If, of course, Slip Casey was still alive.

"Well, I've been up much of the night. Lots going on in this small town. You may have heard there was a shootout." Charley turned away, leaving him with his oats.

Before she could make it out the door, Randall came through it, scowling, as usual. "Miss Hawthorn," he said. Jasper could almost hear his teeth grinding, though he wasn't sure if it was because he was forcing himself to be polite when he clearly wanted to bellow at someone, or because one of his deputies had let someone in he wasn't supposed to.

"Sheriff," she said, dipping her head in a nod and leaving the room.

Though Jasper had seen thunder on Randall's face, he didn't start talking as soon as Charley left the room. Instead he paced.

"How's Valdez?" Jasper ventured.

Randall's attention snapped to him. "Better. He woke up for a little longer. I think it's that dog that did it. You bring her back?" Slip brought her back, but Jasper nodded anyway. "Well, it did him a world of good. Fool."

"She's a good dog."

Randall rolled his eyes. Jasper remembered feeling much the same before Tabitha had faced down a cougar and bitten a man's fingers off. "He says you're telling the truth. That Valdez sent you into the woods with Westin and Casey. That the men who ambushed you wanted everyone dead."

He couldn't see any hint of it on Randall's face when he said Slip's name, so he asked, "Casey make it?"

"For now," Randall replied. "Doctor says he's stubborn. Might pull through." He *was* a stubborn sort, that was true enough. "Stop changing the subject, Duncan."

"Yes, sir," Jasper muttered.

"You say that ambush was all mine men, Brady and the like?"

"It was Simmons who sent them," Jasper said, gently as he could.

"I know that," Randall snapped. He took a breath, quieted. "I know that now." He took off his hat and ran a hand over his nearly bald head. "The question is, what do we do about it?"

Jasper smiled. "I think I have an idea."

CHAPTER TWENTY-NINE

"And you're really certain about this?"

Jasper looked over at the shotgun rider beside him. The time to ask that would have been before they had left Sonora, not when they were six miles out from Long Barn. But he supposed the man hadn't been given much of a choice but to come along. He worked for the mine, and the man in charge down in Sonora was the one who had sent them up with this stagecoach, set Jasper on as its driver. This was as good a place as any to have second thoughts.

"Sure as a man can be."

He'd answered plenty of questions down in Sonora. Yes, sir, he'd been with Westin when he died. No, sir, he didn't have it straight from *Alec* Casey's mouth that he was due to hit the payroll run, but the information was as good as the gold that Buck Simmons was stealing from the mine. Yes, sir, he was certain about that as well.

Westin's papers had helped convince them his word was simon-pure. Jasper supposed they had Alec Casey to thank for that. He'd been able to read Westin's strings of numbers better than Jasper could.

"How'd you find out what Casey was planning?" the shotgun rider asked.

"His brother told me."

Jasper didn't have to turn again to see the surprise on the man's face. He wondered if maybe he should have left that part out, if he wanted the man to trust him.

"How'd a jehu get mixed up with the likes of Slip Casey?" the man asked.

Jasper let out a chuckle. "Well, that's a long story."

The man tensed beside him. "I don't think we have time for that."

Jasper had seen it too — a cloud of dust and, inside of it, riders. There were six of them, coming head-on.

The Casey Gang.

The shotgun rider beside Jasper turned around and thumped the coach. "Heads up!" he called.

They were being attacked.

Jasper picked out Alec Casey in the middle of the group. He'd been right, he thought. Casey wasn't the type to hide away up on a cliff or come from behind to shoot.

Jasper wondered if they had cleared roads from their camp to get to and fro here in the mountains, or if they'd just trotted off road from Sonora. That was where Alec had been, Slip had said, and just on time, he was here.

These horses didn't bolt at the sound of gunfire. They stayed steady, and Jasper gave a silent thanks to whoever had picked out the team. Jasper reacted just as any jehu would have reacted to a surprise attack: kept the team steady, trusted the man beside him to take some shots, and hoped that they could make it through this.

What he wouldn't do, if the attack was truly a surprise, was divert off course.

They were five miles from Long Barn. A jehu would have normally sped through the ambush and tried to get to the town where lawmen might have guns at the ready if they had heard the shots. Jasper had to hope that what they'd planned to do didn't read too obviously like they were trying to lead the Casey Gang into a trap of their own.

Five miles west of Long Barn was where that shortcut they'd taken a few days ago would have let them out. The stage was fast approaching the turnoff. He could hear the pounding of the horses' hooves and the crack of gunfire. Close to his head, the wood of the stage splintered. He drove the horses as hard as he dared so close to a turn.

There it was right in front of him, as unremarkable a path as the other side of it. He turned the team as narrowly as he could, but surprise course changes weren't the purview of a stagecoach. The riders saw it coming, and they'd drawn closer when the stage lost some of its speed in the turn.

He hoped this was going to go the way he wanted it to go. If not . . . Well, he'd almost died twice in the last week running this route. They said the third time was the charm.

This part of the road was as rough as the other end was. It was narrow, and Jasper kept to the center, trying to give the riders as little space as possible to pass. Two of them did, drawing even with the stage and shooting at the carriage, then taking a shot at the driver's box. Their aim was off, and Jasper was glad Bell wasn't among them. Casey had wanted him for his aim, after all; Jasper couldn't imagine him missing.

In the distance, Jasper could see the rocks in the middle of the road, the ones he'd nearly crashed into last time he rode the route. Knowing they were there, even before a sharp turn like that, he could have gotten by them without trouble. He was certain of it.

But this time, he didn't want to.

He pulled back on the reins, hard enough that the jar of the horses rushing to a stop caused the stage to shimmy and jolt. It must have looked like he had stopped in a panic. It certainly felt like it; he felt the shuddering through his teeth and down into his bones.

The two riders who had gotten ahead of them turned around, trotting back toward them, one of them giving a whoop of laughter.

And then Jasper heard his voice.

"Boys, seems to me it's payday!" Alec Casey sounded as pleasant as when he had said it was good to see Jasper, and twice as cheerful.

Jasper wasn't sure if it was the cheer that was the signal or the words themselves, but after Alec was done speaking, the outlaws opened fire.

Jasper and the shotgun rider ducked down into the driver's box. There wasn't much protection there, certainly less than from the heavier wood of the coach itself, but they didn't have to hold out for long. Just a few more minutes.

"Alright, alright, don't waste the ammo,"

Alec called, and the shooting stopped. "We can get the rest up close."

Jasper couldn't see them swing down from their horses, but he knew that was what was happening. Boots crunched on gravel; an open hand thumped the door of the stage-coach.

"Might as well open up if you're alive in there," said a voice, the same one that had let out the laughter.

No one replied. Not with words anyway.

The man inside replied with a shotgun blast.

By then Jasper could hear the horses. They thundered closer from both sides of the road.

Alec Casey had led his men right into an ambush.

As soon as the deputy inside the coach took his shot and Jasper heard the hoof-beats, he moved. He grabbed his father's rifle and slid out of the driver's box. His eyes found Alec Casey almost immediately like there was no one else on the road but them.

He didn't look upset. He'd read the situation already and was halfway back to his horse. A couple of his men were too. Two got on; one managed to wheel his horse around, get off the road, and the other got shot, fell from his horse.

Before Alec could get to his horse, some-one shot it.

The horse gave a scream and fell. Alec's eyes scanned the line of deputies and found the one who'd shot her. He raised his revolver, found his target, and shot. The deputy fell from the horse, and the horse bolted, running into the one beside it, breaking the line of fire. Alec didn't go for another horse. He stood in the midst of the firefight, finding a target, shooting at it, always moving, but never in a hurry. It almost looked like the bullets didn't want to hit him.

Well, Jasper always knew Alec Casey was never going to make it easy for them.

"Casey!" he called, his voice as loud as he could make it so it would carry over the bullets, the shouts, the sharp whinnies of the horses.

Alec heard him. Jasper saw the moment he realized who it was. He hadn't recognized him while he was driving, but Jasper had kept his hat pulled down. It had been knocked off when he took cover in the driver's box, and now that Alec saw his face . . . Of course he recognized Jasper, had recognized him after six years. Maybe the face of the one person he'd ever let go had stuck.

Jasper had hoped that seeing him would draw Casey over. He was right to hope. Casey started toward him, walking leisurely, taking the occasional shot at one of the deputies around him. He usually hit his target, though it didn't seem to bother him when he didn't.

Jasper was standing where the road bent, just out of the heat of the fight. He watched Alec come, walking right through the firefight, until he felt something slam into him, hot, stabbing into his left arm and leaving him gasping.

Someone had shot him.

Jasper hadn't seen it coming. Barely saw who had done it. Hot pain ratcheted through his left arm and it was all he could do to keep a grip on his rifle with his right arm.

Jasper staggered a few steps backward. It reminded him of the first time he'd faced Alec, dropping backward on his rear, then falling from the porch. Then he hadn't had a hole in his arm. Then he hadn't had ahold of his rifle. He started to raise it, but did just what he'd done so many years ago, and fell backward.

A rock, he realized distantly as he hit the ground. He'd tripped over a rock.

Alec stopped his advance, turned to his man who'd shot Jasper, and volleyed a bullet back at him. Dead straight between the eyes. The outlaw fell over.

He had to get up. He had to. Jasper forced himself to his feet, made his arms lift the gun where he'd need it.

"Why'd you do that?" he asked Alec.

"Plenty of people to shoot," Alec said with a wave of his hand. "And I was obviously coming for you. I can't countenance stupidity."

Jasper let out a laugh. "Of course you can't."

"How'd you get out?" Alec asked, his head tilted to the side and eyebrows raised like he was trying to work it all out. "How'd you know what I was planning?"

"Your brother."

"Slip? What'd you do to him?" Alec asked, but before Jasper could answer, he seemed to put it together. He almost looked grudgingly respectful. "He let you go. I never thought he'd do it."

"Honestly, neither did I."

Alec nodded a couple of times. "Is this what you aimed to do?" he asked, jerking his head back toward where the shooting was still going on. "Bring down the Casey Gang?"

"I never much cared about the Casey Gang," Jasper said. He shifted, changed his grip on his rifle. His left arm felt like someone had stabbed him with a hot poker, but his right arm was steady. "Mostly, I wanted you."

Alec nodded again like he had known Jasper was going to say that. "I should have killed you myself back there." Somehow that didn't sound like a regret; it sounded like Alec was sorry he had underestimated Jasper for Jasper's own sake. Like killing him back in that camp would have been an honor.

Jasper didn't think he'd ever understand Alec Casey. After today, he didn't think he'd ever need to try.

"You said the Casey brothers pay their debts. Well, so do I."

Alec gave a slow nod. "I suppose you do," he said, raising his revolver. "Assuming you can —"

Jasper's shot rang out before Alec could finish his sentence. Alec dropped to his knees, just like he'd done so many years before when Jasper's father had given him that scar on his shoulder. His hand still held the gun, but even though his fingers twitched against the metal, he clearly couldn't raise it.

His eyes were cloudy with pain and confusion. He didn't seem to understand that he was dying. Jasper took a step closer, reached down, and pulled the gun out of his hand. Alec's fingers put up a fight, and it took whatever strength he had left right out of him. He slumped over onto the ground, his eyes still open, life leeching out of him just like the blood from his body.

"You're a little bit too much like your brother," Jasper said. "Shouldn't talk so much."

Jasper might have been fooling himself, but he thought he saw a little spark of laughter light up Alec's dark eyes before leaving them entirely.

Jasper took one breath, two, and Alec Casey's chest didn't heave in time with his.

He'd done it.

Jasper felt the rifle slip from his fingers and hit the ground. Hitting the ground sounded like a good idea, so he lowered himself down as well, taking a seat on the stone he'd tripped over.

Alec's body lay in the dirt in front of him, and Jasper had the passing thought that he would probably have hated that. Or maybe not. Maybe he'd wanted to die this way, shot through the heart on a warm spring day, facing an enemy who wanted nothing more in this world than to kill him. As ways to die went, Jasper supposed there were worse for men like Alec Casey.

Around the bend, the gunfire seemed to have stopped. A strange stillness settled on Jasper. Quiet. Even the pain in his shoulder seemed more distant.

He'd spent six years chasing Casey, and now it was over. He'd breathed the idea of revenge, drunk it down like his whiskey. It had been the last thing he thought about at night, and usually the first thing he thought of in the morning.

And now it was over.

Should he have felt happy? Jasper thought of the outlaw whooping with laughter when he shot a man down and realized he didn't feel like doing that. He remembered again what the sheriff told him back then — *You could kill Alec Casey a hundred times and it won't help you feel better about losing your pa.* He'd needed to kill Alec, yes, but in the end, it wasn't going to bring his father back. It wouldn't bring any fathers back.

But then he thought of the man who would have been driving this payroll stagecoach, the one who would have been beside him, and realized maybe that wasn't necessarily true. They were probably fathers. He had saved those sons from the pain he'd gone through.

Maybe the jehu in the parlor was wrong; it wasn't revenge that was sweet, but knowing you'd done some good with it.

Footsteps approached. A set of boots stopped in front of Alec Casey's body. "You alright, Duncan?" a man asked. His shotgun messenger for the day. Jasper recognized his voice.

He looked up and gave a nod. "Yes," he said. "I'm alright."

CHAPTER THIRTY

The payroll stagecoach rolled into Indigo in the late afternoon. This stage didn't stop at the home station; no, this one always continued on until it reached the mine. On the way, they passed Simmons' home, the same place Jasper had gotten the job that had nearly killed him. He wondered now what they'd find inside those clean whitewashed walls.

Jasper hadn't been lying when he said he was alright. The wound in his shoulder had hurt like hell, but it wasn't anything the doctor at Long Barn couldn't stitch up. He'd be uncomfortable for a while and had to watch out for infection, but he was better off than some of the men in their party who'd been badly wounded or died, or the Casey Gang, most of whom had seemed to want to go down fighting. They'd taken only one into custody.

They'd met the actual payroll stage at

348

Long Barn, which carried more than just the miners' pay, and that stagecoach continued on to Indigo. The mine men had been willing to let Jasper drive them all the way until the doctor pitched a fit about the stress on his arm. He settled for riding shotgun. As long as he was on that stage. After all, he'd started this with a run that had brought an accountant to Indigo. Now he wanted to bring the ones who would call to account the men responsible for that accountant's death.

This sort of stage, carrying payroll, always had a shotgun messenger up front with the driver, unlike some, and usually another in back with the money. Jasper was used to being the driver, but if Charley did decide to get back into the life of a jehu, he might not mind so much riding shotgun for her.

As it was, pulling up to the mine building on the opposite side of the coach felt odd. He hopped down, his rifle slung over his good shoulder but still at the ready, and pushed his hat lower on his head.

Simmons walked out to meet the coach. Jasper didn't know if this was a custom of his or if he did it only because he'd gotten wind of the Casey Gang's plan. But even if the latter was true, Simmons didn't look like he had a care in the world.

Until the stagecoach door opened and the Pinkerton who'd been escorting Sam Westin appeared. He, for one, had been glad Jasper wouldn't be driving when they met the payroll stage at Long Barn, even though his anger over Westin's murder had overridden the anger about the black eye Jasper had given him.

Simmons looked like he was about to ask what the Pinkerton was doing there but stopped before he said anything. He took a step backward. "*You* brought the payroll?"

The Pinkerton gave a nod. "The payroll and something else."

The man who stepped out after him was dressed like Sam Westin, but built like a bull, thick shoulders and chest and hands that looked like they could snap Simmons in half. "The boss wants to have a talk with you, Mr. Simmons. Told him we'd bring you right back down the mountain."

Simmons must have known his time was up, though his face didn't show it. He took another step backward. "Of course. There are things I'll have to do first. I —" He stopped talking when he slammed into Jasper.

Simmons hadn't noticed Jasper as he'd moved around the stage to stand behind him. Simmons hadn't noticed Jasper at all until now. The collision caused a jolt of pain in Jasper's shoulder, but it was worth it.

Simmons pulled away from Jasper and stared up at him. "You're in jail," he said as though it were certain, not something belied by the very fact of Jasper standing in front of him.

"I'm not. Matter of fact, I've had a busy day. Had a run-in with the Casey Gang, shot an outlaw or two, and made a delivery." He smiled. "Sam Westin made a request, you see. So I brought your boss what he asked me to deliver, and he sent me back here with them."

Both of the other men stepped forward. The bull dressed as an accountant might have been the bigger one, but Jasper bet on the Pinkerton doing more damage. Westin had been his charge, after all, and he didn't seem the type to forgive so easily.

"You got some good men killed, Mr. Simmons," Jasper said. "Was the gold worth it?"

The look Simmons gave him was colder than any look Alec Casey had given. "It's the only thing that's worth it."

The doctor wasn't used to having two patients staying in his house. That much was clear when Jasper arrived two days later. Instead of ushering Jasper inside, he stepped out to stand on the porch, breathing deep, like he hadn't gotten air in days. Maybe he hadn't. Jasper imagined that Slip Casey would be a hard patient to care for, and never, ever quiet.

"Deputy Valdez is the one you're here to see, I gather," he said all in a rush like there was no possibility of anyone stopping by to see the outlaw.

Jasper nodded as though he didn't see that possibility either. "I would like to talk to him."

"Try not to get him riled up about anything. When we told him Deputy Hatchett didn't make it, he nearly tore all the stitches I put in with his fussing." The doctor straightened his coat, then gave Jasper a prim nod. "I'll just be next door," the man said, "if you need me." His tone said not to need him.

Jasper didn't blame him. The doctor's home was small, with a bedroom in the back and an examination room in front. Jasper wondered where the man had been sleeping. On the floor with a bedroll? The doctor had stretched a screen across half the room, and Jasper could see two sets of feet, one human, one canine, at the end of a low bed, half hidden behind the screen.

He poked his head around the screen to

see Valdez reading a dime novel, Tab curled up beside him. She raised her head and looked at him, thumping her tail once or twice before settling back down. "Hey, ya," he said, and Valdez looked up. "I wasn't sure how to knock on a screen."

The deputy set his book aside and pushed himself up in the bed, wincing as he did. "Jasper. Good to see you."

"You too."

"I hardly believed it when Randall told me. Simmons?" Valdez shook his head, then gave a small smile. "You know, Hatch would've believed it. He hated him."

"I'm sorry about Hatch." Jasper hadn't counted the man as a friend, but maybe he should have.

"Me too." Valdez looked away from him.

Jasper wondered what he was thinking, whether he'd been beside Hatch as he died. Even if he had been, Jasper supposed there wasn't any knowing what was in a man's head when he passed out of the world.

Then Valdez slapped a hand down on his book and said, "I hear you brought my dog back."

Tabitha looked up again like she knew they were talking about her.

Jasper smiled. "It wasn't me, actually. Slip Casey."

"Slip Casey took a shine to Tabitha?"

"I think by the end, it was mutual."

Valdez looked down at Tabitha like she'd betrayed him. "Where did I go wrong?"

Jasper wanted to say that Slip wasn't such a bad sort, after all, but Valdez was a deputy, and an honest one at that. Plus, there was that fat lip Slip had given him to consider. Instead, Jasper said, "I do not believe you did. She saved my life a time or two out there."

"I wish dogs could tell stories," Valdez said with a laugh.

"I'll tell you sometime," Jasper said. "She bit someone's fingers off. It's a story worth telling."

"I'll buy you a drink for that one," Valdez replied.

"Glad you're doing well," Jasper said, stepping away from the bed.

Valdez picked up his book. "Getting there anyway."

Jasper hoped the same was true of Slip.

The sheriff had made sure to put a latch on the outside of the doctor's bedroom door, a thing the man was probably none too pleased about. The window was shuttered too, and nailed from the outside.

Jasper knocked lightly on the door before unlatching it and walking inside.

354

Slip Casey was lying on a bed that was too short for him, feet hanging off, with a hole in one sock. Jasper wanted to laugh at the sight of him.

"I think this time you really did turn that luck around."

Slip looked up at him. He didn't look particularly surprised to see Jasper. "Lucky in how I got shot. I don't know if that counts as good luck."

Slip might have looked happy to see him beneath the frown. Jasper couldn't be sure. He had a bandage stretched across his chest. The bullet had gone in near the shoulder, glanced off the collarbone, and exited somewhat messily. The doctor had told Jasper if Slip had been facing the sheriff full on, he'd probably be dead. Instead, he'd live.

At least until they got him down to Sonora, the sheriff had added.

"Come to say your goodbyes?" Slip asked.

"Something of the sort, yeah," Jasper said.

"Your sheriff says I'm the last member of the Casey Gang around. They cleaned up the folks at the camp, and Alec . . . Well, I guess that was you."

Slip's jaw was set and his eyes shadowed, but Jasper didn't think he was angry. Not at him anyway. Or maybe he was, but it wasn't the kind of anger that needed to strike a blow. Just the kind that needed to exist.

"It was me," Jasper confirmed.

"Did it help?" Slip asked.

Jasper shrugged a little. "It helped that I was stopping him. That he wouldn't kill anyone else. That's what I should have wanted all along."

"There is that."

Jasper remembered Slip saying that Alec had killed a lot of fathers, and remembered that Slip had tried to stop him. Maybe that was what *Slip* had wanted all along.

"You got yourself shot too," Slip remarked suddenly.

"I did," Jasper replied. "Could have been worse."

Jasper saw the question lodge itself in Slip's throat — was it Alec who had shot him? But then he swallowed and he didn't look like he wanted to ask the question anymore. For his part Jasper didn't want to answer it. Maybe it would be better to let Slip believe Alec had died in a shoot-out, both of them drawing their pistols at the same time.

Jasper cleared his throat. "I did come to say goodbye."

"So you won't be the one to take me down to Sonora? But what about the reward?"

"I think I'll forgo the reward. I'll be working off my debt here in other ways. And I
think I'll go check in on those kids, see if
their father came back. Then one day make
my way back to Nebraska."

"Back to that mother of yours," Slip said.
"I hope she cooks better than you do."

"She surely does."

Jasper didn't know what to say after that.
They weren't friends, and after this visit,
they'd never see each other again. Slip
wasn't likely to forget Jasper had killed his
brother, even if there was nothing else angry
and hard between them. But it also couldn't
be denied they'd saved each other's lives.

Perhaps Slip didn't know what to say
either, because after a long moment of
silence, he blurted, "Your deputy friend's
alive and he took my dog."

"She's his dog," Jasper reminded him.

"But we thought he was dead. She was
my dog, fair and square."

"Well, maybe where you're going you can
get a dog of your own."

Slip laughed, his voice bitter. "What, the
great beyond?" The laugh turned into a
cough.

"Sounds like you could use some fresh
air."

"Don't be rushing things," Slip said, groping for the water on the nightstand. He found it and drank some down. "The second they let me walk around, that's when I'll be fit enough to —"

He stopped talking as soon as he looked up. Jasper had opened the curtains and pushed at the window. The shutters swung wide, a little awkwardly, a little broken from being nailed shut and then forced open again.

"Hang," Slip finished, then looked over at Jasper.

"Yes," Jasper said, "I do have some debts to work off around here."

"Look at that," Slip said with a grin. "You're down one already."

"Good luck," Jasper said. "I hope I never see you again."

"Back at you," Slip Casey said.

Jasper left the room, latched the door behind him, and told himself he was done with the Casey brothers.

Chapter Thirty-One

The day before his father had died, he took Jasper fishing.

They went to the pond at the edge of the property. It stretched along a wooded slope, some of the trees coming all the way down to the water. On hot days, Jasper would shinny up one of them, climb out onto one of the branches that stretched over the pond, and leap down, sinking, sinking until his toes touched the muddy bottom before rocketing back up to the surface.

But this day hadn't been for swimming. They brought their poles down to the water and set themselves up on a flat rock that jutted out into the pond like nature's own dock. They hadn't talked about anything really. For the first hour, Jasper had been too tired. He'd slept poorly the night before. His father asked if anything was the matter; he remembered that. Jasper had said nothing was the matter, but the truth was he'd been thinking about Delilah Burke, the neighbor girl, and wondering if her father would let him court her or if they were too young.

He wondered if his father knew that.

They fished until the early afternoon. Sometimes they had great luck on the pond, pulling enough bluegill or carp to feed them for a couple of days, with extra to salt for winter. This day, no matter how nice it was out, was a poor day for fishing. They pulled only a few crappies out of the water, one too small. Jasper threw it back.

In the years after Ben Duncan's death, Jasper rarely thought about that day. He thought about the following one, where guns blazed and outlaws sneered and there was blood in the street. But Jasper didn't think his father would have wanted him to dwell on that. His father would have wanted him to think about them fishing, feet in the pond, their meager catch disappointing Jasper's waiting mother, but not so much that she didn't have lunch waiting for them after they'd washed up.

Jasper tried to think of that now. The three of them sitting at the table, light coming in from outside. His mother would fry the fish later, with salt and pepper and nothing else, and they'd eat them as the sun set.

Jasper thought of that, sitting in the driver's box of his — Charley's — stagecoach, and opened his mother's latest letter.

ABOUT THE AUTHOR

Ralph Compton stood six foot eight without his boots. He worked as a musician, a radio announcer, a songwriter, and a newspaper columnist. His first novel, *The Goodnight Trail,* was a finalist for the Western Writers of America Medicine Pipe Bearer Award for best debut novel. He was the *USA Today* bestselling author of the Trail of the Gunfighter series, the Border Empire series, the Sundown Riders series, and the Trail Drive series, among others.

D. B. Pulliam is a bookstore manager from Northern California.

The employees of Thorndike Press hope you have enjoyed this Large Print book. All our Thorndike, Wheeler, and Kennebec Large Print titles are designed for easy reading, and all our books are made to last. Other Thorndike Press Large Print books are available at your library, through selected bookstores, or directly from us.

For information about titles, please call:
  (800) 223-1244

or visit our website at:
  gale.com/thorndike

To share your comments, please write:
  Publisher
  Thorndike Press
  10 Water St., Suite 310
  Waterville, ME 04901